Mystic Wolves

Copyrighted work is illegal. Criminal copyright infringement, including infringement without monetary gain, is investigated by the FBI and is punishable by up to 5 years in federal prison and a fine of $250,000.

Mystic Wolves

Accidentally Wolf

Copyright © 2014 Elle Boon

First E-book Publication: November 2014

Edited by Larriane Barnard

Proofread by Mike Hoffa

His Perfect Wolf

Copyright © 2015 Elle Boon

First E-book Publication: April 2015

Cover design by Dawné Dominique

Edited by Tamara Hoffa and Mike Hoffa

ISBN: 10-1519416180

ALL RIGHTS RESERVED: This literary work may not be reproduced or transmitted in any form or by any means, including electronic or photographic reproduction, in whole or in part, without express written permission.

All characters and events in this book are fictitious. Any resemblance to actual persons living or dead is strictly coincidental.

Dedication

I'd like to first thank the readers for liking my stories as much as I love them. Thank you, thank you, readers!

A huge thanks to my friends Desiree Holt and Debbie Ramos who helped me get this story published by reading the very raw version. Thank you Valerie Tibbs, Margie Hager, and Janet Rodman for all your help along the way. Y'all are amazing ladies that I am blessed to call friends. You ladies are the best friends a gal can have. I wouldn't have been able to continue on my journey without all of your support. I'd also like to thank all the amazing authors I can call friends. Thank you all for your support and help.

And I owe Caitlyn O'Leary many thanks, for being the best crit partner ever, for pushing me to become a better author and always being there. Thank you soo much lady. Kate Richards and Wizards in Publishing, Y'all rock! Love y'all soo hard, each and every one of ya <3

And last, but not least, I owe many thanks to

my husband and my children. Without their love and support I wouldn't be able to do what I love...Making up stories! XOXO.

Elle

Accidentally Wolf
Mystic Wolves Book 1

by

Elle Boon

Chapter One

"It's okay, little guy," Cora soothed, shoving down her fear for the little wolf caught in the illegal trap. The device had been hidden in a shallow crevice within a couple miles of her veterinary clinic. The way his wound was bleeding she knew, if she didn't get him free, he'd likely die. Inching closer to him, Cora watched for signs of aggression. "I'm going to get you out of there, but you have to promise not to bite me, okay?"

She squatted down until her face was almost level with his. "I'll try not to hurt you."

Cora swore it looked like the little guy nodded. At least Cora hoped that was a nod of agreement. His tiny body shook and shuddered. She prayed she wasn't mistaken.

After carefully looking over the contraption, she realized the jaws were meant for a much larger animal. Luckily for this wolf, his leg wasn't clamped between the steel jaws, only grazed. He was still stuck with his larger paw locked on the inside of the obviously modified bear trap and had a nasty gash that needed tending, sooner rather than later.

What seemed liked hours later, Cora finally got the device forced opened. Sweat trickling down her temples stung her eyes. The wolf lay panting like he'd just ran for miles. His gaze seemed to convey that he trusted her. Although it looked as though the trap only grazed his leg, she still checked to make sure it wasn't broken.

With a glance up at the darkening sky, Cora shrugged out of her jacket, leaving herself in only the yoga leggings and tank top she wore for her daily jog. South Dakota, during the day, could be warm, but as soon as the sun goes down, the temperatures drop dramatically. "Okay, little guy. I'm going to wrap you in my coat, and then I'm going to take you home with me."

Matching actions to words, she gently lifted his body. As she went to place his front right paw inside the jacket, the wolf howled the most pitiful whine, breaking her heart.

"I know it hurts, but I..." Cora jerked back in shock when the wounded animal bit down on her arm.

Once the wolf wriggled out of her coat, Cora watched in amazement as he licked her wound. If she didn't know any better, she'd swear he was apologizing, but thought that would be crazy. She gaped at him and scooted back a step or two, or three, until she stopped herself.

He whined again before trying to stand on his own, falling down when his front leg wouldn't hold him up.

Ignoring her own injury, she grabbed up her jacket and wrapped it around his body, being sure to pay close attention to his bleeding leg. "I know you're hurt, but try not to bite me again." She tried to sound stern when inside she was scared.

The walk back to her clinic took twice as long as normal since she didn't want to jar her patient any more than necessary. Every now and then his rough tongue would peek out and lick her arm. Although she was caught up on all her shots, she still worried about diseases from animals such as the wild wolf. At first glance she thought he was a baby wolf, now with him gathered in her arms and the couple of miles trek back to her home, she discovered he wasn't so young.

"Goodness, you must weigh close to seventy pounds, big guy."

Cora kept up a steady dialogue as she walked. When the clinic came into view, she nearly dropped to her knees in relief. Her arms shook under the stress of holding so much weight for such a long period of time. Normally, the hike would have taken her no time at all, but holding an injured animal that weighed almost as much as she did, the entire way was taxing, to say the least, not to mention the bite on her arm burned like fire.

She stopped outside the back door, adjusting her hold to punch in the code to unlock the back door, and, exhaling in relief, she murmured, "Thank you, technology." Cora's breathing was ragged by the time she made it inside.

Attached to the clinic was her small apartment, with a steel door separating the two spaces. Again, she punched in the code and then used her shoulder to enter the office area.

"Almost there, big guy. I'll have you fixed up in no time." Sweat poured down her chest, soaking her top. Cora ignored it all to focus on getting her patient fixed up. After she'd cleaned his wound, she found he had indeed broken his front leg, which was why he had probably bitten her when she moved him.

Thankful that her training kicked in to tend to the little wolf, when all she wanted to do was curl up in a ball and take a long nap, Cora placed the patched up wolf inside the padded kennel with a sense of relief. He whined when she attempted to lock the gate, his pain-filled gaze breaking her heart.

There were no other patients in the hospital area. She made the decision to leave the lock off, hoping she wasn't making a mistake and headed to take a bath.

Cora wiped her hand across the fogged mirror and stared at her own pain-filled gaze. "How can one little bitty bite hurt so damn much?" She looked at the freshly cleaned wound for what seemed like the thousandth time and stuck a thermometer in her mouth and waited for the beep, promising herself if her temperature was too high, she'd head into town.

Even after taking meds and a cool bath, nothing was bringing her temperature down. Looking at the triple digit reading on the tiny screen she cringed. There was nothing else she could do except head into town to urgent med. Cora really hated to go to the emergency room. She rolled her eyes and shook her head, stopping when the motion made her feel like she was on a tilt-a-whirl.

Wrapping a towel around herself, she decided to check on her patient one more time before she got dressed. The door between her home and the clinic was open, but the lights were out, sending a shiver of fear down her spine. Cora flipped the switch on the wall, illuminating the walkway. Her head felt heavy, the lights overly bright, making her stumble and lose her footing.

"Shit, damn." Rising to her feet, she reached her palm out to the wall to help steady herself and blinked a few times to bring things back into focus.

Standing in the middle of her clinic, with the injured wolf in his hands, was the most magnificent man she'd ever seen in her entire life. At over six foot tall, with short blonde hair and tattoos—lots of tattoos. The man exuded sex and menace. Yes, he definitely looked like he was angry. Even with her head feeling wonky, the sight of the unknown man made her body come alive. A whole different pulse began beating between her thighs, making Cora want to reach out and touch him, and not because she was in fear for her life.

"Who are you, and why do you have my wolf?" Cora was happy her voice didn't come out sounding as scared as she felt.

"Your wolf?"

The big man growled, the sound making her feel things she really shouldn't. Her nipples peaked at his deep rumble. Cora blamed the reaction on the fever.

"Listen, despite the fact you obviously broke into my clinic and I could press charges, I won't, but only if you put the animal down and leave the same way you came. You have less than five minutes, and then my offer is gone." Cora arched an eyebrow at him. "Do we have a deal?"

She waited for him to agree and put the sleeping wolf back down. Instead he quirked an eyebrow of his own, widened his stance, and sniffed the air.

In a move too fast for Cora to comprehend, the hunk standing a good ten feet away from her one moment, was all of a sudden crowding her space, sniffing her neck.

"Hey, have you heard of personal space?" When Cora attempted to push him back, her world spun.

* * * *

Zayn Malik didn't know whether to laugh or growl at the human who tried to tell him what to do, all while she stood in nothing but a miniscule towel. Holding his nephew in wolf form, he opted for the latter. Every member of their pack knew the rules, and he couldn't imagine Nolan, even at the young age of seven, breaking them. He'd wait until whatever drugs the woman gave Nolan wore off, and his nephew could shift back to find out what happened.

The overwhelming scent of antiseptic clouded his senses, making it hard for him to discern the unusual smells assaulting him. When she raised her hand to push him back, he watched her eyes roll back in her head. Zayn shifted Nolan to one arm, being careful of his injured leg, and caught the woman in his other arm.

That was how his alpha found him, holding an injured cub in one arm and a naked female in the other. It wasn't his fault the towel was dislodged when he pulled her into his arm to stop her from face planting onto the ceramic tile floor.

"You want to tell me why you are holding my cub and an unconscious naked human, Zayn?"

The smile his brother suppressed didn't make Zayn happy. He wanted to toss the human to Niall. Only fear of hurting his nephew kept him from following through on the thought. "Fuck off, Niall," he grumbled.

"Give me Nolan. Do we know what happened to him?" Niall reached for his cub, carefully tucking him into his body.

As he handed Nolan over to Niall, Zayn watched his brother grimace at the bandage on his son's leg, then sniff at the offending thing like he wanted to rip it off. The joking man was gone, replaced by the concerned father. Niall stood at over six foot three with more red in his blonde hair, but with the same blue eyes Zayn had. When Niall spoke as alpha, everyone in the pack listened. Although they had pack mates who were bigger than Niall, none could take him in a fight in human or wolf form.

They'd come to the Mystic River Pack in South Dakota when Niall found his mate by chance during one of their annual bike rides to Sturgis. Within a few months they'd found themselves full-fledged members of the pack, and Niall had learned he was to become a father.

His brother's nose then turned to the woman Zayn cradled in his arms. Niall's face got too close for Zayn's peace of mind to a bandage wrapped around her thin arm, making his inner wolf rumble close to the surface.

"Do you smell that?" Niall sniffed again.

"What?" Zayn pulled the woman closer to his chest, using his large hand to cover as much of her bare ass from his brother as possible.

The right side of Niall's mouth quirked up for a moment before he turned serious. He bent to pick up the towel that had been dropped and draped it over the female.

"She's been bitten."

Narrowing his eyes, Zayn ran his gaze over the sleeping woman. "What did you say?"

The woman in his arms stirred, a feverish light in her eyes. That was when he noticed she was extremely hot to the touch. The smell of the clinic and the medicines had masked the unmistakable scent of the marking, which meant his sweet little nephew had bitten the good doctor when she had obviously tried to help him.

"You smell soooo delicious." Cora licked her lips.

"Um, what's your name, sweetheart?" Zayn tilted his head back from her questing lips and tongue. *Damn, her tongue is really long.*

"Mmm. You taste really good too." Another wet swipe from her tongue had him panting.

"Oh, goddess. Baby, you need to stop." Zayn needed to get the woman to stop licking him or he was going to throw her down on the table and fuck her.

How the hell did she go from being cradled in his

arms, to wrapped around him with her legs locked around his hips, and her arms around his head? Zayn swallowed. Jesus, he was ready to come in his jeans with his brother and nephew not five feet away.

"That's enough, Cora." The low timber of Niall's voice reverberated around the room. A shiver went through the woman in his arms, and she swung her stare toward his brother.

Niall held an ID card with a picture of the woman in his arms. The name, Dr. Cora Welch, was at the top for Zayn to see. His brother grinned, his blue eyes dancing with mirth.

* * * *

Cora's pussy contracted. Holy crap, the man was hot with a capital oh-my-lawd H, and she was humping him like a cat in heat, a naked cat in fricking heat.

She unlocked her ankles from the blonde Adonis's waist, hoping her legs would hold her up. They wobbled but didn't buckle—thankfully. "I'm so sorry...I don't know what came over me."

"I know what almost came all over me."

Sucking in a swift breath, Cora crossed one arm

over her breasts and snatched the towel from the red haired man. Not that they hadn't seen everything there was to see, but she was in control of herself now.

"Smooth, Zayn, smooth. I apologize for my brother. He's not usually so crass, but we were worried when we couldn't find our little one here." He indicated the now alert wolf.

Eyes so blue peeked out between the big man's arms, accompanied by the whine she'd become accustomed to from the cub. She reached an unsteady hand toward his head to give a little scratch between his ears.

"Luckily for him, he's going to be okay. I found him stuck in a medieval looking animal trap made for a much larger animal. His little leg here," she indicated his cast, "barely missed being snapped in half by the steel jaws. I set the break and cleaned the wound. He should be right as rain in a few weeks."

Here she was buck-ass naked, carrying on a conversation with two men and a wolf. She was definitely sick. Cora raised her hand to feel her head. The short speech made her breathless, like she'd just run a marathon.

Behind her, she heard something growl. Turning

to see the gorgeous man wearing a scowl, she took an involuntary step away. She looked around, fearing a wild animal had somehow gotten inside her office.

"Thank you, Cora Welch, for saving my cub. I owe you a life debt."

She swung her gaze back to the man holding the wolf. "Who are you? I've seen you in town, but I don't think we've met."

"I am Niall Malik. The man behind you is my brother, Zayn Malik."

Cora's tummy fluttered as she looked behind her at the man named Zayn. Lower down, between her thighs, her sex seemed to swell. A woman could come just from the stare of his blue eyed gaze.

"Well, it was very nice to meet you both, but I'm not feeling the best...so, um..."

Cora stumbled forward. A steely arm wrapped around her from behind. Blonde hair lightly dusted the arm roped with muscles upon muscles. Tattoos covered every available inch of skin she could see.

"Easy," Zayn murmured.

Cora blinked. Her stomach twisted; her pulse beat so loud she was sure even the man not holding her could hear it. Why did she feel like something monumental was about to happen?

"What the hell is wrong with me?"

Around her she saw white flashes. More men seemed to fill her once empty clinic. She wasn't a fan of having people witness her in a towel, let alone if she was going to either hump the man holding her or pass out. Either option seemed possible.

She blinked her eyes a few times to clear her vision. The newcomers pushed and jostled or shoved for prime position to see what the action was, making it the last straw for Cora. The equipment, along with all the instruments, was expensive, and not something she wanted to have to replace.

"Everyone stop!" Cora yelled, stepping forward with her hand out, hoping they didn't see the way it shook.

Zayn pulled her in closer to his body, eliminating the small space she'd attempted to put between them for her own peace of mind. Did the man not understand personal space?

Niall inclined his head. "You heard the lady. Everyone move out. The situation is in hand."

"Zayn's got something in hand."

"Watch your tone, McDowell." Niall warned.

McDowell was easily fifty pounds heavier than Niall, and it looked to be all muscle, but he seemed to shrink right before Cora's eyes at Niall's command. Cora studied all the men in front of her with a slow inspection. Faded denim hugged muscular legs, skin tight T-shirts or sleeveless flannel button down covered equally muscular torsos. Each man looked as if he stepped off the cover of some muscle magazine. She may be new to the Mystic River area, but she was pretty sure it was not normal for so many gorgeous men to be in one place, unless...*Oh please don't be gay*.

The extremely large erection digging into her back gave her hope that the man holding her wasn't, but in this day and age one just never knew.

"Sorry, Alpha. We see you found your cub." McDowell nodded towards Niall.

"Yes, let's head back. I'm sure he's tired from his long day."

Cora pulled her attention from checking out the bevy of gorgeous men to see the look of love shining in Niall's eyes as he looked down into the blue eyes of the wolf in his arms.

"Where did you say the trap was, Cora?" Zayn asked.

After she explained where it was located off the running trail, all the men in the room trained their eyes on her. “What are you looking at me like that for?”

“How did you get him back here?” Niall fired the question at her.

“I wrapped him in my jacket, picked him up, and carried him.” Her arms still felt like Jell-O from carrying him for over two miles.

“You carried an injured, sixty-five pound cub, over two miles?’ Zayn raised his brows.

Cora frowned. “Are you calling me a liar?” She spun out of his arms, nearly falling in her haste. She raised her hand when Zayn reached to touch her. “First of all, he weighs seventy-two pounds.” She pointed to the cub in question. “Second of all, I usually run over five miles every day, not to mention I do yoga and cross-fit. So yeah, carrying him was really hard, and I nearly fell several times. My arms hurt just holding them up right now, but I did it, and I would do it again. I am not a liar. You and whoever else who don’t believe me can go fuck yourself, and get the hell out of my clinic, because I’m tired, cranky, and I really need to lie down.”

“Everybody back the fuck up.” Zayn reached for her.

She took a deep breath. There were half a dozen

men in the clinic, and she had no clue how they'd gotten in, or why they were all there. "Who are all of you, and why are you here? How did you get in?" The sound of distress from the cub stirred her overprotective instincts.

Forcing herself to turn her attention back to the man who seemed to be in charge, Cora smiled at the wide awake cub. "Did all that ruckus wake you up?"

Cora looked up into blue eyes very similar to the young wolf, but shook off the notion. "He may need some more pain meds. I had him on an IV drip, but *someone* took it out. I can give you some in pill form that you can mix in with his food if you notice him having any discomfort."

"Thank you, Cora. These are men from my...ah...family. When a cub goes missing everyone drops what they're doing to search. I'm sorry if we've scared you." Niall inclined his head.

She flicked away his thank you with a wave of her hand, glad to see almost everyone had cleared out, like they'd been waiting for the order. Now, if she could just get rid of the last of her unwanted visitors, she could go to bed. Surely by the time she woke up in the morning, she'd feel much better. If not, she'd go to the doctor, even if she hated the thought of that.

"Do you have someone to take care of you?" Niall asked.

"I don't need anyone taking care of me."

"I'm afraid I can't leave you here alone, Cora. Either you come home with us, or Zayn stays with you. We owe you a life debt."

"That's...that's crazy. I just saved your pet. Now you have him and everything is fine. I just have a bit of a cold. It's fine."

Niall shook his head, and Zayn's scowl deepened. "Seriously, I'm fine," she repeated.

"You coming with us, or is he staying here?"

He was an immovable obstacle. What do you do with an immovable obstacle? You go around him. Cora was glad her wits were still functioning, even though she knew her fever had to be even higher than the last time she took it.

"How about if I take some meds and call you in the morning?" See, she could be reasonable. She nodded.

"Did you grab her bag?"

With a quick glance, Cora gawked at the sight of Zayn holding her overnight bag with more than just a change of clothing. "Yes," Zayn growled.

"Good. Grab the girl."

What were the chances she could make it down the hall to her apartment with the steel door before either man could catch her? And if she did make it, could she get the alarm set and the police called before she passed out?

All these questions became a moot point when the man in front of her turned on his bare feet, which she just noticed, and walked out the front door, while Zayn murmured next to her ear, "You wouldn't make it two feet before I caught you."

"What?" Her voice came out in a breathless squeak she blamed on fright.

"You have very expressive eyes, and they were saying very clearly that you were about to do a runner. Rest assured, nobody, and I mean nobody in our...home would ever hurt you. We only want to see to your safety and wellbeing."

The last bit of strength Cora possessed left her all at once. Fortunately for her, Zayn just happened to be there to stop her from kissing the floor. Still, common sense told her she should let someone know where she was, just in case they planned to murder her—or something.

"I need to let my assistant know where I am in case of an emergency."

"It's Saturday. Aren't you closed on Sundays?"

Her challenge almost faded on her lips, not because she'd lost her senses, but because he'd bent his head so close to hers she could feel his breath on her lips. For a moment she almost forgot how to breathe. Holy buckets, the man was potent.

"I said in case of an emergency."

"Fine. Who do you need to call?"

Cora swallowed. Surely if they were going to kill her, they wouldn't allow her to let people know where she was going. Right?

With a grunt, Zayn waited while she left a voicemail for her assistant, letting her know she'd be staying with the Maliks and to call her cell if she needed her.

"Okay. You can put me down."

"Not gonna happen. You'll fall down, and then Niall will blame me."

Cora gaped at his audacity. "You can't carry me all the way back to your place."

"One of the guys brought my truck. I only have to carry you out front," he grunted.

She was too tired, and honestly too sick, to argue any further. Besides, his shoulder really felt good to lay her head on. "You smell really, really good."

"You said that before."

Cora closed her eyes against the flashes of white light.

Zayn pulled the door closed, engaging the locks. "Any problems on your way back, Kellen?"

"Coast was clear. Everything okay on your end, boss?" Kellen called from his place against the wall of the clinic.

At the sound of the newcomer's voice, Cora turned her head into Zayn's chest.

"Yes. Thank you for bringing my rig. Can you drive while I hold her? I don't think she will let me go long enough to let me drive us home."

She really wanted to lift her head and give him the finger, but at that very minute she couldn't. The steady rocking from his walk was so soothing her body went lax. Instead of fighting sleep, she let it claim her. A sense of security wrapped around her in the tattooed arms of the big man that she hadn't felt in a long time.

Chapter Two

When Zayn woke up that morning, he'd had no clue he was going to be running all over the countryside looking for his wayward nephew, let alone be stuck with a naked human woman. He had nothing against human women, per say. They were good for certain things, just not to become a part of their pack. He didn't want one tainting their bloodlines, accidentally or not. Even if they smelled so damn good his cock was ready to burst the seams of his denim jeans, and his body was screaming at him to take her. His mind was smart enough to say no.

Desperation rode him to ask, "Can't you drive faster, Kellen?"

Kellen laughed. "If it's a hardship holding the female I'll switch places with you."

The urge to growl at his best friend became harder to suppress as he saw Kellen's eyes roaming down the curve of Cora's back through the rearview mirror.

"Eyes on the road, Kellen."

"Yes, sir."

Kellen was openly laughing at him, but at least his eyes were firmly on the road.

By the time they'd reached the subdivision the pack had made their home, Zayn had his libido firmly under control, sort of. Having a basically naked woman in his lap, one who seemed to want to climb inside him and lick him from head to toe, was playing havoc with his hard won self-control. Life was a bitch sometimes.

"Your place or the alpha's?"

Did he really want to have the constant distraction in his home? Did he want his brother to be faced with a woman in heat with a cub in his home? Zayn snorted. He wasn't worried about his nephew's virtue or his brother's for that matter.

Looking up from the sleeping woman, the object of his desire, he met Kellen's amused look. "Mine." It wasn't lost on him he'd used the possessive word, nor Kellen.

The Mystic River Valley was right outside of the bustling town of Sturgis, within an hour's drive. Far enough away they could escape the craziness, but close enough for their business. Zayn and his brother owned a shifter run bar that catered to not only shifters, but also to humans who loved all things bikes. During bike week and the weeks leading up to bike week, they were busier than normal, which they loved, but this year something felt off to Zayn. It could be the woman who was now sleeping in his bed.

"How's your guest doing?"

"Damn, Niall. Don't you know how to knock?"

"What's up? You look...a little freaked." Niall raised his brows.

Zayn laughed. "What makes you say that?" He pushed away from the counter needing something to do with his hands. "You want a beer?" A nod of Niall's reddish head was his answer.

After he pulled two bottles from the fridge, he tossed one to his brother. Twisting the cap off his own, he downed half the contents in one swallow before he looked at Niall again.

"I'm fine."

"Liar." Niall adjusted the beer to his left hand, holding his right hand up in a stalling motion. "You've been on edge since the moment I walked in on you holding a naked Cora Welch. We have decisions to make, and if you aren't level, then I need you to take a step back. Let me take the woman." Niall took a deep breath as if the statement pained

him.

"She stays here," Zayn growled pointing to the floor at his feet.

"Is she your mate? Are you planning to finish the marking my cub started?" Niall's words were asked in a grave tone.

"I don't want a fucking human for a mate. She's so damn skinny she'd break if I fucked her the way I like. You know I like women with curves and meat, something to grab onto for a long hard ride." Zayn emphasized the type of woman he liked with his hands, making exaggerated shapes of breasts and hips.

Niall let out a snort. "You're a bastard." He smiled before he dropped his gaze to the floor, running his thumb over the sweat dropping off the bottle of beer. "Seriously, you need to understand the ramifications of the situation. If we let her ride out the one marking, then she will come out of this with the memory of one of the worst colds of her life." He looked up. "But you gotta keep your dick in your pants and your fangs to yourself. If you don't think you can do that, then you need to let me take her to my place. I can guarantee me and my dick won't have a problem resisting her."

Chest tight and stomach a churning mass of conflicting emotions, Zayn frowned at his brother. "She'll be fine here. My dick and I are in complete accord."

Niall, the bastard, had the audacity to look at Zayn from head to toe. "I'm glad to see the dick in question isn't standing at attention the way it was back at the vet's office."

Rolling his eyes, Zayn adjusted his stance and crossed his bare feet at the ankles. Like most wolves they liked to run barefooted. "I had a naked woman pressed against me, licking me for fucksake. I'd like to see any man, or wolf, not get hard."

Niall fixed him with a steady stare. "For as long as the fever lasts and she's in your house, you keep it platonic, unless you want her as a mate. It shouldn't be too hard to keep your cock in check for forty-eight hours."

To Zayn that seemed like a lifetime, when every time he thought of Cora he had an urge to crawl in beside her on his big bed.

Niall finished his beer and fixed Zayn with his alpha gaze, the one Zayn had come to recognize as meaning *don't mess with me.*

With their eyes locked, the bad ass alpha cupped

the back of Zayn's head, pressed a brotherly kiss to his forehead and walked out the back door.

Alone with the alluring scent of the human and nothing to do but check on her, just to make sure she was okay—not because he couldn't stay away—Zayn made his way down the hall to his room. Lying in the middle of his California King bed she looked tiny, although he knew she wasn't short by human standards. Maybe five foot five, with dark red hair, almost brown. He'd have sworn it was a dye job except the same color graced the small patch between her thighs. Damn, she was thin. No, thin wasn't an accurate description. She was muscular, or, well, fit was the appropriate description. Leanly sexy as sin is what she was. So not his type. He was such a liar.

The second he got his first look at Cora Welch in all her naked glory, he'd wanted her more than he could remember wanting any other woman or wolf. Goddess, did he want her in the worst way possible. He wanted to run his hands over the sleek muscles of her shoulders. The taunt yet surprisingly rounded globes of her ass drew his eyes like a moth to a flame. He knew she'd been turned on by the sweet scent of her arousal at her clinic, before the other wolves had shown up. She'd all but vibrated with want. However, he couldn't be sure if it was from the marking or because she wanted him.

He studied her. Even in sleep she looked serious, a bundle of feisty, indignant, ferocious, takes no shit woman.

Zayn raked his hand through his hair, not liking the way he couldn't stop thinking about Cora. Maybe he should've sent her to his brother's. "I don't want you," he muttered, turning on his heel, he retraced his steps. The erection tenting his jeans made the statement a complete lie, one he was glad his brother wasn't there to witness.

Dinner needed to be cooked, and if nothing else, it would take his mind off the woman lying in his bed. Tonight was Niall's night at the bar, and his nephew Nolan would be arriving within a couple hours. His unwanted house guest would undoubtedly be hungry too. He defrosted several steaks, prepared a handful of baked potatoes and pulled out the fixings for a salad.

The sound of the shower coming on had his head turning toward the master suite. Several times he was sure he'd heard her breathing change, indicating she'd woken up, but each time he'd checked, she appeared to be asleep. Either she was a really good faker, or she was extremely exhausted. The last time he checked, her fever had gone down. It had only been a few hours since they'd arrived at his home, which meant she'd only been marked a handful of hours. Usually the first bite's effect lasted for up to forty-eight hours unless the next bite occurred, or the appetite for sex was appeased, or both. But, in the words of his wise brother, he was keeping his fangs and his dick to himself, or he'd have an unwanted, accidental wolf mate.

He could still send her to his brother's or one of the other pack member's houses, but he'd be damned before he'd allow another wolf, or man, to touch what was his...or what he was protecting, he silently corrected himself.

Cora walked into his kitchen, shattering his hard won self-control.

Goddess, she was sexy. She obviously had no clue how good she looked in a pair of cut off jean shorts with their frayed ends and ribbed tank top, sans bra. She'd towel dried her hair, but left the wet mass down, the ends still had drops of water he longed to reach out and catch with his finger.

"Um, can I help with anything?" Cora asked.

He closed his eyes and shook his head.

"Okay then." She turned to walk out on the patio.

"No, I mean yes. You can make the salad if you want."

An expression of puzzlement flickered over her beautiful face. "Yeah. Sure. I can do that."

It took monumental effort for Zayn to move back and make room for Cora to step up to the center island where all the salad fixings were laid. All he wanted to do was walk up and rub against her. Mark her with his scent and then his bite.

His brother's admonishment rang in his head, keep dick and teeth to self. The smell of her heat was making him crazy. He told himself any woman would do, but knew it was a lie.

Body stiff, arms firmly against his sides, jaw bunched, he stepped away from the alluring scent of Cora Welch. "I'm going to check the coals, make sure they're hot enough."

Without another word, he spun and stomped out of the house onto the patio, spine as stiff as his raging hard on.

Nolan bounded up onto the back patio. "Uncle Zay, is the lady doctor okay? Dad says she's staying with you, but I want her to stay with us."

"Whoa, little dude." Zayn picked his nephew up.

"Where's my hug?"

At seven, Nolan was like all other wolves, they loved and needed affection. His childish arms wrapped around Zayn's neck and squeezed for all he was worth, along with a grunt that made Zayn smile.

"Where's she at? Can I see her?" Nolan pressed his mouth close to Zayn's ear. "Is she mad at me for biting her? I didn't mean to Uncle Zay."

The last bit was said with tears choking Nolan's voice. Zayn patted his back and whispered words of comfort. Nolan buried his face into the crook of his neck, soaking the collar of his T-shirt with his tears. Zayn didn't care. He wasn't sure how long they stood there. It could have been a minute, or it could have been an hour, but finally Nolan lifted his face.

Using the end of his tear stained shirt, Zayn wiped Nolan's face and reassured the little boy that nobody blamed him. Zayn knew his brother would have reminded Nolan the need for secrecy and the fact that Cora couldn't be told the truth of their identities, unless they finished the marking. Which he wasn't going to do.

He looked at his brother over his nephew's head. "Why don't we go inside and see her, hmm?" Zayn sat the sturdy kid on his feet, looked down at his shirt and shrugged his shoulders. "What's a little snot and tears?"

"I've definitely had a lot grosser things on my clothing than that." Cora indicated the front of Zayn's shirt.

Her sweet voice eased over Zayn, and from the look of worship on Nolan's face, it was doing the same to the little boy.

"Hi, my name's Nolan. I'm sorry I…I mean, I'm sorry my wolf bit you." Nolan, the future alpha stood tall. With his thin shoulders squared, he held himself as erect as any proud member of the pack making an apology would. If Zayn didn't already love the boy, he'd have fallen hard right there and then. The good doctor didn't stand a chance against the kid.

Niall came up behind him, sadness clouded his expression. His large hand landed on Zayn's shoulder. "He's so much like his mother."

"She was a wonderful woman." Zayn knew his brother still missed his mate even after so many years. Theirs was a true mating, and to find a true mate once was a miracle. Zayn couldn't image facing the rest of his life knowing he'd lost the one woman meant for him like Niall had.

They both watched as Nolan charmed Cora with

his exuberance. If she'd had her arms free, Zayn was sure there was no way his nephew, in all his cuteness, would still be standing on his own two feet.

Already so in tune with the woman, Zayn could see the feverish light in her eyes, the way her well-toned arms shook from the minimal weight of carrying a bowl of salad. Had he not been paying such close attention, he might have missed her eyes rolling to the back of her head. He was glad his brother was as quick on the uptake as he, when he quickly grabbed Nolan and the bowl of salad before either became a casualty.

Zayn wasn't sure why she was reacting so differently to the first bite. A human hadn't been bitten in so long, their records didn't give detailed descriptions of what to expect. They anticipated a fever, high sexual need after the first bite, and then, if no second bite, all should return to normal. There were no records of the human constantly fainting.

Setting the bowl on the counter Niall nodded toward Cora. "I'll take Nolan to Dev's for the evening. Do you need help with her?" Niall proved why he was the alpha with his immediate response to the situation, taking charge without pause. Since losing his wife, he wasn't the laughing man he used to be, but he was still the solid rock everyone depended on.

"No, I got this." Zayn knew he was growling, his beast reacting to her scent, her heat, the feel of her soft lips, and tongue moving along his jaw.

Zayn killed the unwanted need and carried the object of his desire back inside his home. If she would just keep her tongue to herself, maybe, just maybe, he could get her back to his suite and run her a nice cool bath and order her to take a long soak. *Fuck. Alone*

"I'm so hot. Why am I so hot?"

Each word was asked against his neck, her hot breath had licks of desire rushing over him.

"It's the fever. We need to get you cooled down. I'm going to run you a bath. Do you think you can get undressed and in the tub by yourself?"

He prayed she said yes. He hoped she said no. He feared she'd say no.

* * * *

Cora had heard Zayn talking to his brother when they thought she was sleeping. He'd said he didn't want her, that she wasn't his type and knew he wouldn't be overcome with desire at seeing her naked, but she wanted him—with every fiber of her being. It had been a long time since she'd been with a man, a really, really long time. She ached to feel Zayn's hands on her body. She wondered if he would be as rough as he looked or gentle. His callused hands running over every inch of her were surely something every woman should experience at least once in their lifetime.

Hearing him say he didn't want her hurt at first, but she didn't want him, either. Not for the long haul. When she settled down it would be with a nice, well-mannered man. Nobody could call Zayn Malik anything other than wild. Cora wasn't sure why that word came to mind when she thought of the man.

Twenty-four hours ago she'd have said she was fine with her no sex life. That was before she was faced with over six feet of *good-god-all-mighty they really do make them this fine.* She got her first look at Zayn Malik in the flesh and wanted him. She wanted to lose herself in him. She wanted him to do all the things she knew he could do, and she wanted to scream his name in ecstasy while he did it. The best way to accomplish that goal was to unsettle him, seduce the big man set on not wanting her.

"I think so, but could you just stay to make sure I don't fall? I'd hate to bust my head on all this tile." It took all her self-control not to smile at the low growl that came from Zayn.

Earlier, she could've sworn the brothers had mentioned something about wolves and mates, but her mind kept going back to the fact she needed Zayn.

Determined to get under his skin, she didn't wait for him to turn his back. She pulled her shirt over her head, dropping it to the floor with little care. Her breasts may be on the small side, but they were high and firm. The men—okay, the two men she'd been with, one in high school and one in college—didn't seem to mind. In fact, they both said they loved them.

The snap on her shorts came undone with a loud pop. She pulled the sides apart, did a little shimmy to help the denim fall to the floor. If the little devil in her put a little extra wiggle in her hips, well, it was his fault for saying she wasn't his type. Of course, that extra movement made her world spin a little too much, making her lose her balance. Luckily for her, she had a big strong man to catch her.

"Stop shaking your ass and get in the tub, woman."

Pressed up against him, she felt the unmistakable proof that he did indeed want her. He may not, but his body did. She loved the feel of his muscled chest against her already oversensitive nipples. His arms felt like steel bands wrapped around her, making it hard to move the way she wanted.

"This tub is big enough for two. You wanna get in with me?" Cora stood on her tiptoes, stared up at eyes so blue she could get lost in them. For a moment she thought he was going to agree, but then a look of tension fell over his face, there one moment and gone the next.

"In you go."

Cora squealed as Zayn lifted her up and deposited her into the cool water without further ado. Before she could sputter a word, he spun on his heel and practically ran from the bathroom. A laugh bubbled up at the absurdity of the situation. There she sat in water too cold to be considered comfortable, in a pair of sheer panties that did nothing for modesty, while the big bad wolf ran from her. The last thought made her laugh. She sank further into the cool water. It really did feel wonderful on her overheated body.

A shiver wracked her frame sometime later, followed by another and another. Her teeth began to clatter, but she'd be damned before she yelled for help from the scaredy cat Zayn.

She sat as long as she could in the cold water with her knees to her chest, hoping it would help while time ticked by at a snail's pace. By the time her fever was either down or she was close to hypothermia, she pulled herself out of the water.

The sopping wet underwear joined the rest of her clothes on the floor. Her stomach growled, reminding her she hadn't eaten in what seemed like forever.

Not one to hide, Cora wrapped an extremely large towel around herself and headed back to the kitchen, a little upset to see it empty. The whole house had an air of emptiness.

In the fridge she found the steaks and baked potatoes, along with the salad all wrapped up like they were put there for her. She pulled them out and made herself a heaping plate after warming the steak in the microwave and carried it out to the back patio. The sun had set some time ago, but she felt safe, even though she was basically naked and sitting on a stranger's deck—a man who said she was not his type. And didn't that hurt? She sniffed back a tear, refusing to let him or any man ruin her meal.

The sound of leaves crunching off to the side

brought her gaze up to see Zayn staring at her from the side yard. She narrowed her eyes, remembering the way he'd dropped her in the water and left her. Something told her he was running. From what, she didn't know. He gave off a *don't touch me* vibe that suited Cora just fine.

She waved what was left of the T-bone steak she held in her hand, which was basically just the bone. When she realized she'd been chewing on the bone like a dog, she tossed it back onto the plate. *Gross. What is wrong with me?*

"Out for a run, Mr. Malik?" Cora asked with a bite.

"You could say that." Zayn bounded up on the back deck. "I'm glad you found the plate I left you."

"Yep."

"Why are you mad at me?" Zayn stood with his hands on his hips in a pair of jeans and nothing else, glaring at Cora like it was her fault that he was angry.

"Why am I mad at you? You're the one standing over me like a bull with smoke coming out of your ears. You're the one who dropped me in a tub of subzero water."

"No, you're mad because I didn't fuck you. Isn't that right? If that's what's got your panties in a snit, then I can fix that. All you gotta do is ask." Zayn rubbed his crotch.

"Fuck you." Cora jumped up from the table. "Oh, by the way…I don't have panties on."

"That's not asking, baby."

His mocking words had Cora wanting to smack the smug look on his face. Only the fact she was scared she really would climb him like a bitch in heat, kept her from turning back to face him.

* * * *

Emerson Glade got up from his favorite chair to stare out at the landscape of the Black Hills. He could hear his mate stir in their bedroom, missing his warmth, but the feeling of impending change was in the air. He may not be the leader of the pack any longer, but he was still a dominant. He'd given up being the alpha without a fight to a man he knew deep in his soul was right for the position. He'd been ready to hand the reins over to his own son when he'd become a man, but that time was snatched from them. Emerson, Jr. had made too many foolish mistakes. His son and heir had died during a fight with another shifter, and because it was a fair fight,

Emerson could do nothing but bury his son.

His daughter, Emma, had been his last hope for their line to continue. When she fell for a shifter not of their pack, there were many who had protested. Niall Malik had proven he was more than worthy of his baby girl and every bit the alpha they needed. Emerson credited the increase in their numbers to Niall and his men. They had moved to Mystic River, and within a couple years their pack had grown by leaps and bounds. Now he had his grandson, Nolan, who was so much like his beloved Emma. Sadness gripped him at the thought of his daughter, who died so foolishly. A hunter, illegally hunting on pack lands, had shot and killed his beautiful girl.

He wiped impatiently at the tears streaming down his cheeks. An alpha who didn't cry was not a man, in his opinion.

A warm body stepped up behind him, wrapped him in a tight embrace. "Why are you up so late?" His mate Payton rested her chin on his shoulder.

"I feel something in the air." He pulled her around to stand in front of him. The big picture window faced the moon, bathing them in its rays.

"Me too, although I believe it's my fey-half telling me something. Maybe I'm rubbing off on you."

The humor in her voice relaxed him like nothing else. Like most shifters Payton was close to six feet tall, even though she had fey blood in her, she took after her father's people. Her mother, Magdelyn, was fey and even though she was tiny in comparison to a shifter, Emerson was even more scared of her than he'd been of her dad, Archie, who was all wolf.

"My mother would never have hurt you."

He snorted. "Bull crap."

"Well." She laughed. "She only hurt those who hurt her babies."

Emerson turned his mate around in the circle of his arms. "I'd never hurt you intentionally. You know that, right?"

"Of course I do. That's why you're still a functioning man, my love." The twinkle in her whiskey colored eyes sent blood surging south of his waist band. He began walking backwards, careful of the furniture. Without pausing, his wife used her abilities to turn off the few lights that were on, as he fused his mouth over hers. His only wish was they could still have cubs, but at close to eighty, that ability wasn't in the cards for them, even though they didn't look a day over fifty. No matter their age, he suspected they'd be making love well into their hundreds. The lifespan of a typical werewolf could be hundreds. He pressed his lips to his mate's mouth, claiming her all over again. Their bodies moved together, reaching the heights of pleasure as if it was new.

Lying with his mate in his arms, Emerson should be sated, should be ready for sleep to claim him, but a nagging sensation that something was coming, something that was going to change everything, and they needed to prepare, pounded at his head.

"You can feel it too, can't you?" Payton rubbed her hand over his chest.

"Do you know what it is?" He laid his much larger palm over his wife's.

"I get a glimpse of a young woman running, being chased by a pack of wolves."

"Could be the doctor," he murmured.

"No, this woman will come to mean something to Niall."

"Our grandson did bite her. Maybe his father will turn her?" Even though he said the words, he didn't believe it. He couldn't see things the way Payton could, but his gut wasn't telling him the good doc was his son-in-law's. No, she was meant for someone else, the other man just had to get his head out of his ass and realize it before it was too late. That was something that Emerson planned to tackle in the morning.

"You need to rest. Tomorrow will take care of itself." Payton yawned, a jaw cracking yawn.

"I know you're right," he agreed.

"I'm always right."

He pinched Payton's still firm backside and settled more firmly into his pillows. His mate was always right, but he wouldn't tell her that. Her husky chuckle let him know she was aware of his thoughts. As a mated shifter pair, telepathy was as normal as breathing.

Chapter Three

Cora woke up screaming. The dream seemed so real she could feel the sharp teeth tearing into her flesh, ripping into her, shredding her apart as they feasted on her like she was their last meal. Her throat felt raw, and she was soaked from head to toe with sweat.

After she had run from Zayn, she had found the bag with her clothes and put on a pair of basketball shorts and a tank top with a built in bra, not that she needed any. Still a girl wanted a little protection. Now she needed a shower, but a cold glass of water was first on her list of must haves.

She turned her ear towards the closed door to listen for any sounds, like she could pick up any noise. She shook her head at the absurd action, before flinging the damp sheets off and grimaced at the thought of climbing back into the bed with distaste.

On silent feet, she tiptoed into the kitchen, happy when she didn't encounter her unwanted host. No, happy wasn't the correct word if she was being honest. When she thought of Zayn, she was intrigued, horny, and angry. For the most part she was horny. All she had to do was picture him and her body went hot—well, hotter than from the fever—and wet. God, she was wet and ready.

Cora held the cold glass to her forehead and imagined what it would feel like to have Zayn want her like she wanted him.

After several glasses of cold water, feeling marginally better, she looked across the kitchen counter. The large leather sectional in the living room looked a lot cooler than the damp sheets she'd just left in the room she was allocated. With a quick study of the clock, she decided she'd take a quick nap for the remaining couple of hours before sunrise and be up before Mr. Asshat even knew she was there.

A sigh escaped her lips at the feel of the cold material beneath her. It felt so good against her overheated flesh. She knew she probably should've taken a shower before lying back down, knew she'd rest better not being all sticky with dried sweat, but the leather was soft like butter. Another sigh escaped her lips as her eyes drifted closed.

She was on fire again. The bite on her arm throbbed. Everywhere her clothes touched irritated her flesh. With impatient hands, she shoved her shorts off, sighing when an immediate sense of relief washed over her. The leather couch hugged her, welcomed her, or maybe that was her imagination. Her pussy throbbed, and her nipples ached. The top chafing, making her want to take it off, only a sense of modesty kept her from acting on the impulse.

No stranger to touching herself, Cora needed relief. For every beat of her heart, she felt an echo between her legs. She sucked two fingers into her mouth and swirled her tongue around each digit before reaching under her lace briefs. Her body jerked as she unerringly touched her swollen clit. "Oh, yes," she whispered.

Trailing her fingers down farther, she gathered more of her own juices and rubbed in small circles, not wanting to come too quick.

A male groan shattered the otherwise silent room. Cora stilled her fingers, and her head turned toward the hallway leading to the bedrooms. Standing in a pair of loose sweats was Zayn. His eyes seemed to glow from the moonlight shining through the huge picture window, but his gaze didn't meet hers. No, they were focused on where her fingers were.

Instead of being embarrassed, she decided to give him a show. With her free hand, she pushed the lacy fabric down, exposing what she was doing to his rapt attention. She used one hand to open herself up, showing him how wet she was, then retraced her fingers to her opening, plunging two fingers into her pussy. She couldn't hold back the cry from how good it felt to be filled by anything, even her own fingers. Her eyes slid closed, unable to watch to see if he enjoyed the show. She pumped in and out with one hand, using the heel to rub her clit.

"Fuck," she panted. She was on the edge of orgasm when her hand was removed to be replaced by Zayn's tongue.

"What are you doing?" Cora asked, near the edge.

"You taste so good."

Even though he didn't answer, she didn't care. She wanted to come. God, when was the last time she needed to come this badly? She ran her hand through his hair, amazed at how soft it was. "Don't stop, please, don't stop."

A rumble was her answer, and then he pressed two of his fingers into her. She forgot all about his hair or hers. She was all about sensation. She screamed as she came harder than she'd ever come in her life, but it wasn't enough. She wanted, no, she needed, more than his fingers filling her.

"Zayn, I need you. Please, please, don't leave me. I'm begging you to fuck me. Now."

In the bright light of the day, she knew she was going to kick her own ass for the whining and begging, but at that moment she didn't care. Her body was like a living flame, ready to burst into a million pieces if he didn't fuck her.

"You don't know what you're asking. It's just the fever. Here, let me take care of you."

When Zayn rubbed his fingers on her oversensitive clit, Cora tried to pull away. With strength that shocked her, she flipped their positions, sitting astride Zayn with only a thin pair of sweats separating their bodies.

She grabbed the hem of her tank and jerked it above her head, loving the way his blue eyes riveted to her breasts. Her nipples had always been sensitive to the touch, but with his gaze tracking her fingers as she pinched them into tighter points, they became hard peaks. She ground her wet core against his extremely hard erection, an erection that would've scared her if she was in her right mind, but she was hornier than she'd ever been.

"If you don't want to take care of me, then I will just go out and find me another man who wants me, Zayn." With each word she rubbed up and down his shaft.

He growled and reversed their positions so fast her head swam. "Mine," he growled.

The deep rumble had her pussy quivering in need. The impatient way he shoved his sweats down and kicked them off had excitement flooding her system. The vision of a naked and erect Zayn made Cora wetter, if that was even possible. She spread her legs wider in a display of wanton need. "Then take me, Zayn."

She wasn't sure what she'd expected. Being flipped on her stomach and onto her hands and knees wasn't it. Again, she didn't care as long as he filled her.

The sound of foil ripping open almost made her whimper at the loss. She wanted to have his seed bathing her insides and shook her head.

"Are you changing your mind?"

Cora looked over her shoulder. "What? No, hurry for the love of God."

With that, Zayn wasted no time, and for that

Cora was pleased. If she had more time to think on her irrational thoughts, she wasn't sure she'd have wanted to continue. Of course that was before he began.

Zayn surged into her in one thrust, filling her to the point of pain.

"Damn, you're so fucking tight. Don't move."

That was a truly laughable thing for him to say. Cora felt like someone had shoved a two by ten into her. She literally froze, hoping he'd back out slowly without ripping her in half. Her arms shook from the strain of holding herself up. How long would it take for him to go soft and get out?

"I'm sorry I hurt you. Just hold still. Your body will adjust," he grunted.

"You're not the one with a fucking baseball bat shoved up your hoo-ha."

Zayn laughed. "Relax, baby. I promise to make you feel good." He reached between their bodies and touched Cora's clit, but she jerked away. "Don't do that, honey."

The endearment made Cora feel special and eased some of her tension even though she knew it was silly.

"That's it." Zayn strummed her clit.

He was so much larger than her, his body blanketing her much smaller one, she felt sheltered. His hand between her thighs, his cock inside her, waiting for her to be ready for him to move, and she was ready. Her hips swiveled, pulled away enough to feel the slide of his cock against the swollen tissue of her inner walls.

Two of his fingers traced where his dick was buried inside her and then his body seemed to shake all over, he sucked in a breath. Just as she opened her mouth to question him, he pulled back and slammed back inside. She straightened her arms, her body more than ready for the pounding Zayn was giving it. She met his thrust with one of her own, climbing the peak of bliss she was coming to recognize only Zayn could give her.

She pushed toward the ecstasy, the orgasm so close she shook with the need to let go. When it finally struck, she let free a keening cry, feeling so liberated with him it increased her pleasure. She turned her face into the arm so close to her head, the urge to bite the roped flesh riding her, one she was unable to resist.

The man behind her howled his own pleasure, or possibly from pain, she wasn't sure. She tasted the copper taste of blood, not a lot, but enough to let her know she'd broken skin. Zayn's grip on her hips tightened moments before his hot breath fanned her neck, and his own teeth gripped her shoulder. He bit down, making another orgasm washed over her. The contractions of her pussy squeezed him, milked him, his hips continued to thrust long after he should've stopped. They were locked together physically.

Her foggy brain tried to work out the irregularities of the situation, but exhaustion claimed her. The last thing she remembered was the feel of Zayn finally slipping out of her body and away from her neck. She thought he murmured something about accidental wolf, but wouldn't swear on it. She was just happy to sleep.

* * * *

Zayn carefully slipped from his mate's body, wincing at the word *mate*. He should've let her go to his brother's house when he'd offered, but just the image of her in Niall's arms sent a red-hot rage over him. Now, there was no going back, not for him or her. She was his mate whether he wanted her or not.

The memory of her tight, wet heat enveloping

him sent fresh blood to his recently softening cock. The knowledge that he'd been too rough with her kept him from joining her on the sofa, that and he now needed to tell his brother what he'd done.

He lifted Cora into his arms and carried her to his bed. The sight of the twisted sheets told a story of her fitful sleep. "Damn it." He detoured to the room he'd been sleeping in with the standard king bed. At least it had clean sheets. He hadn't slept in it after he brought Cora to his home.

She made a soft sound that brought out his protective instinct as he laid her in the middle of the bed, leaving the comforter off until he was able to wipe her down. After he made quick work with the use of a cool wet cloth over her body, between her thighs, he found semen. When a shifter mated, their wolf would also mate, knotting them together. Obviously a condom can't hold up under all that strain. "Fuck," he rumbled. He didn't sense her wolf yet. Would they have a full bond if only part of her mated him? He needed answers.

Now he had to face his alpha, not as a man, but as a wolf. He stepped off his back deck naked and faced the moon letting the change take over. Unlike in the movies, his bones didn't pop and crack. One moment a man stood, and then next a wolf was in his place. It was the same for a human who was turned wolf, only they had to be shown how to complete the change.

He went through the woods separating their homes, taking his time like a prisoner being led to the gallows.

The larger wolf met him in the clearing made for pack meetings, the sacred circle where marriages of sorts were performed, sentences, and even punishments were meted out. Now it was where he would tell his brother, his alpha that he had taken a mate. Although it wasn't strictly against the rules and he wasn't the first to bite her, Zayn still worried there would be some elders on the council who wouldn't be happy with what he'd done.

Niall stood tall on four legs, waiting for Zayn to enter. Behind him the other members of the pack had gathered. Zayn should've known his brother would've called a pack meeting. Their bond was strong, and as alpha he had to have sensed a shift when a new member joined their ranks. It was up to the council to decide if Zayn and Cora would be welcomed or outcasts.

Whatever their decision, he would not cower like

a pup. He jumped over the ring of boulders and faced Niall like an equal, causing a chorus of growls from the council. He wasn't challenging the alpha. Zayn proved this by turning his head to present his throat.

Their old alpha Emerson and his mate Payton were the first to take a place around the center fire in human form. That seemed to be the signal for the rest of the council members. While Zayn respected most of them, there were several who still didn't believe Niall was the right choice for alpha. When Niall's wife Emma had been killed, the council wanted Emerson to resume the position. Niall had to prove in this very circle that he was top alpha, defeating several of the enforcers and killing one of them. It wasn't a job Zayn envied, but he had his brother's back then, and knew Niall would have his now.

Zayn waited until the last of the council shifted, until just he and Niall were the only two wolves, and then he shifted, followed by Niall.

"As alpha, I felt a shift in the fabric of our pack. As many of you elders, I'm sure, felt also." Niall looked around the gathering. "You all have been informed about my cub biting the local vet, Cora Welch, yesterday." Niall waited for the murmurs to quiet down. "She was brought to my brother's home for safety reasons and has since become his mate."

"Does she know about shifters? About what she will become?" Leon, one of the elders, asked.

"What about her job?"

"What about her family?"

Niall held his hand up to stall the questions being fired at him by all sides of the clearing. "They are a newly mated pair. I'm sure there will be growing pains and issues that will need to be worked out. But they, Zayn and Cora, are Pack, and as such they are under my protection." Niall's eyes glowed, the bright color blue that marked him as an alpha, the alpha of the Mystic Pack.

All members of the pack lowered their eyes and presented their throats at the display of power, including Zayn. As brothers they had a bond stronger than just pack, and Zayn knew he could count on his brother, but he was prepared to leave to save Niall from having to choose. He still would if it came to it. This was not just Niall's home, but Nolan's.

The pack filed out of the clearing after Niall's declaration, once they wished Zayn the best and offered their help if needed. Zayn had asked for time, and in no uncertain terms told them he'd let them know when he and Cora were ready and not a moment sooner.

"You do know it's not gonna be easy, right?" Niall stood next to Zayn.

"No shit, Sherlock." Zayn smiled.

Niall shoved him with his shoulder. "Have you told her?"

Zayn shook his head, and then explained to Niall about the marking, glossing over the amazing sex without looking at his brother. He wasn't sure what he expected, but Niall's large arm grabbing him in a headlock wasn't it.

"Being locked inside your mate is the best fucking feeling ever. Goddess, I remember the first time with my Emma." Niall choked on the last word.

Zayn grabbed his brother in a hug. Since he'd lost his mate, Niall had sealed away many of his memories of her, not sharing them with anyone. To hear such an intimate memory brought a wave of sadness and happiness to Zayn.

"It was pretty great, but scarier than shit man. I wasn't expecting her to bite me. I thought I could wear a condom, keep my fangs to myself just like big brother told me. Then, my world was rocked right on its axis."

"You're lucky. I was lucky. So, why are you still

hanging out with me? You need to get back to your mate." Niall squeezed his shoulder one last time, and then stepped away.

"I'm outta here." Zayn shifted and ran full out for his home and his mate.

What he found was an empty house. The smell of their lovemaking still fresh, but her bag was gone, along with his truck.

* * * *

Cora woke alone. She was pleasantly sore between her legs, but for the first time in what felt like forever, she didn't feel hot and achy. She looked around and didn't recognize the room she was in. "Zayn," she whispered. Fear snaked down her spine. Did he ship her off somewhere after they had sex?

She slipped out of the bed, wincing a little at the pain. A quick look around and she recognized some of Zayn's things. Slightly relieved that she wasn't in some stranger's home, but still disappointed to be alone, she tiptoed to the door. Again, the house seemed eerily quiet.

The door to the room she'd slept in was open, and she didn't see any sign of Zayn. She spied her bag and without thinking too hard, she quickly got dressed. She wasn't an idiot. Here was a man who didn't want her. However, when a woman comes on as hard as she did, he couldn't resist. What man would? So now he left and obviously wanted her gone. Heck, he hadn't even kissed her or even wanted to look at her when he fucked her. A sob escaped, but she shoved her fist in her mouth to keep the sound from being any louder. His words rang in her head like a dull knife to her heart. *I don't want you.* He'd thought she was sleeping when he'd come to check on her the first day. She wasn't his type he'd said to his brother, and she knew from the talk in town he liked voluptuous women on the taller size—the complete opposite of her.

There were two vehicles in the garage. The truck she remembered riding in and a huge motorcycle. She may hate herself right now, but she didn't have a death wish. Zayn kept the keys on a hook inside the garage. It was only a matter of grabbing a set that went to the truck, pushing a button on the inside to lift the bay doors, and she was driving out of his garage.

It wasn't stealing, just borrowing. She planned to leave him a message telling where he could pick his truck up, but he knew where she lived for crying out loud. Of course, she had no plans to be there when he did show up.

She didn't take time to go inside the clinic, thankful she had a bag of clothes and her purse along with her phone. She called Zayn thru his OnStar and left a brief message. "Thank you, technology." The switch of vehicles took less than ten minutes, just long enough for her to grab her car keys.

Even though she didn't think Zayn would come looking for her, she still wanted to get out of town as fast as her Charger would take her. She needed a day or two to lick her wounds, and then she'd come back and pretend nothing ever happened.

It's not like she and Zayn ran in the same circles. With that, she spun the fire-red car in a circle and headed out of town. Bike Week was in a few days and inevitably there were always an influx of injured pets that found their way to her clinic, not that she minded. It paid the bills, and she loved her job.

Still thinking of where to go, Cora crested the hill leading to Sturgis. The sun was high in the sky. She knew Zayn had probably realized she had left, had probably already heard her voicemail. "Good for him. Hopefully he had to walk all the way to pick his truck up."

The uncharacteristic meanness gave her pause. She had no way of finding out if he'd found his truck, but she reassured herself. It wasn't like Mystic River was huge. Barely containing the desire to turn her car around, she continued through town, past Deadwood, knowing she preferred to get a few more miles between her and Zayn. Licking wounds needed more than one town.

Her car Foxie did a little jerk and sputter, making Cora look at the digital dash to see the little sign that normally had hundreds of miles before empty. It said low fuel instead. She hadn't heard the annoying dinging with the music blasting. Foxie did another rabbit type of jump before shutting down in a very precarious place. The twisting road leading out of town had more winding turns as they led upwards without much of a side for stalled vehicles. She let her car coast the farthest that it would go. Pulling her cell out, she prayed there was service.

Cora reached breaking point when her phone beeped showing she did indeed have service, but then her phone died. "Noooooo," she screamed.

Jerking the door open, she pushed the trunk button. Inside she found a backpack along with the kit she always kept for emergencies. This was what she considered an emergency. She shoved a change of clothes from the duffel into the backpack along with the emergency kit. By her calculations, the hike up would be a lot further than the hike back down, or she could cut through the woods.

The story of Little Red Riding Hood popped into her head, only she had on a purple jacket. She was wasting time and knew it. "I'm more likely to kick the wolf in the nuts than be eaten by him, anyways. Besides, I obviously turn guys off." She rolled her eyes and shook her head.

She'd stick with the highway. Chances were good someone she knew would pass by, and she could hitch a ride, or she'd make it to Deadwood and get some gas for her car.

The sound of a wolf howling didn't usually scare Cora, but the one that sounded too close for comfort made her wish she'd stayed in her car. She glanced over her shoulder to see if she could see the red Charger, but she was a lot further away than she'd realized. The sun beat down on her head, only she feared if she took her sweatshirt off she'd get sunburned. Better to sweat than get burned.

Another howl split the air, closer than the last,

shivers danced up her spine.

She ran her tongue over her teeth. Did they feel sharper? Her skin itched, like something moved beneath the surface. "I'm losing my ever loving mind. Maybe it's heat stroke?" She stopped and pulled the bottle of water off the side of the pack. She drank sparingly and ran the somewhat cool bottle over her forehead.

The sound of something running full out in her direction had her spinning to look toward the woods.

With her hand on her chest, Cora held her breath and held perfectly still, like that would save her from whatever was coming. The sight of a cute little bunny scurrying through the underbrush made her giggle almost hysterically.

Cora walked on shaky legs to one of the huge boulders that lined the roadway, still laughing like a hyena. Leaning against it she wiped the sweat from her brow with her forearm.

"What do you find so amusing?"

Cora nearly fell off the rock at the deep voice rumbling behind her. "Jumping Jehoshaphat, don't scare me like that!"

"What do you call what you did to me, Cora? I come back from meeting with my brother to find you gone, my truck gone, and no word as to where you are," he growled. "What do you call that?" He moved to stand in front of Cora, both arms caging her in.

"I didn't think you'd notice, except for your truck...and I left you a message." She leaned backward, without actually lying back on the rock, trying to put some space between an obviously angry Zayn and herself.

"Oh, I noticed. I noticed a lot." He licked her neck, up to her earlobe to tug on it. An answering tug woke between her thighs.

"What are you doing?" She pressed her palms against his rock hard chest.

He leaned closer still with his body, erasing the small space between them. "Do you know how much I have fantasized about tasting you?" Zayn licked the seam of her lips and hummed.

"I think you should..." Whatever she was going to say was swallowed up by Zayn's questing mouth.

He fused his mouth over hers, brushing back and forth teasing her with soft caresses. He didn't just kiss her. He claimed her lips as his own. His hands cupped her face in his palms as he traced his tongue over her bottom lip.

For a split second he pulled away, making her

stiffen in his arms, but then he pressed his hips more firmly into the V of her legs and nipped her lip. She groaned a low keening sound she would've been embarrassed about making had she not been so turned on.

He dipped his tongue into her mouth, licking, sucking her tongue, kissing her like none other ever had as more wetness soaked her panties.

She met him passion for passion, sliding her fingers into his hair, down his back to cup his ass. The denim rode low on his hips, making it easy to slide her hands under the waist band to the firm globes she wanted to bite. She dragged her nails back up. Pushing her pelvis up into his, the hard press of his cock provided a warm pressure against her sex. The pulsing organ in his pants thumped a steady beat against her, reminding her of the sensation of having him inside her.

The sound of a horn blaring had Zayn lifting up with a deep rumbling growl.

"What the—" Cora stumbled over her words. She licked her swollen lips, ready to orgasm from his kiss alone. To say the man could kiss was a major understatement.

Zayn had his back to her facing the highway and

whoever had honked. She sat up realizing her sweatshirt had been raised at some point in their heavy petting session.

"I'll be right back. Don't move." His warm breath fanned over her lips as he gave her a brief kiss.

Cora lifted her hand to her mouth. She really needed to stop being such a hussy when it came to Zayn Malik. She snorted.

"Why are you laughing, my mate?" Zayn walked back and reached out to help her off the boulder.

She ignored his words and took his outstretched hand. "Do you know them?" She indicated the jeep on the other side of the road.

"They belong to another...family. They've offered us a ride back to town."

"Oh, that's great. Why are we waiting?" Cora looked at the idling jeep. Two men who looked to be as big as Zayn stared at her and Zayn with smiles on their faces. "Come on, big guy. I'm hot and tired. The faster we get gas for Foxie, the faster I can get my car back on the road."

"Who is Foxie?"

Zayn looked so cute when he had that puzzled look on his face, Cora couldn't help but grab his shirt and pull him down for another fierce kiss.

"She's my car. Come on, big guy, let's go." Cora grabbed his hand and led him across the road.

Chapter Four

Zayn didn't like the way those from the other pack was looking at his mate. He knew his scent was all over Cora and was glad they'd made out like they had. The fact she still had no clue what he was, what she was, burned like acid in his stomach. To top it off, he had two of the biggest assholes this side of the Black Hills who turned up to be their saviors. *Great.*

There was no other choice except to gracefully accept their help, or make his already overheated mate walk the long trip back to town or teach her how to shift.

His mate made their decision, marching across the road, dragging him along in her wake. Lust rode him hard, jealousy a close second as they got closer, and he saw the unmistakable want reflected in the other men's eyes.

"Was that your beauty broken down up the road there, gorgeous?" the driver asked Cora, completely ignoring Zayn.

"Um, yeah...I completely spaced getting gas when we headed out for a drive."

Zayn fell a little more in love with his mate for including him on her impromptu trip and for not stumbling in her lie. Shifters could smell a lie a mile away, and even he believed what she said.

"You need to take better care of your woman, or someone else will," the passenger said.

Zayn knew his name was Tom, but refused to acknowledge him or his taunt. He'd lived long enough to know the other man was trying to get a rise out of him. Zayn helped Cora into the back of the open topped jeep, blocking the other man's view of his mate's incredibly fine behind in the process. The growl from the front was music to his ears.

Hatred burned in the eyes staring at him through the rearview mirror. He met the flinty look with one of his own. The other man was the first to turn away, showing him his profile. Tom hopped in and crossed his arms over his chest with utter disdain etched on his features. Both men could kick rocks for all Zayn cared.

Cora seemed unaware of the undercurrents running between the three shifters in the vehicle. "Could you please just drop us at the Circle C station?"

"We can wait and give you a lift back."

"My brother should be there within a few minutes of our arrival. We appreciate your offer, and your generosity." It took every ounce of control for Zayn not to the growl words.

Cora turned to him. "How does Niall know where we're going to be?"

He held his phone up, careful not to show her the screen and the no signal. As wolves they were able to communicate, even at a distance. He knew once she started thinking, she'd wonder how he came to be near where she'd ran out of gas. He just hoped they'd be somewhere private he could explain about her new abilities.

That place wasn't going to be in the backseat of another pack's jeep and certainly not on the side of the road.

"Very convenient," Tom answered with a smirk.

"Isn't it though?" Zayn said with a bite in his voice. The two in the front of the jeep were not high in the hierarchy of their pack, unlike Zayn who was second in command of the Mystic River pack.

"Hey, gorgeous, when you want a real man, all you gotta do is come on up to Whitewood. We always make sure our women are taken care of."

She shook her head. "Are you hitting on me?"

"Why yeah, I was," Tom chuckled.

"Shut up, Tom," Zayn growled.

"You mad I asked first, Al?"

"I don't have a death wish, Tom," Al muttered.

The other man ignored Zayn's warning even knowing Cora was Zayn's mate. By asking her out, Tom had just challenged Zayn. Wanting to answer the challenge, Zayn's claws threatened to burst from his fingers, and his gums ached with the urge to allow his fangs freedom to rip Tom's throat out.

"Sorry, I'm not interested." Cora placed her hand on Zayn's thigh.

She diffused some of his tension, though not enough to save Tom. The pup in front of him had signed his death certificate when he asked Cora out. The Mystic River pack had an agreement with the other packs in the area. They didn't encroach on each other's territories and all was well. If you had to pass through lands that were not your own, you let the alpha know and didn't disturb what wasn't yours. He'd been doing a lot more than passing through their territories.

Heads up, Niall. Tom from the Whitewood Pack just challenged me for Cora.

What the fuck. Are you sure? Maybe it's just the

newly mated hormones, Zayn. Let me handle this. Niall's tone was completely calm.

Niall, there is no mistake. My scent is all over her, and she wears my mark any shifter with eyes can see. Nor did I mishear. He asked her out in front of me.

Don't do anything rash. Let me talk with his alpha. He's a pup. Nothing.

Zayn cut the connection to concentrate on the road ahead. He could see the town in front of them and didn't trust Tom or the other man not to do something stupid.

The sight of Niall, along with several other pack members standing next to Zayn and Niall's trucks, made the driver of the jeep clench the steering wheel. Zayn wasn't sure why the two in front didn't expect his pack to have his back, or why they thought he wouldn't have contacted Niall as soon as he got in their vehicle. That was the way of his pack. He shook his head. Maybe their pack didn't speak with the lower ranked members the way the Mystic River pack did. Whatever. What they did or didn't do as a pack wasn't his problem. Only Tom, at the moment, was. However, he'd allow his brother to speak with the alpha first to set up the challenge.

"Thanks for the ride, Al. Let your boss know we'll be in touch." Zayn kept the sneer out of his voice by sheer force of will. When he turned to Tom, the pup had the audacity to meet his eyes. He had a yellowish cast to the whites of his eyes which concerned Zayn. He wondered if maybe Tom was on drugs. Al turned to face him with the same tinge of yellow in his eyes.

He wasted no time hopping out of the vehicle, lifted Cora out, keeping his body between Tom and Cora's. Drugs, to humans, were toxic. To a shifter they were deadly to all involved.

"See you around, Cora." Tom leaned one hand out the window. His parting words ringing out the window, their tires left marks on the pavement as they sped off.

"Oh, goody. I can hook up with creepy dude up the road." Cora shuddered.

Zayn all but roared. "The only dude you'll be hooking up with is me!"

Cora jumped back. "Are you trying to scare the crap out of me?"

Zayn raked his hand through his hair, staring at her where she stood, next to his brother near his truck. What does that say about him, that he's scaring his own mate?

It says your emotions are high, and you need to chill.

His composure recovered with a few deep breaths. Zayn held his hand out to Cora in a placating gesture. “Forgive me, Cora. When I came home and found you gone, I lost it. I’m sorry.” He hung his head. Cora may not understand the meaning of the move, but his pack did.

“Well, since you happened by when I needed someone…which is something I’ve been thinking about. How did you happen to be in the woods there anyway?”

Cora watched him with eyes too smart for her own good. Niall saved him from answering with half-truths. “We were out trail riding, scouting to see if we could find more traps.”

The four-wheeler in the back of Niall’s truck added an element of truth. They had sent half the pack out looking for more traps, but when Zayn had found Cora gone, he’d shifted and sent a call out for help in finding his mate. Had she not run out of gas, he feared he’d not have found her. His gut twisted, but he pushed it aside.

“Niall, can I get a ride back to my car? I stupidly let her run out of gas.”

Zayn saw red. Cora was new to their world. He knew that, but he still couldn't control his wolf. He grabbed her arm and set her behind him, showing his fangs. His voice came out a deep rumbling growl. "She's mine."

"I'm conscious of who she is, Zayn. You need to get control, now." Niall brooked no argument.

Zayn shook his head, aware he was being completely unreasonable.

"Are you hell bent on being an asshat?" Cora tried to step around Zayn.

"Maybe. Or possibly I'm just hell bent on shooting myself in the foot. I think I may have foot in mouth disease. Do you think you could cure me?" Zayn turned to wrap Cora in his arms. He gave into the urge to sample her lips. They'd become a new obsession, one he had no desire to resist.

He bent his head and brushed his mouth across hers, sipped at the corner of her lips. She'd applied some type of lip balm on the drive down, but he preferred Cora's natural flavor. Zayn traced the seam of her lips with his tongue, dipped inside, swallowing the shaky sigh she made.

"I think I could cure you of that disease with my fist, but only if you two disengage said mouths.

You're drawing a crowd." Niall indicated his truck. "Why don't you both ride with me, and Jett can drive your truck back to your house, Zayn?"

Next to Niall, Jett was Zayn's best friend. They'd come to Mystic River together years ago. Growing up they'd called themselves the three amigos and had stayed as close as three brothers, even though Jett was no relation. Jett had a way of looking at a woman that said he knew every dirty way to make a woman come and could do it in under ten minutes, and if you were one of the lucky ones, he'd be glad to demonstrate it for you. Of course he wasn't too discriminating. He said he liked to make the ladies happy, and the piercing on his tongue helped, or so Jett said.

"I'll take your girl, and by girl I mean your truck. Keep your shit level, man." Jett flashed his pearly whites, hands raised in a placating gesture.

Cora cocked an eyebrow at him, a flush covering her cheeks. Zayn didn't miss the fact her hands still gripped his arms or that her tongue darted out to lick at her lips.

That's a win for him.

He held her gaze, her face turned up to his. "Can we get my car before something happens to her, please?" She blinked up at him.

He was so screwed.

"Ahh, and...just like that it's happened." Jett snickered.

Zayn lifted his hand and flicked Jett the middle finger. "Let's go, luv." He tapped her on the tip of her nose with his index finger.

The way her eyes widened at the endearment made his solar plexus ache. He may not have wanted a mate, but what he had was a beautiful woman he was proud to call his.

His mate's smile stretched wider.

With ease he lifted his mate—and didn't he love that word more with each passing moment—into his brother's truck. He didn't even mind that she was in the middle of the front bench seat, especially when she scooted closer to his side.

By the time they'd reached the place she'd left her car and filled it with the fuel his brother had brought along, he was harder than he could remember being, ever. The more than hour drive back to Mystic was going to be the longest of his life.

Cora thanked his brother who waved her thanks away with 'you're family,' which made heat fill her cheeks. Admittedly, Zayn didn't know much about

Cora's family, something he planned to rectify soon.

They watched Niall pull away, executing a U-turn with a salute as he drove off at a sedate pace.

"Can we go back to my place? There are things I need to talk to you about, things you need to understand. I'm sorry for the way I treated you, for making you run." Zayn backed Cora against the driver's door of her car. He knew he could be risking bodily injury with his arms braced on either side of her head, his legs outside hers, but he wanted to inhale her scent, wanted to be as close to her as possible.

She dropped her gaze to his waist, her eyes jumping back to his face.

He shook his head, knowing she couldn't miss the evidence of his arousal. Hell, all he had to do was be within sniffing distance and he was hard. "Ignore him."

She snorted. "Kinda hard, pun intended."

Zayn planned to at least get them to his place before he mauled her again, but his body had other plans. His head descended, crushing her lips with his. She whimpered, digging her hands into his back pockets as she opened up to him without hesitation.

The unmistakable sound of a V-twin engine

broke through the lust filled fog, bringing him back to their surroundings. He pushed away breathing heavily.

"Woman, you need to get in the car before I lose all sense of where we are and fuck you where we stand."

Her tongue swept out to lick at her mouth, almost making him lose his last bit of control. She fumbled with the door handle and stumbled into the driver's seat. Her eyes never left his, like she was afraid of the big bad wolf, which gave him the extra push to gather more control before he did something he'd regret, like screw his mate for any and all to see on the side of the road.

The deft way she handled her car impressed Zayn. He loved muscle cars, especially the older models and hadn't been in the newer versions until now. Although he still preferred the originals, he was glad Cora had chosen one with speed. It made the drive back to his house a lot quicker than if she'd driven something more compact, something that would've made the drive take a lot longer than he wanted.

They spent the drive talking about their likes and dislikes. He found she had an eclectic choice of music, just like him, although they both despised the twangy country songs and couldn't stand the popular pop music. Neither could choose which version of *Turn The Page*, either by Bob Seger or Metallica they liked best, because they felt they both were awesome. They both loved pasta in all its forms and agreed it was better the next day, and she hated slasher movies just like him, but loved action movies. Of course when she said, depending on what movie she was watching, her "hubby" changed. He asked for clarification.

That was when he decided he was firmly a romantic comedy type of guy. No way in hell was his mate going to sit next to him and pretend she was married to Riddick or The Rock. Then the other shoe dropped. They were never watching anything except animated films. He could compete with animation he'd declared, which caused his mate to laugh like a hyena and almost caused them to wreck.

By the time Foxie rumbled into his drive he was completely in love with his accidental mate. He just had to figure out how to explain to her what he was. What she now was. Easy, right?

He sat back in the leather seat and exhaled a loud sigh.

She unbuckled and turned in her seat to look at him. "Okay. So spill."

"Not here. Inside." He gave her his best boy scout grin.

"Does that look usually get you what you want?" Laughter lit up her face.

"Is it working?" Her unique scent mixed with the spiced apple lotion she wore had his mouth watering.

Cora blinked. "Your eyes are like glowing...and it's not th...the sun."

"No," he answered. There could be no lies between them. "Please come inside. I will tell you...show you everything." He reached over and took the keys out of the ignition, but instead of pocketing them he held them out to her. Trust was something earned.

Her hand hovered over his, and then she surprised him by curling his fingers over the keys.

"That's my girl," he murmured, kissing her knuckles.

Once inside his house, he wasn't sure where to start.

"Would you like a drink?" At her nod, he went to the fridge and pulled out a bottle of water for them both. After their discussion, he may need to hit the hard stuff, but he'd save that for later.

"Why don't you just spit it out? It can't be worse than what I'm thinking. I mean you can't be a vampire, cause you've been out in the daylight." She turned to face him, the bottle of water gripped tightly in her fist.

"What!" he exploded.

She jumped nearly dropping her drink, but Zayn was there to catch it, jerking her into his body. "You thought I was a bloodsucker?' He laughed, caught the fist holding the bottle before it connected with his stomach. "Oh, luv, I'm no bloodsucker. I'm...let's go into the living room where we can be more comfortable. I promise to explain everything."

At Cora's nod against his chest, he lifted her chin with his index finger. "Everything will be fine. I promise." Because he couldn't help himself, he brushed his mouth over hers.

Lacing their fingers, he led her into the living room with the leather sectional where he'd made love to Cora for the first time.

Sitting on the edge, she looked so small.

Instead of prevaricating or mincing his words, he figured he'd just get them out. Taking a deep breath he squatted down on his haunches. "What I'm about to tell you is going to sound crazy, and you're not going to believe me, but I want you to let me finish before you say anything. I will prove it to you after I'm done. Again, I'm going to need you to trust me. You will want to scream, maybe even run. Above everything else you believe, you must trust that I will never, ever hurt you, or allow anything or anyone to hurt you. Do you think you can trust me?"

"You're really scaring me. Why don't you just say it and get it over with. Kind of like a band aid. If you just rip it off, it hurts a lot less than if you ease it off."

He let out a wry chuckle. "Damn, I love you. Okay. I'm a werewolf. My nephew bit you first by accident and then I did, which in turn has made you one of us. I'd say I was sorry, but honestly, baby, I'm not. I'm sorry I...Fuck!" Zayn choked. His breath wheezed out in a gasp as he fell on his ass with a pissed off she-wolf standing over him.

"I asked you for the truth, and you make up some lame ass story. Well piss off."

Zayn pressed a palm to his chest. "Wow, you pack a punch." With his free hand he grabbed onto one of Cora's ankles when she tried to step over him. "I can prove it to you. Just give me a minute to catch my breath." She obviously had no clue that as a new shifter her strength was increased.

Uncertainty flashed in her eyes. Doubt clouded her beautiful features, tension in her body never lessoned, but she nodded.

"Will you sit back down?" He didn't let go of her ankle.

Exasperation flickered over her face. With a huff she sat, caught her bottom lip with her teeth and had her eyebrows drawn into a deep frown that Zayn wanted to erase.

He stood in a fluid motion.

The magic that allowed them to shift also gave them the ability to do so with or without their clothes on. Usually when they knew they were going to shift they removed their clothes, not because they needed to in order to shift, but because it was freeing. As a wolf, they didn't need clothes, so when they became their wolf, the clothes just disappeared. When they returned to their human form, whatever they had on before the shift is how they returned. He had never questioned how or why, it just was. For as long as shifters had existed, that had been the way it was. Though he wasn't sure if that was the way it would be for a human made shifter. Cora was his first. He really needed to speak to the elders or Niall.

Cora's gaze locked with his, as if telling him to get on with it.

He let the magic pour over him, keeping his gaze locked with his mates.

A shriek, loud enough to wake the dead, flew from Cora as she threw herself backward on the couch. He opened his mind to hers, another benefit of being a shifter, hoping to calm her fears. *Cora, calm down, honey. It's me, Zayn. I'll never hurt you. I asked you to trust me, remember?*

Her eyes bugged, and the smell of her fear overwhelmed to his senses.

"How are you talking to me?" she demanded.

The same as you can now. As a shifter we can communicate telepathically in either form. Do you want me to shift back?

She sucked in a swift breath, straightened from the sofa, and reached out her hand to touch his head.

He lowered his head to rest on her thighs.

"So, are you saying I can do that too?"

Yes. If she kept scratching him the way she was he was sure he'd roll over like a domesticated pet and beg for her to rub his stomach.

"How?"

He scooted back, missing her touch immediately.

With ease, he shifted back to his human form.

It was hard not to jump his mate and make her forget, for a little while at least, what he knew she needed to know.

Zayn gave her an abbreviated description of shifters and how he and his brother, along with Jett had come to Mystic. The compassion she couldn't hide for his nephew made him all the more happy that she was his mate. Being born a shifter from two parents who were shifters, he wasn't sure what to expect for one who was accidentally turned.

"So where are your parents now? I thought wolves were pack animals?"

A genuine smile crossed his face. "They are pack animals. We are pack animals. My parents are still with their pack, our old pack. I don't know how to explain it. We were restless, Niall, Jett, and I. There just didn't seem a place in the pack for us." He shrugged his shoulders.

* * * *

"So do I have to wait till the full moon and then, you know, like turn all furry?" Cora tried to make light of the situation, when inside she was a little freaked. Okay a whole lot freaked out.

Zayn grinned. "We don't need the moon, full or not. All you need to do is picture your wolf in your mind."

She wasn't ready. The thought that her...boyfriend—or whatever he was—turned into a wolf was enough to take in at the moment, thank you. She had a thousand other questions that needed answered. "How do you know I'm one, if you haven't ever met a human who was, you know, bitten or whatever? How do you know I don't need to be naked? And why do you call me mate? And what does this mean for me and my life?" The questions swirling around in her mind frightened her.

"Hey, calm down. Listen to me. I know that humans have been turned and are fine. Our life expectancy is longer than the average human. No, we are not immortal. We don't live for hundreds of years without aging. Our oldest elder is a hundred and fifty-one, but don't quote me on that. We can go see him and his mate. They will have answers to your questions. If they don't, we will find someone who does. As for mate, you are it for me. Don't you feel it? It's an unmistakable pull with a scent only a mate has."

She sniffed. "Are you saying I smell?"

Cora wasn't sure if she should knee him in the nuts, push him away, or pull him closer. Now that he'd mentioned it, he did smell really good. Truth be told, no other man she'd met, before or after she'd made love with Zayn, had done anything for her. Although in her defense, she hadn't really dated anyone after college. The need for Zayn was a little disturbing, a compulsion that was far beyond what was natural, or what used to be normal for her.

"I'm saying that when a shifter finds his or her mate, nature lets them know by their scent. I was confused because when I first scented you I wanted you, but you were human. Hell, want is too tame a word."

"And you didn't want a skinny human." She had little doubt he regretted his words.

"Oh, baby, I was running scared. I didn't mean it. You're the perfect mate for me. I'm the one who doesn't deserve you, and I will work for the rest of my life to make it up to you."

She was drawn to him, whether it was because of the shifter thing or not. She steeled herself against her heart's reaction to his impassioned speech, pulled in a deep breath, and waved a hand between the two of them as she spoke. "I need some time to digest all this."

He nodded, sadness and resignation etched on his handsome features.

"I understand. I was supposed to work at Chaps tonight, but I got Jett to take my shift. That's the bar we own in Sturgis. The weeks leading up to Bike Week can get pretty crazy. We all try to be on hand, but I was going to stay here and help you adjust."

She swallowed the lump in her throat. He was giving her space. "I think you should work, and I'll go home—back to the clinic and get some rest," she corrected. "Catch up on some...laundry and stuff."

"Yeah, okay. I'll follow you home. Make sure you get there safe."

"You don't have to do that."

"Don't argue, baby. I'll just follow you even if you protest." He leaned down and rested his forehead on hers. "Damn, I'm sorry I fucked up."

God, she wanted to wrap her arms around him and tell him everything was okay, that she'd stay, but she needed time to deal with everything. "You didn't fuck up. I just need time to process. When the bar closes, why don't you call me? If I'm still up, maybe you can stop by."

His eyes, which had been closed until that moment, popped open. The electric blue that had scared her a few hours earlier made her heart beat faster for a whole other reason now. She wondered if her eyes would change color too. Then she thought of Jett and his black eyes and realized that would be an absurd thing, or would it? More unanswered questions.

Chapter Five

Zayn looked at the clock behind the bar again, wishing all the people in the place would just go for fuck's sake.

"You know if you keep looking at everyone like that, you're either going to scare the shit out of them, incite a riot, or entice the ladies to drop their panties. I'm all for options one and three, not so much for number two. Why don't you take your scowling self on home? You're not doing us any good the way you are." Jett slid a beer across to another customer.

He knew his best friend was right, but Zayn didn't want to look like a whipped pup. He mixed another Jack and coke, popped the cap off two more beers before handing them off to one of their waitresses. All the waitresses wore leather chaps and leather vests as part of their uniforms. What they wore underneath was their choice. Most of the ladies chose to wear a pair of boy short briefs, but some of the more adventurous went for a thong. In the past Zayn had loved to watch them as they walked away. Now, he only wanted to watch one woman, and she wasn't here.

Diane, one of their veteran waitresses, sidled up to the bar with a sweet smile on her face until she locked eyes with Zayn. He tried to temper his emotions, obviously failing when she side-stepped to place her order with Jett instead of him.

"Maybe you're right," he conceded, filling two mugs with draft beer for Jett. It was getting harder not to growl at some of the customers. A niggling fear for his mate had the hair at the back of his neck standing on end. With their mating being so new, he wasn't sure if he could connect with her so far away, but he had to try.

"I'm going to go out back and see if I can't reach her. Can you handle this?" He indicated the bar. Jett nodded, making Zayn exhale before he called Teal over to help out.

Once outside, he breathed a little easier. Even knowing it might be impossible, he opened his senses and searched for the mating bond to Cora. The trail was faint but there nonetheless.

Cora, are you okay?

There's something not right, Zayn.

What do you mean, baby?

I hear howling, but it's scary. Not like...I don't

know how to explain it, but not like you or family.

Is there a safe place in your clinic you can hide till I can get there? Even as he spoke he was climbing on his Harley. He feared it was the wolves from the Whitewood Pack, but didn't want to scare her even more.

There's an old walk-in freezer that I've never used.

Go in there. Can you lock it? Zayn could hear her fear even through the miles separating them.

No...Oh God, I'm inside. There's no light.

Zayn did his best to stay calm, knowing his next instructions were going to be the hardest he'd ever given. He linked with Niall while he was talking with Cora, hoping his brother who was closer could reach her in time.

Cora, I need you to listen very carefully to what I'm about to say. The shifters that come in there aren't friends of mine. If they were, I'd know about it, and they wouldn't be there. That can mean only one thing. Zayn took a calming breath. *Honey, they are there to take you. I want you to go with them. Don't fight, even when that's what your instincts scream at you to do. A wolf loves a fight. Don't run. That's like waving a red flag at a bull. Do you understand what I'm saying to you?*

The silence that greeted him had his heart nearly stopping in his chest.

You want me to just go with them like a sheep to slaughter?

His breath burst from his lungs, reminding him he needed to breathe, or he'd pass out and be no use to Cora. *I'm saying I need you to live, so I can find you and kill the sons of bitches who dared to take what's mine.*

What if...what if they r-ra... She didn't continue, but Zayn knew what she was asking.

Cora, I will love you no matter what happens. I just need you alive. Don't shift. Don't fight. Please, baby. I'm on my way. Niall is on his way.

I'll try. I can hear them in the clinic. Panic laced her voice.

Keep our link open. Don't shut me out. Zayn put as much authority into his tone without scaring her as he could.

I don't even know how we are doing this.

Her fear was almost overwhelming him. *All you have to do is think about a line that goes directly to me and talk to me.*

I hear scratching at the door. I'm so scared,

Zayn.

The scream that filled his head was one he'd hear for the rest of his life. The lost connection to his mate was even worse. No matter how many times he yelled for her through their bond, he kept hitting a wall. Thankfully, the link wasn't severed so he knew she was alive, which meant she was unable to contact him because she was still too new, or she was incapacitated. Neither possibility made him happy.

Niall, how close are you to Cora's clinic? A lump the size of a golf ball was lodged in Zayn's throat.

Almost there, I rounded up several other pack members, but didn't want to leave the cubs unprotected.

Although he wanted everyone racing to save his mate, he also understood Niall had to protect the rest of the pack too.

I'm still a good thirty minutes away. That chafed Zayn's ass. He should've insisted on staying with Cora or had her come with him to the bar. Anything other than leaving her alone and at the mercy of other shifters to do whatever they planned to do to her.

You need to stay focused, bro. If you lose your head and get yourself killed before you get here, you won't be able to help find her. I don't know her scent as well as you.

The surge of alpha power whipped across their bond as if his brother was standing in front of him, instead of miles away. Zayn was never so glad to have Niall with him as he was then.

It usually took over an hour to get from Mystic into Sturgis, a drive he normally loved, but with his mate in trouble he cursed every mile. He kept his senses open for danger along the long winding road, while keeping his mind open in case Cora tried to contact him.

When Niall reached her clinic and found it empty but trashed and relayed it all to Zayn, he pushed the gas on his custom Harley to the limit without any thought to his own safety. If he lost his Cora, he would gladly go to the other side to be with her. His brother Niall had Nolan to live for. Without Cora, Zayn had nothing.

By the time his Harley crested the last hill to the clinic, he was having problems keeping his beast in check. The scent of Cora's fear rushed him within seconds of him pushing the kickstand down on the bike. His senses were more acute in wolf form, and he allowed the change to take him without a second's hesitation.

Niall, along with four other pack members, stood in their shifted forms. All were waiting for Zayn to catch his bearings and lead the way.

He let his nose sift through all the different smells, zeroing in on the one scent he most wanted to find. The cloying scent of one of the men he recognized as Tom overlaid Cora's. All around the building he was able to differentiate over four other shifters. Meaning five shifters had been there, five men he would have to kill. The scents shifted and left three different trails leading away from the building.

Niall, Torq, and Bronx waited for Zayn to point out which trail to follow. Afraid that the other wolves had done a bait and switch, Zayn decided they should split up. He'd follow the one with Cora's scent, and his pack mates would follow the two other trails.

At the last moment, he reminded them of the traps that had injured Nolan. The possibility that there were still more out there waiting for a victim, or a wolf, made his hackles rise. While the cub had escaped without real injury, the adult wolves wouldn't. Upon further inspection of the trap, Niall had found it wasn't an ordinary trap, but one with a silver core, meant to kill werewolves. Luckily they could scent silver if they knew to look out for it.

Each group turned in opposite directions, taking the other trails.

Zayn kept his nose and senses on Cora's scent, kept calling out to his mate to answer him. He came to an abrupt halt. The tiny almost nonexistent whisper of sound off to his left had his hackles rising. He dropped into a crouch, ready to pounce.

Paul, a member of their pack, stalked into the underbrush. *You were right. The trail led back into a circle this way. They tried to fake us out.*

Zayn reached out to Niall. *Did you send Paul out to search for Cora?*

No. Paul was supposed to be helping watch the cubs.

He's here pretending you sent him. I'm going to allow him to think I believe him and see what he does.

Zayn fed him a line of bullshit, hoping he was in turn relaying it to the bastards who had his woman, hoping it would buy them more time. *Thank you, Paul. I appreciate your help. I'm fucked in the head, thinking what could be happening to my mate right now. She can't even shift.*

I'd be the same way, man. You lead the way,

and I'll follow you.

Now that he was really listening, he could hear the sneer in Paul's voice. Paul had a thing for Niall's mate Emma before Niall came along, even though she hadn't returned the feelings. When Niall and his brother came to Mystic with Jett, Paul and several other pack members had tried to scare them away, which was normal in shifter societies. They'd challenged, all three of them, Niall, Zayn, and Jett in not so fair fights, and lost each time. Again, it was normal in their world. Niall had to prove he was alpha enough to be mated to the previous alpha's only daughter. He was.

Up until that moment, Paul had never shown any signs of not being satisfied with Niall being the alpha. Never did Zayn think Paul, or any other member of the Mystic pack, would ever harm a woman or child considered part of their pack. Now, he had to wonder if others from his pack were part of the attempt on Nolan's life, and who else he was going to find holding his mate who were part of his pack too.

Gods, this was going to kill Emerson and Payton. They loved each and every man, woman, and child like their own flesh and blood.

Zayn blocked his thoughts from Paul, other than

showing the man a mass of confusion. The other man on the other hand, didn't have the same control, and Zayn picked up his sense of triumph. Zayn wanted to turn around and rip out the man's throat. Unsure what kind of connection Paul had with the other pack was the only reason Zayne didn't follow through on the impulse. A loss of life could alert the ones who had Cora that Zayn was onto them.

Once he had Cora safely in his sights, all bets were off, and the first he'd kill would be who was closest to Cora, followed by Tom.

* * * *

Cora's stomach rolled. Being hit over the head with what felt like a sledge hammer and then waking up, face down over the shoulder of some stranger did that to a person. She swallowed bile for the hundredth time. The last thing she wanted to do was throw up all over his ass, unsure if he'd hit her again or kill her. The man jumped over something, jarring her more, and she gave up the pretense.

"Oh, God, I'm gonna be sick." Hot tears poured from her eyes.

He either didn't hear or didn't care until she

gagged and everything she'd consumed moved up her stomach.

"You fucking bitch," Tom roared, throwing her off his shoulder.

She closed her eyes, landing with a sickening crunch on the hard ground, too undone to pretend indifference. The kick to her side made her curl into a ball, a whimper of pain escaped before she could call it back.

"Don't kill the bitch, Tom. She's worthless to us dead."

Cora cracked one eye open to see who the other man was. He had a scar that ran down one side of his face, and the same yellowish tinge to Tom's eyes also burned in his. She didn't recognize him from Mystic.

"She threw up all over me," Tom whined.

If she wasn't in such a dire situation, she'd laugh at his cry baby voice. She thought back to her time with Zayn. How he'd told her he loved her. With shifters maybe it was instinctual, or whatever, but now she wished she'd told him she really felt deeply for him. She wasn't sure if it was love, but she wanted to find out. All they needed was time. It wasn't fair that just when she found someone to love her, her world was tilted on its axis and destruction was left in its wake, again. Life wasn't fair.

Her first thought was to get up and run, or fight. Zayn said those were two of the worst things she could do around shifters, and he would know. She trusted him with her life. With her heart though was a whole different thing.

She kept her eyes closed trying to get control of her raging heartbeat. Knowing they could hear her every breath, she didn't want them to aware she was scared shit-less. She pretended to be asleep or knocked unconscious, when the man with the scar came to check on her. Even when his hands touched her breasts, Cora didn't make a noise. Not even when he grabbed one of her nipples and twisted, so hard she was sure he was going to rip it off, did she make a sound of protest. She centered herself with deep breaths.

You're doing so good, Cora. When I get there I will make that man pay. This I promise you.

She focused on Zayn's soothing voice without responding other than sending him thoughts of needing him.

"How hard did you hit her anyway, dickweed? If we can't get her to wake up and give us the information we need, she's going to be utterly useless to the boss."

"Fuck off, Shane. She'll be fine once we get her back to our pack."

If Zayn didn't get to her before they reached wherever they planned to rendezvous, she'd be damned before she'd go meekly where they took her. She wouldn't sacrifice herself, her body, or mind for anything. She knew what she could take and what she couldn't. A beating, yes, but a violation of her body? No. Even if Zayn said he would still love her, she didn't think she could love herself.

Don't think like that, baby. I'm going to get to you before that ever happens.

Zayn, I will hang on and do as you've asked, but I will not sit or lay idly by while they do whatever they choose, if it comes to that. You have to understand. I just can't. Grief for what might be welled in her heart as she imagined being raped by these beasts. She couldn't let it happen, but how could she stop it? How soon before Zayn found her? How much time did she have before they began moving again?

"Did you hear that, Shane?" Tom asked.

"I had the other guys spread out to lead the pack, should they try to follow, in other directions. This is our meeting place. You need to calm down."

Cora watched Shane pass what looked like a hand rolled cigarette to Tom. The sound of a lighter being lit and then the unmistakable sound of someone inhaling were overly loud in the quiet night. A scent that reminded her of the last time she'd been to her dad's house drifted through the air.

Son of a bitch. Shifters on drugs? What did that mean for her? For Zayn and his pack?

Zayn, Tom and some guy named Shane have me and are doing drugs. I'm pretending to be knocked out, but...shit. Men on drugs do messed up things. What about shifters?

I noticed something was off when they picked us up. Just try to not catch their attention. I think I'm close. Your scent is stronger.

What Cora hadn't noticed was how close to the road they were. The sound of a vehicle pulling into the clearing sent alarm down Cora's spine. The doors to the large van slammed open with several men jumping out, shouting orders at her two captors. She went against all her natural instincts and lay like a doll, pretending sleep. Even though it was against the grain, she knew it was the right choice.

What's happening?

Zayn's frantic voice calmed her, gave her a focal point inside her mind. *We must be by a road. There's a white van that just pulled in, and now we are being loaded into the van.* She shuddered as one of the men who picked her up took advantage of her supposedly incapacitated state to reach between her legs to grope.

I want you to find out his name too, baby. He will be another that I plan to kill with my bare fucking hands.

This time she shuddered for another reason.

"Hey, I think the little bitch might be coming around. She's shaking a little."

"You better watch out, Bart. She tends to throw up on men who carry her." Shane laughed.

She wanted to punch Shane in the throat after she kicked the one named Bart in the nuts. After Shane's words, Bart dumped her in the back of the van inside a cage made for animals, uncaring if he hurt her. He sniggered when she moaned, but she didn't allow any other sound to escape. No way in hell was she going to give them any more entertainment if she could help it.

"Did you lock the cage, Bart?"

"Nah, the bitch is out for the count. What did you

do, fuck her silly?" Bart's voice held way too much glee.

"I like my women conscious, you sick bastard," Shane said.

"You can't get a conscious woman," Bart sneered.

"Shut the fuck up both of you. We ain't got time for your bullshit. We are right in the middle of their territory. Did your boy lay out the traps like he was supposed to?"

Cora wasn't sure who the newest speaker was, but his voice alone scared her. The deep baritone sounded like he'd been gargling with sandpaper.

"He said he laid them all around their borders, but—" Tom stopped.

"Spit it the fuck out, boy. I ain't got all night."

"I guess a young cub, the alpha's boy, got caught in one. I don't know how many they found."

A roar split the air. Several windows in the van shattered. If Cora had been closer to the one who did the roaring, she was sure she would have peed her pants. As it was she trembled in the cage.

"Well, I guess that's one way to get rid of some excess baggage." Shane said.

"Keep it up and you're next."

"Sorry, Keith. I'd say that Paul—he's our inside

guy—would know how many traps they might have found. Once we reach our territory, I'll try reaching him."

Cora listened to Shane placate the other man named Keith who was obviously in charge.

Zayn, the van is moving, and they said they had a guy named Paul who was inside, whatever that means.

Paul is with me and a member of our pack, he growled.

Are you okay?

She didn't know what she'd do if he wasn't all right.

I already figured out that Paul was a traitorous bastard. Niall is following the van and we've got eyes and vehicles on the road waiting to see where they take you. Relax. I'm fine.

She wanted to laugh at his command, and she had no doubt it was a command.

Are you laughing at me? Do you know what happens when a mate laughs at her mate? He paused, his voice sounding huskier in her head as he said, *They get lucky.*

Locked in a cage, being driven off to some hell hole with a bunch of drug addicted shifters and she really wanted to find out what he would do to her. The only thing that kept her from imagining what he would do to her was the knowledge that the shifters up front had an amazing sense of smell, and they'd think it was an open invitation.

I'll hold you to that, Zayn, but I'm really scared. The one named Keith is really, really scary. I mean like he sounds like Freddy Kruger type scary.

Zayn tried to cut off his thoughts, but she caught the flash of fear.

Who is he? What is he? Knowledge is power, Zayn.

I need to share this with Niall, baby. I won't keep anything from you. I promise.

A huge leap of faith is what it took for her to say the next three words. *I trust you.*

The van picked up speed, taking her farther away from where she knew Zayn was.

Thank you, Cora.

She was still reeling from the hit to the head and tossed to the ground. Now being thrown around in the back of the van, it was all she could do not to throw up all over herself. That was one reason she'd never been on a cruise before. She knew she wouldn't make it even one day, let alone seven days at sea, without getting sick. Cora didn't think she had anything left in her stomach to come back up, and the last thing she wanted to do was gag on stomach acid, thank you very much.

"Boss, I'm seeing all kinds of glowing eyes following us in the woods."

"I don't care. Let the dogs chase us." Keith said.

"But, you don't understand."

Whatever he was going to say was cut off by what Cora assumed was Keith's fist hitting the man.

The vehicle began to slow, and Cora braced herself against the back of the cage to keep from being slammed around again. Just as she was preparing for the inevitable increase in speed, something slammed into the side of the van, followed by another.

Shouts from the men in the vehicle sounded from the front, but Keith's voice stayed calm as he issued orders. Cora knew she'd promised Zayn she'd not run, not fight, but he hadn't met Keith. He didn't hear the absolute sound of death in the man's voice. She did.

If it was any other man or beast that had her, she would have kept her promise to Zayn. But the man they called Keith wouldn't keep her alive if he didn't want to, and she didn't think he'd want to. His anger was so palpable every person left in the van was shaking in fear, waiting for his instructions, fearful of making the wrong move.

"Shift and kill. Whoever comes back to me without someone's head will die by my hand."

Oh, yeah. It was time to go.

Metal doors were no protection from an angry shifter, and obviously a metal cage wouldn't be either. Cora worked the slider door open, grateful she had opposable thumbs.

She sighed when the door swung open. Her head pounded out an angry rhythm as she crab-walked out of the small space.

"I can hear you, little lamb."

Cora froze with her body half in and half out of the cage. Indecision warred within her. He could leap over the space separating them and kill her, or...he could leap over the space and kill her. Basically she was dead if she didn't get out. She tried the latch on the back door, unsurprised to find it locked.

Calling on the extra strength she knew all shifters had, that she'd yet to tap into, she prepared to aim her feet at the back doors. She'd have one chance to get out with surprise on her side, and hopefully, the good guys were winning on the outside.

Keith taunted her. "You can stop pretending to sleep. I can hear you breathing, and your heart is beating much faster than someone who is sleeping."

While his sandpaper voice grew in volume, she took the time to place her body flat on the metal floor in the best position.

I see the van, Cora. Where are you? Zayn asked.

Zayn, I'm getting ready to kick the back door open. Keith, the leader, is still inside here with me, but he's different. I don't know how or what he is. Just...different in a very bad way.

Wait for me. I'll get you out.

I can't, Zayn. He's getting ready to do...I don't know what. I can guarantee you I don't want to find out.

Cora heard the movement of fabric closer than it was before and without hesitation, she kicked out with both feet. Pain shot up from her toes to her knees. She used her hands to push her body out of the opening, nearly freezing at the sight of a dozen or so werewolves fighting.

An inhuman roar behind her sent her feet in motion toward the fighting, instead of away. A wolf with a gleaming red coat and glowing blue eyes caught her attention as he snapped the neck of his opponent, before he dropped him to the ground. Niall. She knew the wolf was Zayn's brother by his coat.

Cora, head toward my brother. I'm coming up behind him.

She loved that they were so connected and how he seemed to know exactly what she needed to hear.

By the time Zayn reached the road where they'd stopped the van, the pack had killed two of the other pack members. She watched Zayn meet the red glowing eyes of Keith. The chilling smile, like he'd orchestrated the whole diversion, made Cora shiver. She knew he was trying to get a rise out of Zayn.

Keith whistled an ear splitting sound. The remaining men jumped back from their fighting and limped or ran back to the van.

Before any of them could stop the other pack from leaving, they filed inside the beat up vehicle and left, leaving no doubt they'd not seen the last of them.

Niall, Torq, and Bronx still stood, although they had all sustained severe wounds. Against the odds, Cora was happy they were walking away, only she felt like they'd played into the other man's hand.

"Where's Paul?" Torq asked, after he shifted to

his human form.

Zayn shifted too, wrapping his hands around Cora. "Paul was working with them. Did you notice he had a yellow tinge to his eyes?"

When they all shook their heads, he explained his theory on the drugs and what Cora had told them about Shane and Bart. She was glad she didn't have to tell them herself.

"Fuck," Bronx growled.

"So what do we do? Call a meeting and check everyone's eyes out? A shifter is dangerous period, but a shifter on drugs? Man, they could expose us to humans. We'd be hunted down and, at best, killed, or worse, made into science experiments." Torq ran his hands through his hair.

"Let's shift. I'm calling a meeting with the elders and the rest of the council. Obviously there's a lot more going on here than just a little pack rivalry." Niall's words calmed the aggression they all were feeling.

Chapter Six

After Keith realized he was outnumbered, instead of staying and fighting, he left his fallen, called his wounded, and fled the scene. Even the thought of that eerie howl sent shivers down her spine hours later. To make matters worse, Zayn deposited Cora in his home and then left for some meeting she couldn't attend.

Life wasn't fair. Cora was coming to recognize this reality. First she tried to save a young wolf, who just happened to be a shifter, who then bit her. Then she gets the worst flu of her life, only it wasn't the flu. Oh no, Cora couldn't do anything normal. Nope, she finds herself surrounded by a bunch of hot well-built men, who all turn out to be, of all things, werewolves. They 'insist' she go stay with one of them. At this point, surely there should've been some creepy music playing somewhere. Now, one of those hunky shifter guys claims he's her mate.

As far as men went—or mates—Cora couldn't have picked a more perfect specimen. Zayn would tick off every box on her dream man chart, except the getting hairy part. Even in her wildest dreams she didn't think they were real. She couldn't utter the words in her mind, let alone comprehend the fact that she was supposedly one too.

"What are you thinking so hard about?" Zayn slipped his arms around her waist.

Cora knew when Zayn had entered the house, kinda like her *spidey sense* kicking in.

"You don't have *spidey sense,"* Zayn chuckled.

"Get out of my mind." Cora jabbed her elbow into Zayn's stomach.

The sound of his grunt made her giggle. His fingers dancing up her sides had her squirming to get away. Even with her added strength, she couldn't break free from his questing fingers. When those fingers went from playful to downright skillful between her thighs, all thoughts of giggling flew out the window. As he wiggled them against her panty covered sex while they both stood looking out at the backyard, she realized he definitely ticked every box and even some she didn't know she had.

"S-sex doesn't s-solve everything," Cora stammered.

"I need you, mate." Zayn and his talented tongue traced whirls around her ear.

She had to admit the man was talented on so many levels. "I need some explanations, *mate.*" Although her body screamed a protest, she stepped out of his embrace. His palm sliding out of her panties left a wet trail up her abdomen, which she was sure he did intentionally.

She turned her back to the counter and hopped up with very little effort. Score one for the extra werewolf strength. Still keeping her eye on the predator that was her mate, she picked up an apple from the bowl and leveled him with a glare. She was good at the waiting game. Eyes still locked with his, she took a bite of the fruit chewing slowly before swallowing.

And repeat. Cora was almost finished with her snack, and Zayn still stared her down without answering.

"Fine. What do you want to know?" Annoyance laced his tone.

"First off," she held up her index finger, "I need to know how to shift, just in case something like that ever happens again."

"Nothing like that will ever happen again," he growled.

She held up her hand. "You can't guarantee that.

Keith is still out there, for one." She held up another finger. "I need to know how to protect my mind." She tapped her head, realizing she still held the apple core in her hand which she tossed into the bin with accuracy.

Zayn grabbed her palm, licked her fingers and then her hand, all the way up her wrist, making her shiver with need. God, the man really was extremely talented.

"I think you've gotten all the juice," she whispered.

"Oh, baby. You've got so much more juice I want to lap up."

"Aren't cats the ones who lap up?"

Zayn covered her mouth with his hand. "Don't ever compare us to them damn cat shifters." He shuddered dramatically.

"Are you saying there are cat shifters?" Cora knew her eyes looked like they were ready to pop out of her head, but she was just getting used to werewolves. Now, cat shifters too?

He waved his hand in the air. "Cora, there are many different shifters. Most stay away from those that are not of their kind. There are, however, special circumstances. As for how to shift? Remember, I told you to picture yourself as a wolf?"

She nodded. "Right, but how do I know what I would look like as a wolf? I mean for you, it's easy because you know what you look like. How do I know what I'd look like?"

Zayn raked his hand through his hair, making Cora almost feel sorry for him. Almost.

"Let's start with something easy. Picture building walls up around your mind, like a fortress of sorts."

Cora thought of Cinderella's castle and used bricks similar to build her walls. She blocked the sound of Zayn's chuckle, made sure no light could seep between the bricks as she meticulously placed them all around her mind. By the time she felt her thoughts were secure, she opened her eyes. Time had no sense of passage while she worked. To her it had only been minutes, but when she looked at the clock, it was over an hour later, and she no longer sat on the counter.

"Don't ever do that to me again," Zayn growled, his hands shaking.

"How the hell did I get on the couch?" Cora touched her head. "Did it work?"

"Did it work? Are you fucking kidding me?" Zayn jumped up and began to pace.

Cora swung her legs over the side. “Zayn, please calm down. Your eyes are going all wolfey like, and you’re scaring me. Come. Sit.” She patted the place beside her.

He turned, electric blue eyes flashing. “Come? Sit? Little girl, I am not a dog you teach to do tricks.”

“Oh I don’t know. I think you know all kinds of cool tricks.” She winked.

He stalked towards her. “Now you want to talk all sexual? Baby, you are playing with fire.”

“If you answer my questions, I’ll reward you.”

“Fine,” he sighed.

He was so cute she leaned forward and kissed him, just a light brush of her lips over his. She blinked up at him when he just sat there. “I’m waiting.”

“I thought you were kissing me.” He tried to deepen the kiss.

Cora pulled back. “Let’s do this like a game. Do you like games?” She sucked his top lip into her mouth.

Dressed in a pair of borrowed sweats that had belonged to Niall’s mate and one of Zayn’s T-shirts, Cora smiled.

His eyes narrowed. “Why am I a little scared?”

"Is the big bad wolf scared of little ole me?" Cora leaned back into the soft cushions with one knee bent, the other with her foot planted on the floor. "For every answer you give me, I'll take off a piece of clothing. Once I'm down to the skin, you can have your wicked way with me."

For Cora it really was a win-win situation.

Zayn moved closer so their knees were touching. "Think of something, anything."

Keeping the image of her imaginary wall firmly in place, she kept her naughtiest thoughts behind it. However, the things she pictured made her nipples hard and had a flush covering her pale skin.

"Damn it, that's not fair. You're thinking of sex. You can't think of sex," he growled.

She slapped his thigh. "You could read my thoughts still?"

"No, your body told on you. I couldn't read or see a thing. Now off with something." Zayn waggled his eyebrows.

Cora looked down at her bare feet, chewed on her bottom lip, and then decided to take the oversized top off. She still had her bra on, much to Zayn's dismay. The borrowed T-shirt dropped between them soundlessly. She watched Zayn look at the white T, then her chest, and back again. He bared his teeth in a grimace, and then knocked it off their legs.

"No fair. Girls wear too many clothes." His eyes however gleamed with appreciation.

She took a breath. "How will I know how to picture my wolf?" That was a question that really bothered her.

"While you were out, I texted my mom. She says for you to picture a smaller version of a dark brown wolf. Your wolf is inside you and will know what it needs to look like. However, she...ah...she said the first time for a turned werewolf isn't the same as for us born."

She waited, and when it didn't seem like he was going to go on, she waved her hands. "And?"

Zayn raised an eyebrow. "I answered a question. I'm waiting for my reward." He sat back and crossed his arms.

Oh, he was so going to pay. She reached behind her, pretended she couldn't quite get the catch of her bra to come undone. "Can you help me?" As she turned to give him her back, she accidentally brushed the bulge straining the front of his sweats with her palm and pretended not to notice his swift intake of breath.

* * * *

Zayn loved the way his mate wanted to play with him. Wolves as a whole were a playful lot, unless their families were attacked. He shook off the fear and anger, not letting anything intrude upon the game Cora had begun. After he unhooked the bra, he helped her remove the article of clothing, tossing it behind him, accidentally brushing her nipples.

Cora rolled her eyes and shook her head like he was a petulant child. "So what did she say was the difference?"

"She said because you are already a full grown adult you shouldn't trip over your paws. Our young tend to stumble just like toddlers do when they first learn to walk."

He watched her mouth drop open, and then her small body launched forward, knocking him on his back. Zayn caught her arms to her side. Her laughing and calling him names amused him like nothing ever had.

Yes, he'd played with his brother and Jett when they were cubs, and he loved playing with the kids of the pack. But wrestling with a half-naked Cora was on a different level completely. He'd had lots of sex, more than he cared to admit. Not that he was ever callous or didn't make the women feel important, but they hadn't been his mate. The bond between him and Cora was like a living breathing thing he never wanted to do without.

"You cheated. Now you have to take something off." Cora rested with her elbows on his chest, staring at him in earnest.

"Since you seem to be making up these rules, is there a certain item I need to take off or is it my choice."

She tapped her finger on her chin. "I say a shirt for a shirt."

As she went to get up, he held her down with one hand on her lower back. It took some maneuvering, but he was able to get his own shirt up and off in no time.

"Now what?" Zayn asked enjoying the feel of Cora's breasts against his chest.

"You said you weren't sure if I'd have to get naked to shift. How will we know if I don't try with my clothes on?"

Zayn thought for a moment, and even though he

hated to lose Cora on top of him, he knew this was important to her. He tapped her ass. “Hop up, luv.”

Rising to her feet, she ran her palms down her thighs. “Now what?”

“Let’s have you try it with just a pair of panties on. That way if they don’t magically shift when you do, then they’ll easily rip off without doing any damage to your body. When you shift back, we will know if they come back with you.”

Cora threw up her hands. “You make it sound so easy.” She turned away from him.

“It is that easy.” He reached his hand out to turn her back to face him. “Calm down. You need to center yourself.” Zayn slipped his hands under the waistband of the borrowed sweats. He helped her pull them down and put them over the arm of the couch. Had he been a dog, he was sure his tongue would’ve been hanging out over the sheer panties she had on.

Letting out a nervous sigh, Cora stepped back. Her eyes closed.

Zayn held his breath. Time stood still while he waited to see what her wolf would look like, what his mate would look like as a wolf. He took a step forward, wanting to help, but knowing nobody but Cora could do this for her.

A gasp was followed by a shimmer of light, almost too quick for the human eye to see, and then there stood the most beautiful she-wolf Zayn had ever seen. Her coat matched Cora's dark brown hair, with tips of red he couldn't wait to see in the sunshine or moonlight. When he told her his mom said she shouldn't have issues walking due to her paws, he hoped it was true.

Zayn squatted down, held his hand out in a gesture for her to come to him. With her walls built up, he couldn't reach her through their bond.

"Cora, honey. I know you don't want me reading your thoughts, and as your mate I will respect your privacy, but in your shifted form, the only way we can speak is through our bond. Do you understand what I'm saying?"

Her wolf body slowly crept forward.

He feared she wasn't able to understand him. Her green eyes studied him, and then those walls came down stone by stone. Her excitement level was eclipsed by a sliver of fear that she wouldn't be able to shift back.

Just picture yourself as human. Zayn silently prayed her panties were gone, but then realized that was selfish. He'd just strip them off her as soon as she shifted. Forcing himself to step back, he gave her room to shift.

The same shimmer as before happened, only this time where once stood a beautiful brown wolf with red tips, now stood a gorgeous Cora in a pair of tiny panties.

“I did it. Oh my God, it worked!” Cora squealed, launching herself into Zayn’s arms. “Whoa!”

Zayn grabbed Cora before she fell. “Easy does it. It takes a lot of energy to shift, especially for newbies.”

With one arm behind her back and the other under her knees, Zayn did what he’d wanted to do as soon as he’d walked in after the pack meeting. He carried Cora to his bedroom, only this time he’d hold her. He enjoyed talking with his mate, learning all the details of her life. There was so much he still didn’t know about her.

“That was really cool. Does it always feel that way?” Cora laid her head on his shoulder.

Her voice sounding slurred. He was sure she’d be asleep before her head hit his pillow, but that was okay. He’d be there when she woke up, and he’d be there every time she woke, if he had his way.

Careful not to jostle a sleeping Cora, he pulled

the covers back and settled her between the sheets. He discarded his own sweats before walking to the other side and sliding in behind her, tugging until Cora was nestled in front of him, her back to his front. Nirvana. He let sleep claim him, knowing his mate was where she should be, in his arms.

Beside him, a moan escaped the woman who was his mate. As though that was his cue, he shifted his pelvis to rub his cock against the firm globes of her ass. He was definitely an ass man. Hell, when it came to Cora, he was anything that came to her, as long as he was her man. There was absolutely nothing he would change about her, on the inside or the outside.

"Mmm, something is poking me," Cora murmured.

"He is just saying hello," Zayn teased.

She used her elbow to poke him. "Are you one of those people?"

Zayn raised an eyebrow even though she couldn't see him, her tone warning him. "Um, what would one of those people be?"

"You know? Morning people. The ones who are all talky and stuff before coffee."

This time Zayn couldn't help but laugh, her pointy elbow hitting him with a little more force. "Are you one of *those* people?" he countered.

"I need coffee. It's not a want," Cora growled.

Knowing that he was facing a losing battle, Zayn placed a kiss on his mate's shoulder. "Don't move." He rolled out of bed, navigating the semi-dark house to his kitchen, happy he had a coffee pot that was the fastest on the market. Within minutes he had his grumpy mate a cup of coffee made the way she liked it and one for himself.

He walked back into his bedroom to find Cora with her eyes closed. The closer he got to her side of the bed the more she stirred, her gorgeous green eyes popped open, and she reached for the cup. "You made me coffee?" She took a sip and sighed.

Zayn shook his head before climbing back in bed. He waited until she'd finished her drink, and then he took the empty container and set it on his nightstand next to his half-finished one. "Okay, where were we?"

Cora wiggled closer to him. "I can think of a few places."

Whatever he planned to say flew out the window, along with several brain cells, when Cora covered his mouth with hers. She licked at his mouth, sucked his lower lip, and then let it out with a pop. Her hum of appreciation echoed inside his head.

Lust was a living, breathing beast inside him, tempered with the softer emotion he knew was love. He reached for her, wanting to claim her. Her head shook as she climbed on top of him, slid down his body, kissing, licking, sucking as she made her way past his hips.

Her name exploded from him. “God, Cora!”

Her lips traced the head of his cock, and Zayn prayed he would last longer than two point three seconds with her lips surrounding him.

The sweet scent of her arousal hit his nostrils, ratcheting up his own need. “Cora, flip around and let me taste you.”

“Zayn.” His name was a gust of air over his cockhead, a plea, a promise.

After an awkward shuffle, he finally had her where he wanted her. Her pussy was swollen with need, pink and slick with her arousal dripping down her folds.

He spread her pussy lips with his thumbs, licked from her clit to her ass and back up again. Cora’s thighs gripped his head and she gasped. He stroked over her folds again and again, enjoyed the humming she made around his dick. The sweet sensation made his balls draw up tight at having his mate sucking

him.

He circled the bundle of nerves begging for his attention, slipped his finger inside her pussy and gathered up her juices to drag against the tight rosette at her rear. She froze. “It’s okay, I’m only playing. You’ll like it.” He tongued her clit and then sucked her folds into his mouth, humming as her hips began to gyrate.

Cora screamed, tightening her thighs around his head, and then slumped across his legs.

Zayn did indeed lap at her cream. He could become addicted to Cora’s unique flavor every morning. He’d just have to remember to wake her with coffee first.

His dick twitched where it was trapped between them. “Oh, you poor thing. Did I forget about you?” Cora kissed his thigh.

He swore her tone was sinfully dirty, and then all rational thought fled. Cora maneuvered herself so that she was crouched over his thighs, with his dick in her hand. She looked at him with passion filled eyes.

“Cora,” he warned.

She leaned forward and licked the slit on his cockhead. Her tongue traced the rim, before she opened wide and wrapped her lips around him.

It took all his control not to grab her by the hair and fuck her face like a beast. He sifted his fingers through the silky strands, counting backwards from a hundred. Cora gently cupped his balls, tugged slightly, followed by a suction of her mouth which he didn't think she was capable of, and he gave up control to his mate. His eyes slid shut.

Her mouth came off his cock, leaving him panting. She blew a puff of cold air over his heated flesh. "Cora," he pleaded. His body bucked toward her. Fuck, he was ready to come and she had barely put him in her mouth.

She licked her lips, pumped her fist up and down his dick.

"I've never done this to the-to-th-the end before," she stammered.

Her confession gave him the strength to ease back from the edge. He didn't want to blow his load all over her hand or on his belly. He also didn't want her to do something she didn't want to do.

"Cora, you don't have to. I love being inside you. Fuck, babe, being inside you is my favorite place to be."

"I want to." Her voice was a whisper of sound.

She took his cock back into her mouth, his hips

slammed forward before he could stop himself, driving his dick deeper into the wet heat of Cora's mouth. "Fuck, Cora. I'm...I can't..."

Zayn gripped the sheets next to his hips, lost to the exquisite pleasure of Cora's lips surrounding his dick. "Please...If you don't want me to come in your mouth you gotta..."

Cora's cheeks hollowed out, her hand joined her mouth and her tempo increased. She sucked down his length and back up again and again. Zayn wanted to warn her for a second time, but lost all ability to do anything but feel.

His eyes shuttered closed, groaning from the pleasure of her mouth on his flesh as she sucked him to the most amazing orgasm. She continued to move her hand on him, long after the last splash of his come spurted from the tip.

Opening his eyes he saw her upturned face, utter happiness reflected in her warm gaze, giving him hope that someday she may come to love him too. For wolves it was instinctual and happened whether they thought they were ready or not. Even if they tried to fight it, their wolves knew when they'd found their mate.

However, humans didn't feel that instant bond

the way shifters did. He feared even one who'd been bitten, and then turned may not feel the same overpowering need, the same instinct for a mate as a shifter born. He needed to talk to the elders. Fuck, he was so in love with a woman who may never feel the same for him as he did her.

Grabbing a fistful of her hair, he pulled her up his body, his lips rubbing hers, their breaths mingling together. "What you do to me," he swore.

Before she could utter a word, he reversed their positions. Already hard for her, he covered her body with his.

She wrapped her legs around his waist, moaned into his ear, and dragged one heel down his thigh. "Fuck me, wolfman," she whispered in his ear.

He groaned, kissing her, hard. Wanting to take his time, wanting to savor every second of being inside his mate, his body demanded he take what was his. His beast pounded at his mind to claim what was theirs. Now!

Her slick heat licked at his cock nestled between them. He rolled his hips, sliding inside Cora in one swift movement.

She arched, taking him deeper.

He ate at her mouth, the mix of both their

arousals blended between them. He loved the way she opened for him in every way, except the one he really wanted. Her nails raked down his back, her beast coming out to play. He separated their mouths, the little mewl from her made him feel like a king.

He pulled back, looking at her puckered rosy nipples begging for attention. Bending, he sucked one into his mouth. Her back bowed off the bed, her pussy contracted around his dick. He released her nipple with a pop, his hips pistoning in and out of her.

Pulling her knee up to her chest, he plunged deeper. With a growl, Zayn kissed her, claimed her, loved her with everything that he was, driving his cock back and forth, until she called out his name. The feel of her pussy spasming around him had him on the edge of insanity, but he held onto his own orgasm. He waited for her to open her eyes, to see the love in his gaze, and then he came.

His seed erupted from him, leaving him powerless to do anything but collapse in a boneless heap. He had enough sanity to roll to the side and pull her with him, to stop from squishing Cora, but still keeping his spent cock buried inside her.

"Zayn, that was...Oh God, Zayn," Cora cried.

Wonder filled her voice.

The exclamation gave him hope that she felt something for him, but he feared to push for more so soon. He found he had infinite patience when it came to Cora.

"Niall has asked a few of the pack members to help clean up your clinic this afternoon, if that's all right with you. We're supposed to give him a call when we get up." His hands traced patterns down her back.

"Is that right?" She raked her nails across his spine. "We've been up for some time." She pushed her hips against his.

He slapped her ass. "Stop that, you hussy, or we'll never get out of bed." Zayn disengaged their bodies. The wet sound of their combined fluids made a suctioning sound.

"Ewww," she giggled.

He jumped out of bed, tossed the covers back, and then tossed a laughing Cora over his shoulder. "Ewww?" There is nothing *Ewww* about you and me." He pinched her on her left butt cheek, making her giggle as he carried her into the bathroom.

"No, there's nothing about you and me that I don't love."

His breath stilled in his throat. His heart thumped so hard and fast, he feared he might have a heart attack. "What," he gasped.

Cora slapped his ass. "Put me down, Wolfey."

"You can't nickname me *Wolfey*," he growled. He set her down in front of him, keeping his hands on her hips.

She rose on her tiptoes. "I think I could love you, Zayn."

He closed his eyes and rested his forehead against hers. Hearing Cora say she could love him wasn't as good as her saying she did love him, but that was okay. At least she was thinking about them in the long term. That was something. "Cora, I know this has been a lot for you to take in, but I've wanted you since I first scented you. I think my wolf knew you were meant to be ours."

Cora raised her eyebrows. "Are you trying to tell me something?" She sniffed her armpits.

Zayn chuckled. "No. I'm saying it works differently for us wolves. I don't know how to explain it. Although we are one and the same, we have this inner instinct that's our wolf. When I first saw you, I wanted you like I've never wanted another. My heart and my beast knew you were it for us before my mind did."

"I definitely wanted you from the moment I first saw you, even though I didn't like you very much," Cora said, scrunching up her nose.

Having his mate tease him was something he'd never thought to have, let alone enjoy. "Why wouldn't you like me?" He asked.

"For one, you broke into my clinic. For two, you were growly."

Zayn licked the mating mark on the side of her neck. "You like it when I get all growly."

Cora shivered. "I must have issues."

"Hmm, I can smell your issues."

"See, there you go again with the saying I stink." She laughed.

"Shower woman." Zayn opened the slider into his large shower stall, and then lifting her over the step, not putting her down until long minutes later.

Their quick shower turned into thirty minutes, with another bout of love making. It was going on his next favorite way to wake up, after making love to his mate in their bed.

Chapter Seven

Cora was devastated at the utter destruction of her beloved clinic. With all the damage, it would take her weeks to get everything fixed and ready to reopen. Her two assistants stood around with shocked expressions on their young faces. She could understand their fascination, as they stared at the men. Debbie's dark gaze was a mix of trepidation and awe on her pixie face. Zayn and his brother Niall were both gorgeous.

"I better be the only man you are checking out." Zayn came up behind Cora and wrapped his arms around her waist.

She relaxed into him for a minute. "What am I going to do?" Cora indicated all the damage in the clinic with a sweep of her arm.

"Can you make a list of all the things you need?" Zayn kissed her shoulder.

She was glad she'd pulled her hair into a ponytail after their shower, otherwise she'd probably be pulling it out right about now. The cleanup would take days, let alone the inventory.

"It's going to take weeks, Zayn. I don't know where to even start." She stepped away from him.

Her two assistants, Margie and Debbie, seemed to come out of their shock and awe at seeing so many amazing specimen of men in one room and walked toward her with eager expressions on their young faces.

"Cora, I know it looks really, really bad, but I think if we get these big guys," Margie's cheeks turned a fiery red, but she continued, "to pick up the large pieces of furniture, we can get this place set to rights in no time."

Debbie nodded her head, her cap of short black hair bobbing in agreement. Cora loved them dearly, but she couldn't see it happening.

"Listen to these obviously very intelligent young ladies." Jett flashed his pearly whites.

She rolled her eyes when her two very resourceful, super smart assistants, began giggling. "Fine."

She grabbed her tablet. The most efficient way to figure out what was needed was to take inventory. By the end of the day, with the help of several men from Zayn's pack and Margie and Debbie, they had the clinic cleaned and set to rights as good as possible.

Once they had all the wreckage removed, it wasn't as bad as Cora had feared, luckily for her and her future patients.

With overnight shipping she would have most of her destroyed supplies in the next day or two, depending on stock issues with her suppliers. What furniture had been ruined was going to take a little longer. All in all it could've been much worse. What she was most upset about was her home. They destroyed things she couldn't replace.

Cora sat on one of the only pieces of furniture that hadn't been trampled beneath the paws of werewolves on a rampage. Zayn and his pack had left to attend to their regular jobs, either at Mystic Lodge, the ski resort owned by some of the werewolves, or at the bar in Sturgis, owned by Niall and Zayn.

She'd brushed off Zayn's concern at leaving her alone, telling him she needed to grab some personal things and the promise she'd head to his home before it got dark. What she really needed was some time to come to grips with the loss of her things.

A tear slid down her cheek unchecked as she stared at the box in her lap. It held pictures and mementos from when she was a child. She picked up a small frame, the broken glass blurring the picture inside. She remembered the day the photo was taken. Turning the silver frame around, she popped the edges out to remove the picture, sighing when no damage was visible. The silver frame was cheap, but she had memories of buying it for her mom. With care, she sifted through the box that had been stomped on, but otherwise been left alone.

Looking around at her little apartment, she realized home isn't where you put your head at night, but where your heart is, and her heart was wherever Zayn Malik happened to be. She wiped the last of her tears from her face and stood with the box in her arms, amazed that the things that had been a heavy burden just a few months ago, was light as a feather now. She would've needed help doing most of the heavy lifting she'd done in the last twelve hours. Now she marveled at her strength. She really did like being a werewolf.

Cora drove to Zayn's with her windows down, enjoying the beautiful drive. She hadn't noticed that while she was taking inventory of the clinic, her wolfman had decided to pack all her clothes. Not that she minded. All her furniture had pretty much been smashed, except for the box in the back. She needed to explain her family to Zayn before they went any further. What she would do if he decided he didn't want anything to do with her, after he heard about her less than stellar family, she had no clue. A chill made goose bumps race up her arms.

The sun was setting, making the trees lining the winding road cast shadows that sent a shiver of fear over Cora. "I'm a freaking werewolf." She slapped the steering wheel.

Over the next rise, she spotted the turn off for Zayn's private drive and the fear slid away. She let off the accelerator and turned into his driveway, a familiar howl pierced the air. Her mate was on his way home. She wondered if he'd put her clothes away and smiled at the domesticated image. Zayn was many things, but domesticated wasn't one she could picture.

Pulling into his drive, she noticed for the first time the garage door opener clipped to her visor. The man truly was too good to be true. With a simple press of her finger, she had access to his home.

Inside the garage there was a note taped to the door that read '*I know you like games. So this is a game of follow the signs. Love Z.*' Cora tapped the card against her palm and entered the kitchen.

Next to the coffee maker was another note.

'*Please feel free to make a cup. Don't want a growly mate. Then follow the trail. Love Z.'* She looked down to see a trail of purple petals. In one of their conversations she'd told him her favorite color was purple. The fact he remembered, had tears coming to her eyes.

The door to his bedroom was open with the trail stopping next to the big bed. Another card lay on top of a white box. *'Open the box at the end of the bed. And my favorite part…Strip. Love Z.'*

Cora laughed. She could imagine him ordering her to strip or her ordering him. Either way, it made for a really interesting evening. She opened the box to find a gorgeous satin purple nightie and matching robe. Another note was tucked into the bodice. '*Don't get too attached to the nightie. Love Z.'* Hugging the outfit to her chest, she couldn't help but giggle out loud. The man was too much.

The trail of petals continued into the ensuite. Inside, next to the Jacuzzi tub, was another card. '*Take a nice long soak, and when you're done, put the gown and robe on. I'll have one more surprise for you. Love Z.'*

All her favorite body washes were lined up, along with a soothing bottle of bubble bath. Taking him at his word, she filled his huge tub with water, shivering at the thought of what was to come.

* * * *

Niall watched Nolan bound off into the woods, his cast long gone. His brother's new mate had saved his cub and for that he'd be forever grateful. He was happy to see Zayn find happiness. He rubbed his chest over his heart, the loss of his own mate Emma still a huge hole in his life.

"Dad, watch me," Nolan yelled.

His son jumped from the ground onto the top of the six foot fence in one leap, impressing Niall with the ability. He'd make a great alpha one day. "Be careful, son. You don't want to re-injure your leg. What did Cora say?"

"She said I was good as new." Nolan jumped back down, an impish grin lighting up his face.

Niall felt his heart turn over. His son was so much like his mate Emma.

Nolan walked up to him. "When are you going to get a mate like uncle Zay?"

Out of the mouths of babes, Niall shook his head. "I've got work to do kiddo. Go get your stuff to take to your grandparents." Niall tapped his son on the rear as he walked past him. Already at seven he was giving him attitude.

A scent teased Niall's nostrils, the smell made his wolf rise up. He turned his head toward the woods leading to the ski lodge of Mystic. Every winter the lodge flooded with more and more people wanting to become ski bunnies, and more and more found their way down the mountain looking for shit that he had to deal with. He shook his head.

He didn't need a mate. A damn vacation was what he really needed, but that scent called to him. He opened his senses and let the magical wards the Fey had put up to protect their pack tell him if something was wrong. Their boundaries still held, but there was a disturbance the wards recognized.

After he'd talked to the alpha of the Whitewood Pack and was reassured they had exiled the members who had attacked Zayn's mate, their treaty was still in place. The wolves had been kicked out long before they'd attempted to put the traps on Mystic lands. Niall still wasn't sure what the reason was, other than to kill off the males and take over. They obviously didn't realize not all the men would be caught in the killer contraptions. He shook his head at the absurdity. Drugs made men do stupid shit. Wolves on drugs were clearly even worse. His pack had done the best they could to prepare and set up defense structures.

Nolan came out with a backpack, and the strange scent of fear and woman was forgotten. His son and his pack were his life. He was alpha of the Mystic Wolves. That was all he needed. He turned his head back in the direction toward the mountain and the mystery smell.

"Come on, Dad." Nolan tugged on his hand.

Entering the old alpha's home always hit Niall hardest. Here Emma was everywhere.

"Hey, Niall, you got time to visit for a few?" Emerson indicated the recliner next to his. "Nolan, your grandma made you something special in the kitchen. Why don't you go see what she's got for you?"

"You guys have some grown up talking to do?" Nolan asked.

Niall pretended like he was going to swat Nolan, loving the infectious giggle. "Go see your grandma before I eat your special treat."

Emerson waited until Nolan disappeared from sight. The sound of Payton and Nolan talking got fainter as they stepped outside.

"What's bothering you, Niall? Don't try to say 'nothing'. I can see it on your face, and I could feel it when you stepped inside."

"Can I get you a drink?" Niall asked.

"Think we're going to need the hard stuff?" Emerson raised his eyebrows.

He shook his head. Niall loved the Glades like they were his own parents. In the kitchen he grabbed two bottles of beer and headed back for a talk with his father-in-law, stopping at the picture of a smiling Emma holding their son. Every room had at least a picture or two of Emma at some point in her life displayed. Niall traced the outline of her face with the tip of his finger. The cold glass was nothing like the warm woman she was.

"I miss her every day. Her mom still cries when she thinks I can't hear her."

"Nolan reminds me of her." Niall held the bottle out, offering one to Emerson.

"She wouldn't want you to be alone for the rest of your life, you know."

Nearly choking on the mouthful of beer at the other man's words, Niall wiped his mouth with the back of his hand, trying to compose his words. He didn't want to offend Emma's parents, nor did he want them to think he was living like a monk. Damn close, but not exactly. He was a man with needs after all.

"Emerson, I don't...I mean I'm not sure what you want me to say. I loved your daughter. She was my true mate."

Looking into the wise eyes of his son's grandfather, Niall saw acceptance. He finished the rest of his bottle of beer, while standing in the kitchen looking at a picture of his dead mate. At thirty-seven years old, he had a lot of years ahead of him. Those years looked bleak if he didn't start looking for someone to spend them with. Nobody could replace Emma. However, there was room for someone in his bed, just not in his heart. Niall was smart enough not to tell a woman that though.

"I don't like that look on your face," Emerson said.

Niall nodded once. "You're right. I need to move on. Nobody will ever take the place of Emma here." He placed his hand over his heart. "Nolan needs a female in the house too. He asked me when I was going to find a new mate today. This conversation just made me see things a lot clearer."

"Now, wait a minute. I think you need to rethink things. You can't just make decisions based on what a child wants or because your little head is thinking for your big head. What about the woman in question? Is there a woman you have in mind?"

Niall looked out the window toward the mountains in the distance, a vague sense of something coming tugged at him. "There is no woman in particular, yet."

Emerson exhaled loudly. "Niall, think very clearly before you go off halfcocked. You chase after a woman, make her think she's special, and then she finds out you don't love her like she deserves? That's a recipe for disaster. Mark my words."

"Thank you for the talk, and for taking care of Nolan. I need to head to Chaps." Niall squeezed Emerson on the shoulder. He'd make sure the woman he chose never knew his heart was not involved in the equation. If she had to hear the words *I love you* from him, he would do his best to say them, even though they'd be a lie.

* * * *

Zayn knew the moment his mate crossed onto

his property. They'd met with the elders and found out quite a bit about the other pack. What he'd wanted to know was how a made werewolf would feel about their mate. He shook his head at their answers or lack thereof. All that mattered to him now was how Cora felt.

After he scanned the area, he allowed the shift to overcome him on his back deck. His mate's safety was his number one concern, now more than ever. His home, like her clinic, had an electronic sensor locking system, but they also had magic boundaries set up that set off alarms. Thanks to the Fey, they'd stepped up their security measures.

In his kitchen, Cora's scent changed from one of exhaustion, to a much earthier one that let him know she liked his game. Zayn's beast itched to howl, but he suppressed the urge. He could hear the telltale sound of his mate in the tub.

His shirt was ripped in half with little care. He stopped long enough to kick his boots out of the way and pull his socks off. His jeans were barely given any more consideration than his top. By the time he reached the bathroom, he was completely naked and his dick so hard he could hammer nails.

He stopped next to the tub, spellbound by the

beautiful sight she made, her hair, a halo around her head. Several candles he didn't know he had were lit around the bay window, and she looked so peaceful. He sighed.

"Are you just going to stand there, or are you going to join me?" Cora opened her eyes. The green orbs looked like emerald fire in the candle light.

Zayn grabbed his cock in one palm, more than ready. "Why don't you climb out of there and join me?" He reached for the large bath towel over the heating rod, held it out for her and waited.

Cora used one hand to roll her hair up and clipped it to the top of her head. He was always amazed at the dexterity women had to do that, and then she stood.

His mate's body glistened with water and several suds that didn't want to leave her delectable body. He envied those bubbles.

"Fuck, you're amazing."

She smiled. "You're the amazing one."

Zayn wrapped the towel around Cora, and with ease, swung her up into his arms. Unable to wait another minute, he kissed her, swallowing her gasp of surprise, He needed his woman, his Cora, his accidental mate.

He carried Cora to their bed. To him there could be no other option. Wherever Cora was, was where he wanted to be. He put everything he felt into the kiss, telling her without words that she was it for him.

He jerked the covers back, placed Cora on the edge with her knees hanging over the side.

“What are you—?”

Zayn didn’t give her a chance to finish her question. With less finesse and more than a little desperation, he dropped to his knees on the floor. “This,” he muttered. He wedged his body between her thighs, and lowered his head. Sucking her clit into his mouth, he pumped one finger and then two into her tight channel, over and over again. The walls of her pussy contracted around him, the sweet scent of his mate’s orgasm washed over him. He loved the sounds she made, craved the taste of her sweet cream on his lips.

His nuts were drawn up so tight he was shocked they hadn’t erupted. He stood, his dick bouncing against his stomach.

Cora had a slightly dazed look as she stared at him. Her green eyed gaze dropped to his cock, and then she smiled, licking her lips. His damn erection jumped in happy agreement, pre-cum seeping from the tip. “Another time, luv. If you wrap those gorgeous lips around me, I won’t last, and I want to be buried balls deep in you when I come.”

She pouted, but scooted back on the bed, moving to the middle. She spread her legs in open invitation.

Zayn moved to the end of the bed. “Take the clip out of your hair,” he growled.

Her eyes narrowed, but she did as he asked. He climbed on the bed, crawled up and stopped at her feet. Sitting back on his heels, he kissed each foot and continued up her body, paying homage to every part of her.

By the time he planted both arms next to her head, Cora and he were both breathing hard. His entire body covered hers, reminding him again how small and precious she was. She may be a werewolf now, but she was still his to protect.

The head of his cock was lined up to her opening, she was slick with her recent orgasm, but he still pushed forward slowly, her body gradually giving him access. Zayn fought to go slow. He wanted Cora to come around him before he gave into the urge to fuck her like a wildman.

“You won’t hurt me, you know.” Cora’s whispered words startled Zayn.

Zayn took a deep breath. "I just want to love you like you deserve."

She brushed her hands through his hair. "You do."

He touched his forehead to hers. "I love you, Cora. You know that, right?"

"I love you too, Zayn."

Zayn squeezed his eyes shut tight. "Say it again."

"I love you, too. Now if you don't move that fine ass of yours, I'm gonna go wolfey on you."

He couldn't stop the laugh that escaped, nor prevent the tear that slipped from his closed eye. "Woman, you are hard on my ego."

Cora kissed him, and he moved, slowly at first.

Love, his mate loved him.

She squeezed her inner muscles, and Zayn swore he saw stars. He pulled his hips back and slammed forward, again and again. She met him stroke for stroke, her back arched off the bed. The sound of their bodies slapping together was music to his ears. With every downward stroke, his balls hit her ass, his pelvis, and her clit, and she cried out, arousing him even higher if possible. Zayn shifted his hands to entwine with hers.

"Cora, come with me," Zayn whispered, driving

his cock faster, deeper.

Warmth surrounded him. Her pussy spasmed around him. She cried out his name, her orgasm milking him of his own. He thrust hard, gave a yell, and drove deep one last time. His mate clung to him, her nipples stabbing into his chest. He held her, never wanting to leave the comfort of her body. “Ah, my mate.”

The flex and release of his still stiff dick inside of Cora pulsed, wanting more. His beast wasn’t done.

“You’re insatiable,” she teased.

He nuzzled her neck. The mark where he’d bitten her was fading. He wanted to fully mate with Cora. “Will you be my mate, Cora?”

“I thought I was?”

Zayn saw the way she mentally pulled back from him. He’d respected her privacy, even though she hadn’t had her walls up. “I know you’re my mate. When wolves mate it’s for life. There’s no divorce for us, Cora. To make it permanent, it’s not just through words.”

He hated to see the fright on her face. “Wolves are...we are very instinctual. Right now my scent is all over you, but you could shower, and in time it would fade. If you agreed to be my mate, then I would mark you, and you would mark me. The first bite Nolan gave you would have done nothing had I not bit you the second time, and you bit me creating the exchange that turned you. I knew you were mine, but still you could choose to walk away, to find someone else." He ran his finger over the fading wound. "If you agree to be my mate, the mark wouldn't fade like this. Although to humans they would see nothing, to other shifters, it would be clear that you were mine and vice versa." He wanted to mark her for all to see, but would be satisfied that at least other shifters would know she was his.

"How do we mark each other? Please tell me it's not like a dog marking his territory, because I'll tell you right now, I am not okay with that at all." Cora shuddered.

Zayn flexed his hips. "Woman, we are not dogs. Wolves. We are wolves."

"Did you know that all dogs come from wolves?"

He rolled his eyes. "Okay, I give, but no, we don't mark that way. I would bite you here again," he licked between where the neck and shoulder met. "And you would bite me too." At her confused expression he continued. "When the time comes, your fangs will drop, and you'll instinctually know what to do." He hoped.

"Before you mate with me, you need to know about my family. I don't come from the best of the lot. My mom was great, but my dad was a womanizer and a drug dealer. He cheated on her all the time, and one day he screwed over the wrong guy or guys. Long story short." She took a deep breath. "A bigger drug dealer came to my parents' home while I was away at school and decided to get rid of the competition. My dad, however, wasn't at home."

"Oh, baby, I'm so sorry." Zayn rolled their bodies. Making love to Cora took a backseat to holding her while she cried for her mother.

"Anyway, when my dad came home he found the message left for him, cleaned out his *stuff,* and called the police. Next thing I know, he's moved his latest whore into my mother's home. I came home one weekend and packed a box of my mother's things and never looked back." Cora tucked her head under his chin.

Zayn held her tighter. "Where's your dad now?"

She laughed without humor. "The *whore* he moved into my mom's house actually turned state's evidence against him. He was sent to prison for dealing drugs and gun charges soon after. He was killed in a prison riot a couple years later."

"Son of a bitch, baby." Zayn couldn't imagine the pain she must feel at the loss. He, Niall, and Jett only left their old pack because they knew their mates weren't there. They always knew they could go home anytime.

"So, do you still want to mate with me?"

Using his index finger, he lifted her face to his. "Honey, you could be Charlie Manson's daughter, and I'd still want you to be my mate. However, he wouldn't be invited for Christmas dinner," he joked.

A small smile appeared. "Are you sure? You said this was permanent, so you can't just up and leave right? Or decide you want someone else?"

Uncertainty glimmered in her green eyes.

Zayn rolled them, pinned her beneath him. "Cora, it's not the same for us as humans. Like I said, when we mate, it's for life. I'll never feel this way for another. My wolf and I will never want another as long as there is still breath in your body. Our main objectives in life are to keep you safe, happy, and satisfied. Everything else we will work on. Right now, how about I work on the latter?" He rolled his hips.

She quivered under him, her body already primed.

They soared together with him buried deep inside her exactly where he wanted to be, his name flew from her lips, followed by the word *Mate*.

"Okay." Cora turned her head.

Frozen in place, he stared at her exposed neck. Did she mean what he thought she meant? "Does this mean you want to mate with me? This is for life. 'Till death do us part' is not just words, Cora."

Tears swam in her eyes. "Are you having second thoughts?

"Fuck, no," Zayn swore. He licked the precious area. Her shiver was an allover body shake. His fangs dropped down, ready to claim her. He wrapped his lips over the tendon, sucked, and then let his teeth sink in, knowing the enzymes from his bite wouldn't cause her any pain, just the opposite.

Cora shuddered, and he held her in place while he pulled his teeth out, and licked the small wound. Her inner muscles flexing made him smile.

"Oh my God. I had no idea it would feel soooo..." She trembled.

Zayn couldn't help but agree. His own dick was ready to explode. "Your turn." He turned his head to give her better access to his neck.

"What if I do it wrong?"

Had she been able to, he was sure she'd be wringing her hands. "Cora, love, you won't. Let your wolf guide you." He dropped onto his left forearm to hold most of his weight and held her head in his right palm. With his head turned, he guided her to his neck.

The feel of her moist breath made his dick jerk inside her tight sheath. Without warning, she struck. His wolf howled. His hips jerked. His cock grew thicker, if possible. He held her to him as he moved, unable to control himself. He knew, had she been human, she would be bruised from his frantic movements, but as a shifter, the bruises would be gone by morning. The mating bond snapped in place and all sense of taking things slow left him.

Cora met every slam of his body into her with one of her own, until they were both shuddering and moaning. Zayn floated on a sea of pleasure with his mate under him. He nearly collapsed on top of Cora, but turned with their bodies still joined.

With Cora lying on top of him, he lay in silence for what seemed like forever, simply enjoying holding his mate.

"Love you, my accidental wolf."

"And I love you, my wolfey."

Zayn laughed at her absurd nickname, content with his mate.

The End

His Perfect Wolf
Mystic Wolves Book 2

By

Elle Boon

write

Chapter One

"Dad, can I stay all weekend with grandma and grandpa?" Nolan asked.

Niall smiled down at his seven year old son, seeing his wife's eyes looking up at him. It took monumental effort not to scoop up his son and hug him tight, never wanting to let go. When they'd lost Emma, Nolan had been a baby. Even almost seven years later, Niall still missed her like it was yesterday. "Don't you want to spend the weekend with your old man?"

Nolan rolled his eyes. "Me and grandpa are going to campout and fish and grandma is coming along to make sure we don't get into trouble. Besides, you have to work while Uncle Zay spends the weekend with Cora."

"Grab your bag. I'm assuming you packed enough for the entire weekend?"

Nolan nodded, showing Niall that his backpack was indeed bulging. "I'm ready when you are, Dad."

Grabbing his son up and over his shoulder, they headed to his bike parked out in front of their log home. Being the alpha of the Mystic Wolves, he had prime position at the end of the cul-de-sac, each home having anywhere from one to three acres, or more. He had over ten, but the pack had hundreds of acres outside of Sturgis. The Glades, his in-laws, lived within three miles and had several acres. Emerson, the old alpha, had stepped down when Niall mated his daughter, Emma. He handed Nolan his helmet, making sure it was on properly before putting on his own skull cap.

With his son's little arms wrapped snuggly around him, Niall made the short trip to the Glades residence. By the time he was ready to leave his son with Emerson and Payton, a plan was formed in his mind. He swung his leg over the seat, his leathers squeaked as he straddled his Harley. Nolan and the Glades waved from the porch, he smiled at the excitement shining in his son's brown eyes as he revved the bike before taking off at a sedate pace.

Stopping at the end of the road, he looked up at the woods leading to the ski lodge, a mysterious scent teased his nostrils, making his wolf rise up and take notice. The lodge was always flooded with want to be ski bunnies in winter, inevitably they found their way down the mountain into Sturgis and their bar, Chaps.

He and his brother Zayn, along with the rest of the wolves, then had to deal with their shit. It was good for business, so they put up with it, but it was a pain in the ass. Niall shook off the urge to head north, and pointed the bike down toward Sturgis and Chaps.

He'd find himself a mate, and Nolan a mother, that was his great plan. He thought back to the conversation he'd had with Emerson. Since he and Zayn's parents were so far away, he looked to Emerson and Payton as surrogate parents. Emerson had told Niall, according to Payton's dreams, that change was coming and that they understood his need for a new mate, but they didn't understand. He missed his wife and didn't expect to find another truemate. Hell, if a wolf was lucky they'd find one truemate, but many settled. He was a man, a wolf who needed a mate, and a mother for Nolan. Niall knew he was more than blessed when he found Emma and that he wouldn't find that again, but he would settle for companionship, sex and a mother for his son. Niall kept his thoughts to himself, the old alpha still believed in love.

Emerson still teared up when he spoke of Emma, he said that Payton still cried at night, though she tried to hide her sorrow from her husband. Niall wasn't the only one who still suffered.

When he'd looked into the wise eyes of the older man in the kitchen, with pictures of his dead mate hung all around, Niall had made a decision. He was a thirty-seven year old man with a lot of years ahead of him. He hadn't been a monk for the last six years, not by a long shot. However, he hadn't looked for anyone to fill his bed permanently. Truth be told, he'd not had any woman in his and Emma's bed. He wasn't sure he could let another woman sleep in the same place he'd made love to his wife. Niall looked at the bleak years ahead if he didn't make some changes. Nobody could replace Emma. Not in his heart, but a bed was just a place to lay your head and now it would be a place he fucked. Niall was smart enough not to tell a woman that though.

Emerson had known what Niall was thinking and tried to talk him out of it. Even though he valued the older man's opinion, in this instance he didn't think Emerson had a clue. His wife was alive and healthy, while Niall's was not.

Niall opened up the throttle on the bike. The hour drive was giving him time to ponder how to go about getting a mate and mother. He didn't want a tiny petite thing like his Emma, nor did he want someone like her. A blonde with big boobs and no brain would work for him, but not Nolan. Maybe he'd meet her at the bar tonight, or at least find someone to take the edge off his needs.

* * * *

"What do you mean he's found a mate for me? Like I need him to find me a husband, Mom. This is not the...the Victorian age, where the father marries off his girls." Alaina Strop paced in front of the fireplace mantel. Her mother, Adalynn, sat with her legs crossed, looking very much the lady of the manor, but anxiety shown in her chocolate brown eyes.

"Baby, you know how your dad worries about you. Well, after that boy held you at gun point, along with your students, he decided you needed a mate. The council agreed and if it gets you home, then I'm sorry, sweetie, but I agree. You could've been killed."

Alaina narrowed her eyes, horrified to hear her own mother agreeing with the archaic dealings of her dad. "Mother, I'm a twenty-five year old woman for crying out loud. I came home because I took a leave of absence after that incident." Alaina had to take a breath.

Nightmares still plagued her of that day. She'd always wished she could shift, but being part fey and part shifter, she had a little of both her parents. Had she not been in a room filled with thirty, sixteen and seventeen year old, students she could have used her abilities to disarm him, maybe. Instead, she was stuck with a maniac waving a gun around for hours, until he grabbed her by the throat and stuck the gun to her temple. He'd already killed several students in the library before he'd locked himself in her computer lab, bent on exacting revenge on whoever had posted an anonymous letter about him.

Adalynn pointed her finger. "See, you can't even talk about it without turning white. Your dad has found a nice wolf who doesn't care that you can't shift."

Her mother's words brought her back from the past. "Oh, he doesn't mind, does he? How nice." Alaina turned her back on her mom, knowing she'd pissed her off and not caring. Most who were mated with a wolf could be turned, but with her they didn't know what the outcome would be. The familiar mental intrusion she usually welcomed from her mother trying to make her understand only pissed her off more. “Mother, can you hear what you’re saying? There is not a wolf here in the Cascades that I want to marry, let alone mate with. You do know what mating entails right? What if his truemate comes around? Am I supposed to just stand aside, and be oh so understanding then?”

Adalynn stood. Alaina was always amazed at how much they looked alike. Her mother kept her dark brown hair shoulder length, and was a couple inches shorter at five feet five inches, while Alaina topped out at five foot seven. They both had dark brown eyes, and her mother was still slim and curvy.

“That is hardly going to happen Lainey, but if it did we’ll cross that bridge when we come to it.”

“Oh, my gawd. You sound like a Stepford Wife. What has happened to you since I’ve been gone? There will be no we, no bridge to cross, and no damn mating to a wolf I don’t know or love.”

The slamming of a door had them both turning to face the large man in the entry.

“I’m sorry to hear you say that, Alaina, but you don’t have a choice. You’re on pack land and pack law says your alpha has the right to say who marries whom. Since the last time I checked, I’m the alpha and your father, I’ve decided you will mate and marry the wolf of my choosing," Roger Strop said.

Alaina held her breath at the deep baritone of her dad. He'd always been over protective of her, which was one of the reasons she'd gone away to college, and chosen a position half-way across the country after graduation. Seeing him exert his status and his anger toward her, she held her breath. He was never happy with anything she'd done as a child. He'd wanted a son, and since she was a girl, that was one check against her. She couldn't shift, two checks. The list kept getting longer as she got older and didn't fit into his role of the perfect daughter.

"Father, I'm sorry, but that is crazy. I came home to see you and Mom. Not get married off to some stranger. I have a job, a life back in Baltimore with people who are expecting me to return."

Her father's piercing blue eyes drilled her with his alpha stare. "I don't give a flying fuck if the President of the United fucking States is expecting you for dinner at the White House. My land, my pack, my rules. You will be mated, married, and out of my family in forty-eight hours."

She flinched at each of his words, when the last sentence penetrated her brain. Out of the corner of her eye she could see her mother pleading with her eyes. Alaina opened her mind to let her mother in on their private path. Another mark against her in her father's mind was her ability to keep him out of her thoughts.

Don't anger him, baby. Please just do what he says. You will still be my daughter. He is upset at me, not you. Adalynn's voice sounded tear filled.

I don't understand what is going on. Why is he pissed at you and taking it out on me?

Roger strode to Alaina, pinching her chin between his fingers. "Don't fucking mindspeak in my presence, you two. Adalynn, get your ass in the kitchen and start lunch. I have plans to finish up, but I'll be back in a couple hours. You both be on your best behavior this afternoon because I'm bringing your intended over." He released her with a vicious shove.

Alaina was expecting the move and took a step back, using her fey abilities to go with his brute strength.

"You'll learn your place with Rickard. He'll make damn sure to train you proper."

They watched Roger stomp from their home. Alaina could see her mother shaking in fear, and didn't want to add to it with more questions. She knew her mother kept a journal that only another fey could read, and since she was the only other fey, Adalynn felt safe writing her thoughts down. Alaina made a motion with her hand indicating writing. Her mother gave her a brief nod before heading into the kitchen to begin cooking.

By the time she finished reading her mother's journal that had been written just for her, she was shaking. Her father didn't hate her just because she wasn't a boy, but because she wasn't his. He'd thought she wasn't his, but didn't have proof until the school shooting had made the national news. The man Adalynn had loved from her old pack in Mystic had seen the news, obviously put two and two together and came up with his daughter. Clearly, her dad wasn't happy to have had his doubts confirmed. She could only imagine the type of man he wanted her to marry. "I'll take that one-way ticket to hell, please. Not." She closed her mother's journal, putting it back in the bedside table where her mom kept it.

Mystic, South Dakota was where all of her maternal family lived, and Alaina always wondered why they never went back to visit. Now she knew the why. What she didn't know was why her mom didn't stay and marry her real dad? Why did she move halfway across the country with Roger, unless she wasn't sure who was the father. Alaina could imagine the Maury show, with her mother sitting next to Roger and the paternity test coming up negative. Only when Maury did the reading and saying *Roger, you are not the father,* her dad, or the man she thought was her dad, would shift into his wolf and eat Maury before turning his focus on Adalynn. The image was so real Alaina shivered.

She hurried into her bedroom, seeing the bag she'd packed still sitting on the bed, she made a snap decision. Without wasting time, she grabbed it and her purse, opened her bedroom window and snuck out, like she'd done so many times as a teenager. Only then it was to go hang out with her friends, this time it was to escape her father.

Alaina pressed the unlock button, hoping none of the wolves with their super hearing were anywhere near. She held her breath as she tossed her bag in the passenger seat and climbed inside. The entire time she kept expecting her dad, or one of his enforcers, to come charging out of the woods and drag her in front of the council. When she was buckled up and the keys were in the ignition she exhaled and looked around before turning the key. Her cell phone was in her purse, but she wasn't going to risk calling her mom until she was hours away.

Driving at a sedate pace, she pulled out of the driveway, keeping her eyes on the road in front of her and didn't look back. Alaina thought about returning the rental to the airport, but was sure her da...Roger, would look there for her first. Once she hit the highway she'd make a plan as to where she would go. She had two weeks leave from work with pay, but she hadn't planned anything beyond staying with her parents.

The sound of her phone ringing made her jerk the wheel, almost causing her to collide with another vehicle on the highway. Alaina realized she'd already begun driving east, and passed the turnoff to the airport. The ringtone was the one she'd assigned for her mother. Which meant her mom was checking in with her, or Roger was making her call, either way she wasn't answering.

After many hours on the road, and not stopping for anything, she was in need of several things, gas being one, something to drink, and the ladies room were the others. Not necessarily in that order. She pulled into a large truck stop, figuring she could blend in with the other vehicles. Again, avoiding eye contact was her main focus. She filled the tank, and then visited the bathroom, before loading up with bottled water and snacks.

A sign saying free Wi-Fi caught her attention. There was no way she was going to drive across the country with no destination in mind, and the thought of Baltimore held no appeal. Mystic, South Dakota, where her mother's family still lived, was a place she'd always wanted to go. Pulling her iPad out of her bag, she logged onto the free server and google searched the Glade family in Mystic from her mother's journal entry.

"Gah, damn wolves and their secretive hides." Alaina tapped on the route icon.

"Excuse me, are you okay?"

Alaina looked up, startled to see a slender man sitting so close to her. She scented the air, but found him to be one hundred percent human. She may be only part wolf and part fey, but she had heightened senses, and could smell another wolf a mile away. If she was paying attention. "I...do I know you?" she asked.

"You just exclaimed about wolves. I was wondering if you were okay." He smiled, but it didn't reach his eyes. Alaina's creep meter went off.

"Oh, I was just looking at all these...stuffed animals." She hid her screen and stood from the barstool.

Glad that she'd parked the rental close to the front of the building, something she'd learned in one of the self-defense classes she'd taken, Alaina waved at the stranger and held her breath as she walked briskly to the door. She felt him watching her as she left, but he didn't follow. At the rate she was going, if she kept holding her breath she would be able to qualify for deep sea diving. The thought had her giggling as she put the car in gear and pointed it in the direction of Mystic. "At least now I have a destination in mind, even if it's going to cost me an arm and a leg with the rental company."

The song *Something Bad* by Miranda Lambert and Carrie Underwood came on the radio. It used to be one of her favorite songs, only now the words seemed ominous. She was running away from something bad, not toward it. She hoped.

She stopped one more time for gas and had driven almost nine hundred miles. When she'd left her mother was just starting to prepare lunch. The clock on the dash showed she'd been driving for almost fourteen hours, stopping for gas and food and short breaks to stretch her legs. As she passed through the town of Sturgis, she realized it was still filled with people long after closing time for bars and she wondered why. Mystic was still an hour away, but, being so close, she felt excitement and nerves bubble in her stomach.

So intent on getting to her mom's sister, Payton's, house, she missed the turnoff to their town, but saw the sign for Mystic Lodge and decided to continue on up the mountain. She hadn't called to tell them she was coming, and since it was well after two in the morning, Alaina thought the lodge might have rooms.

The dark night seemed to close in on her as she drove further up and away from the town, with the only light coming from her headlights and the dashboard. She looked down at the mile gauge to see how far she'd gone, trying to measure how much farther she had to go.

"Oh, shit," she said as she ran over something in the middle of the road, the sound of crunching glass could be heard through the closed windows. Her stomach clenched in dread and she figured she was halfway between the lodge and her aunt and uncle's house. A trek she wouldn't be scared to make if it wasn't after two in the morning on a dark and winding road. She snorted. "Cue the scary music, Lainey."

Had she not been playing the music so loud, and singing along like she was Adele, maybe she'd have seen the bottle lying in the road. Her rental jerked hard to the right, thankfully she was on a flat part of the road and was able to pull off to the side. The moon overhead gave her enough light to see the lopsided way the car was sitting.

She unplugged her phone from the charger putting it in her back pocket, grabbed her purse and bag and locked them in the trunk. Up or down? Alaina was always cautioned by her mom not to use her fey abilities because it upset her dad, or Roger. She threw caution out the proverbial window and let her fey senses guide her.

The rainbow of colors was awe inspiring, clearly leading back downward. "How does the story go?" She looked through the trees. "Over the hills and through the woods."

With a shrug she followed the trail, wishing she was sitting in her comfy apartment in Baltimore watching Sons of Anarchy. Instead, she was traipsing through unknown territories, to seek shelter from unknown family. Not the smartest thing she'd ever done.

A wolf howled in the distance, followed by a chorus of several others. She'd heard wolves howling before, having grown up in a pack, but these howls had the hair on the back of her neck standing on end. Alaina thought about sticking to the road, but the colors were more vibrant and seemed to go in a straight line through the trees. As the howls sounded closer, she chose to go with her gut and headed into the woods, the thought of climbing one of the trees as a last resort flittered through her mind.

Her enhanced hearing picked up all the sounds surrounding her, and it took her a moment to filter them out and focus on the danger. The wolves were closing in from three sides. She was faster than a normal human, had heightened senses, but up against the odds of several shifters, she knew these were not mere wolves, she was no match. Even if she was to climb the tallest tree, they could shift and climb up after her. However, she did have her fey magic.

"Screw it," she said and started running as fast as she could, following the trail while dodging low hanging branches. Her feet flew over the ground, barely making a sound, but each time she broke a twig it sounded like a gunshot to her ears. She knew the wolves could hear the same thing, she just prayed her Aunt Payton felt her presence. When she'd opened her fey abilities, the welcoming flood of magic was a familial one she recognized. It was very similar to her mother's, only crisper, not as shadowed with sadness. Alaina realized her mother wasn't happy, and she wished she'd paid closer attention when she was younger. She made a silent vow to do all she could to get her mother away from Roger and his pack...if she made it out of her own predicament.

Alaina swerved around a fallen tree, losing sight of her color guide. She stopped, trying to catch her bearings. A huge wolf jumped in front of her, his teeth bared, spittle dripping from his jaws. Another wolf, not quite as big, but just as menacing came at her from the left, followed by another on her right. She knew the tactic they were using, caging her in on all sides. She wondered if there was one behind her, but was too scared to take her eyes off the largest one in front of her. The eerie yellow eyes staring at her held menace and knowledge, a double whammy in her world. She wondered if she'd wandered onto their land.

"Listen, I know you understand me. My dad is alpha of the Cascade pack and would be really pissed if you hurt his baby girl." A complete and utter lie, but he didn't need to know that, she used the extra fey powers to surround her with an utter sense of calm, hoping they believed her.

The leader of the wolves chuffed and took a step forward.

She sent a call out to her fey family, hoping someone was up and near.

You never turn your back on a predator and you never run from a wolf. However, she did take a few steps back sensing there was no other wolves behind her. For every step she took backward, they took one forward, closing the gap between them.

Alaina raised her hands in front of her. They began to glow, magic from the lands infusing her with power she'd never had before. "If you don't back the fuck off, I will blast your asses." The two smaller wolves stopped the pursuit, their heads cocking to the side. The alpha snarled, the hair on his back stood up, indicating he was ready to attack. "I mean it, you prick. One move and you'll be roasted dog meat. Imagine the stink, boys. Have you smelled burning hair?" She made a gagging sound, but never let her arms drop. They seemed to believe she could actually roast their asses, which Alaina wasn't so sure she could or couldn't do. Continuing to back up she didn't take her eyes off of the three wolves in front of her, she didn't realize where she was walking. In that moment her main worry was keeping the animals at bay. The thought made her giggle almost hysterically, but only for a split second.

Arms flailing she screamed as she fell off the edge of a cliff. Her back hit what felt like a tree branch. Instead of a free fall she began sliding, tumbling end over end as she frantically tried to grab onto anything to stop her downward descent. A sickening crunch followed by pain flared down her left arm, making her pull back and then a jarring stop followed by another hit, this time on her head and Alaina saw stars and then blackness swallowed her whole. She yelled out for help just before total darkness encompassed everything.

Chapter Two

Niall locked up after the last of his employees had gone home. It was after two in the morning and Sturgis was still lined with bikes and their riders, along with the street vendors who had yet to close up. He shook his head. They could have the left-overs, all the smart businesses closed up before the local police started making their rounds. Checking his phone to make sure Nolan was okay before he strapped his skull cap on too, he scrolled through the half a dozen pics Payton had sent of his laughing son. *Lord,* he loved that kid. He texted a short message that he was leaving Chaps and heading home so the older woman wouldn't worry, he'd have to text again when he got home. The irony made him chuckle. His own mother didn't have him checking in, hadn't since he was sixteen, and here he was at thirty-seven checking in with his mother-in-law. The instant reply to be safe gave him a sense of home.

He pocketed his phone, straddling his bike he headed toward home. When he crossed his packs boundaries he was immediately assailed with the knowledge he had intruders on his lands. The Harley, with its loud pipes, roared even louder as he twisted down on the throttle. He let his alpha powers tell him where the breach was, let the fey wards Payton had set show him how many there were.

Past the turnoff to his pack's land, the fey colors swirled brighter, indicating where the danger lay. He recognized the area, and his heart froze while his blood ran cold. The Glades home sat close to where the mass of colors were leading, from what he could tell from his bike. He crested the last hill, seeing a sign for the Mystic Lodge. His headlight flashed on a vehicle parked on the side of the road with out-of-state plates. He pulled behind the vehicle, his nose picking up on a feminine scent that seemed familiar. His instincts were screaming at him to hurry, but he pushed them back, walking around the car he felt the hood. It was warm, so either the car hadn't been driven far, or it hadn't been here awhile.

Niall looked up and down the road, seeing the fey colors leading into the woods. "Why would a female go into the woods alone?" Unless she was leading him into a trap. He wondered if she knew the fey would lead him to her. "Only one way to find out." He let the change come over him, calling on his wolf, seamlessly changing. Once he was on four legs, he took off, following the scent as it grew stronger.

When he became aware of three new scents of shifters in his territory from the pack that had sworn to not enter his lands, Niall's wolf snarled. He'd recognize their smell in a crowd of hundreds after the run in they'd had when Cora had been taken. Had Zayn not already turned her—Niall's heart ached at the knowledge he'd have lost more than just a sister-in-law. He slowed his pursuit. The female scent of orange blossoms and ginger turned to fear, unmistakable to him. He knew in that moment she wasn't with the shifters chasing her, and by the tracks in the ground he could see they were most definitely corralling her. His ears didn't pick up any sounds of a struggle, which caused his stomach to clench.

The female's scent followed the fey trail and then stopped. He followed the three wolves' path, taking precious time so he didn't miss anything. He turned his nose up and howled, a warning should they still be in the area. Niall would remember the smell, and he'd exact punishment for being in his territory. For now, he followed the unmistakable scent of the orange blossom and ginger female, its intriguing smell made the man and wolf want to mate with her.

At the edge of a cliff he thought he'd lost all traces until he smelled blood, the sickening coppery scent was something he'd never forget. Looking down, Niall saw the woman lying in a heap twenty or so feet down at the bottom of the hill. Without wasting time or thought for his own safety, he began the slippery decent.

A few times he almost lost his footing, but in wolf form he was much more agile. By the time he reached the fallen woman, he'd prayed to every deity he could think of, hoping he'd find her alive. He'd shifted back to human before he'd completely hit the bottom. With shaky hands, Niall brushed her long brown hair back from her face. His breath caught in his throat. She was drop-dead gorgeous, even with a few cuts and scratches.

He let his breath out when he felt how warm she was. Her chest rose and fell, but her left arm was held against her, it appeared to be twice the size of the right one.

Niall ran his hands over her legs and sides, checking for other breaks. A moan escaped the woman on the ground. Her eyes fluttered open, a dark brown gaze stared back at him. He could get lost in their amber depths. "Don't move, babe. I think you've got a broken arm and maybe a few other injuries. Can you tell me your name?"

"I...I don't know?" Tears welled in her beautiful eyes.

"Hey, listen it's okay." Niall wiped at a tear on her cheek. "You took a pretty hard knock to the head. My name's Niall Malik," he said in a soft voice. "I'll call my sister-in-law, she's a doctor, and have her meet us at my place if you think you're up to the trip on foot. If not, I can call for one of my guys to bring in an ATV, but I think that would be more jarring on you."

She nodded. "Okay.

Her instant agreement worried him. He didn't know her, but was pretty sure it wasn't normal for her to automatically agree.

He placed one arm under her legs, the other behind her back. She kept a death grip on her injured arm, but her pale features worried him the most. He sent a call to his pack, needing his bike picked up and wanting their territory scouted for the intruders. Within seconds, he had several members' affirmations they were on their way.

"You're really strong," the woman in his arms murmured.

She felt right in his arms, her head nuzzling into his neck made his dick stand at attention.

Niall picked up the pace to his home. The last thing she needed was to be mauled by him when she was obviously going into shock and hurting.

The feel of her warm breath fanning over his neck didn't calm his hormones, nor the feel of her teeth scraping over his shoulder. "Careful, babe. You keep doing that and I'm liable to drop you." His voice came out much deeper than normal, his wolf coming to the surface.

A single swipe of her tongue, followed by a gentle nip, and then she said, "You'd never hurt us."

Niall looked down to ask who was us, wondering if she was maybe pregnant, or if there was someone else in the woods with her, but her eyes rolled into the back of her head. Alarmed at her loss of consciousness Niall yelled out to Zayn. *Z, I need you and your woman at my place, like five minutes ago.*

He used her lack of wakefulness to his advantage, putting on a burst of preternatural speed. By the time he made it to his home, Zayn and his mate were waiting for him.

"Holy fuck, Ny, what happened to her?" Zayn asked.

"Damned if I know, Z. Thanks for coming, Cora. I found her at the bottom of a cliff, busted up." He proceeded to tell them about the strange wolves, and her use of the word *us*. He didn't like to admit he felt completely useless, but when Cora instructed him to lay her on the bed in his guest bedroom, he ignored her, taking her into the master bedroom instead. His excuse that the bed didn't have sheets on it was bullshit, but no one called him on it.

As he placed her on the bed, she did that moan thing again. The sound made him think of sex, not something he should be thinking while surrounded by his brother and his mate, and definitely not when it was coming out of an injured woman.

"I asked if you could get me some warm water in a pan and some washcloths, Niall. I know you're alpha, but in this I need to be the boss," Cora said, her green eyes laughing at him.

"I'm always the boss, Cora. However, I'll get you what you need." He smiled.

Cora laughed while his brother kept a protective stance beside her. Niall shook his head and walked out of the room.

In the kitchen he filled up his largest pot with warm water and retrieved several cloths from the laundry room off the mudroom. Zayn was waiting for him when he came out. His little brother was leaning against the kitchen island, arms crossed over his chest, a smirk on his face.

"She smells funny, Ny." He tilted his head in the direction of the hallway.

Niall raised his eyebrows. He thought his mystery woman smelled fantastic. "That's kinda cruel, Z. Maybe you just think that because you got your nose stuck up Cora's fine ass."

Zayn's lips tilted up in a grin. One finger raised to his right eye, the middle finger no less, and he scratched. "It is a fine ass, but that's not what I mean, jackhole. I mean she reminds me of Payton, and—Emma."

Niall's heart skipped a beat. Nobody ever mentioned Emma around him except her parents, and sometimes Nolan. No one ever said they recognized her scent in someone else. She was special, and she was dead.

"Whoa, calm down, Niall." Zayn held his hands up, his relaxed stance gone.

"She does not smell like my Emma," he growled. He tried to remember what his mate smelled like. He swore he'd always know her scent anywhere, but he couldn't remember at that second.

His brother turned his head away, exposing his throat, making Niall feel like a total asshole. It wasn't Zayn's fault he couldn't remember what his own mate's unique smell was. "I'm sorry for growling at you, Zayn." Niall approached his brother slowly, pulling him in for a hug. He didn't want to be the alpha that instilled fear because he was a tyrant.

Zayn slapped him on the back. "No worries, bro, I love you. I'm sorry I brought up a sore subject."

Niall let Zayn go with another pat and then they both went back to check on the two women.

Cora's eyes were misty, making Niall painfully aware she'd heard their entire conversation. Damn wolf hearing. The mystery woman was awake again, and if he wasn't sure she was human, he'd think she had heard as well. There was definitely something different about her, he couldn't put his finger on it, but he wanted to put so much more than his fingers on her.

"You boys okay?" Cora asked.

The sound of his Harley saved him from answering and also gave him a reason to leave the accusing eyes of both women. For fucksake, he was alpha and here he was running away.

"Jett brought my bike back. I'm going to have him tow your car as well." He didn't ask or wait to see what was said. He needed to leave the room that smelled too much like orange blossoms and ginger.

* * * *

"I'm really sorry about him. He's really a sweetheart when he's..." Cora began.

"Asleep?" Alaina asked.

Laughing, the woman touched her arm. "How are you feeling? My name is Cora, by the way, and this is my...fiancé Zayn."

She studied the petite woman who smelled like a wolf. She also smelled like her mate, and sex, which wasn't surprising. When Niall had raced through the woods, she vaguely remembered the trees rushing past. However, the man who stood next to Cora was hard to miss, with his looks very similar to Niall's, she knew they were brothers. She didn't miss the fact Cora wouldn't call him her mate. She tried to remember why she knew they were wolves, and if she was one too.

"My head feels like it was hit by a baseball bat and my arm, not much better," she answered truthfully. Now that she was thinking a little clearer, her arm wasn't throbbing nearly as much.

"Without taking you to my clinic to make sure, I can do a cursory exam. Will that be okay?" Cora asked.

With a nod, she let the other woman clean her up with the warm water and cloths. She enjoyed watching the interaction between the couple as Zayn did Cora's bidding.

Zayn was sent off to fetch a first aid kit, leaving her alone with the woman who acted like a doctor.

"Are you a doctor, Cora?"

"I'm a veterinarian, actually. Before you say anything, I'll have you know that as a vet we go through years of schooling and have to learn the physiology of not just one body type, like a human doctor, but many. I mean, do you know that not many animals share the same internal makeup. For instance—"

Cora's words were cut off by Zayn who came in and placed his hand over her mouth.

"Don't get her started on all the ways the animal kingdom is different. We could be here all week for that lecture." His blue eyes smiled down into his mate's. She felt a pang of jealousy at the obvious affection.

"I just wanted her to know I was more than qualified to take care of her." Cora grabbed the ice pack from Zayn while he set everything else on the side table.

She held up her good hand. "I do trust you, and I also believe if you think I need the hospital you'll take me there." She found herself believing her words, even though she didn't know these people from Adam. Yeah, she probably should get her head examined.

Cora began swiftly cleaning the scrapes and scratches, careful of her arm she'd already placed the ice on and elevated with pillows. By the time she cleaned and checked her over, a good twenty minutes had passed, and still no sign of Niall. Her heart didn't pang from his absence. *Nope.*

"Has the swelling already gone down?" Cora peered down at the arm in question.

Zayn moved closer, making her feel threatened. She scooted to the other side of the bed, falling off the edge with a resounding thud. The pain of hitting the hardwood floors on her already injured ass, made her scream as she reached out with both hands to stop her fall.

An unholy roar shook the very floor she sat on.

A sense of calm stole over her.

"What the fuck are you doing to her?" Niall asked, storming into the room.

She watched the play of emotions cross the alpha's face, and she had no doubt Niall was the alpha. Zayn placed himself in front of his mate, the stance protective, yet submissive.

"Niall, we didn't do anything. You need to chill, man, before you scare her more." Zayn tilted his head, but didn't look away from Niall.

She processed the new information she was witnessing, sure that the alpha she'd known would've torn out the lesser wolf's throat for looking him in the eye. She sucked in a breath as a memory of a large wolf attacking a much smaller, weaker wolf, came to mind. The sound must have caught the enraged man's attention, because the next thing she knew he was beside her. He cleared the bed and landed in a crouch, crowding and protective, with his blue eyes scanning her for injuries. She held perfectly still, trying not to anger him with any quick movements. Not that she was up to any more quick escapes.

Her left arm ached from the pressure of holding it at the angle she'd landed on it, but the thought of moving scared her even more.

“Easy, babe, I’m not going to hurt you. Let me help you back onto the bed. Will you let me help you?”

His deep baritone voice sent a delicious shiver down her spine. Good God, almighty, she was not going to get excited by his voice. Wolves could scent that shit. *Think of anything other than how good he smells.*

Already at eye level, she couldn’t miss the sparkle in his gaze, nor the way his lips tilted up in a grin. Totally busted macking on the hot wolf, who didn’t know she knew he was a wolf. *Oh the something web we weave.*

“Ready?” Niall asked.

She nodded, afraid if she opened her mouth she’d lick him, or ask him to lick her. Jeezus, she was becoming a right hussy.

“I’m sorry for being a pain in the ass, if you could just let me call a cab—” Shit, she didn’t even know her name let alone who she could call, or where she could go.

“Hey, none of that. There’s no reason for tears, babe.”

“That’s easy for you to say. You know your name.

I don't know anything." She cried, a hiccupping cry bubbled up before she could stop it.

Burying her face in his chest, she let go of the tears she'd held at bay, letting the big man wrap her in his arms and hold her. She'd heard the doctor and her mate leave, but couldn't bring herself to lift her head and face him. Niall was the only thing she wasn't afraid of in the world at the moment, even the doctor didn't give her a sense of safety like he did.

A few minutes, maybe more, and she finally lifted her head from his wet T-shirt. His large hand smoothed her hair back from her face, and she swore he looked sad.

"I'm sorry, I got your shirt all wet." She tried to put space between them. His grip on the back of her head tightened for a brief moment.

"Are you feeling better?" he asked, his expression once again passive.

She swallowed the lump in her throat. "Yeah...no, not really. I feel like I'm lost and I don't know what to do or where to go." A thought struck her. "Did I have a purse, or phone?"

Niall shook his head. "Not on you, but maybe it fell out when you took your tumble. I'll go out tomorrow and scout the area. I also didn't find your car keys, so I'll look for those too. I suggest a nice hot bath, and a good night's sleep. Everything always looks better in the morning."

Her stomach rumbled, reminding her that she needed to eat. Why did she think she hadn't eaten anything for a while?

"Why don't I start you a bath and while you take a soak, I'll cook us some dinner. I usually eat after I close up the bar, so I'm starving too."

She should protest, but her gut told her she was safe or as safe as she wanted to be. He didn't wait for her to agree, just got up and went through the door she assumed was the ensuite. She heard him moving around and then the unmistakable sound of water running. He walked back out and into another door, coming out with a shirt and a pair of socks and what looked like sweats.

"These are clean, and way too big for you, but I figure you'll want to put something on after your bath. If you want, I can throw your clothes in the washer if you toss them out here after you undress. I promise to be a gentleman and not look in on you...unless you need me or want me to."

His beguiling smile nearly had her begging him to join her in the bathroom, or the bed. However, she wasn't sure if she was that kind of girl or not. For Christ-sake, she wasn't even sure if she was a card carrying member of the virgin squad. Surely, if she was a virgin, she'd be wearing like a bracelet or something? White panties? *Help, help, I've decided to have sex. Someone help.* Yeah, she was pretty sure she hadn't seen that infomercial. So, no life-alert bracelet for the virgins.

"Thank you, that'll be fine."

"Do you like steak?" Niall asked.

Her mouth watered at the mention of raw meat. Oh lord, she was afraid she was going to drool on him for another reason. At the rate she was going, she would be the worst house guest, ever. Get host wet with tears? Check. Wanna have sex, but not sure if you're that kinda girl, so you might be a tease? Check. Drool on host at mention of meat, and not the one between his legs? Check. She could hear the host calling out her name now. Only she didn't know her name so it would be something like, *and the winner for worst house guest goes to blahblahblah. Come on down.* She laughed at the absurd thoughts and then sobered at the worried look on Niall's face.

"I love steak, I'm pretty sure. Um, rawish or rare, or however you're having yours will be fine." She was babbling, but the flood of words couldn't be stopped.

"Come on. You take a bath, and I'll have supperish cooked in no time."

He was playing with her. She didn't think a man had ever played with her before. He helped her stand, making sure she was steady before he released her.

"Thank you, Niall. You're a sweet man."

Niall's grin lit up his face. "I think you're the second person in this world to ever have called me that. Here you go." He handed her the stack of clothes. "Toss your clothes out and I'll start a load while you bathe."

With a nod she went inside the bathroom. The tub was huge. Like built for five or six football players, which must be why he wasn't worried about it overflowing. He'd added some oil to the water. The scent of ginger filled the room. She loved the smell of ginger. The memory gave her pause. She tried to grab onto it and force more, only to have pain throb in her temple.

Shedding her dirty clothes, she was shocked to see her left arm was no longer swollen. Black and blue bruises mottled the entire arm as she eased the shirt off, exposing the damage, but there were only bruises, no breaks. Quickly, she removed the rest of her clothes, folding them and placing them in a pile outside the door.

She decided to get clean before she inspected the rest of the damage in the mirror, figuring she had maybe fifteen minutes, twenty tops. On the edge of the huge tub she found shampoo and conditioner, and she wondered if he had regular overnight female guests. The green-eyed monster reared its head at the thought. She twisted her hair up and tied it in a knot, praying it didn't fall into the oiled water. Looking across at the glass enclosed shower, she could imagine Niall using it, and she calculated her time.

The warm water felt delicious as she stepped over the side and sunk into the depths. She could've sat in the warm oily water forever, but she had put a mental clock on, and her time was ticking. Through the water she could see more bruises covered her legs and torso. She wondered why she didn't hurt from head to toe. Sufficiently clean and relaxed, she pulled the plug, sighing, wishing she had an hour to spend in the glorious tub. As she stood, she looked out the floor to ceiling windows behind her, figuring if there was someone out there they were getting a great view of her sorry looking ass, which she assumed was just as black and blue as the front of her.

She grabbed one of the towels Niall had left out for her and wiped her feet, not wanting to fall on the tile floor before she made her way to the shower to wash her hair. With the shampoo and conditioner in hand, she stepped inside, marveling at the amenities his home had. She chose the temperature she wanted on the display and within seconds his shower was on and at the desired temp. Five shower heads began spraying from the walls. Decadent was the term she'd call his shower, and again, somewhere she wished she had more time to spend. Untying the knot in her hair she let the overhead rain shower spout run over her.

Sighing, she quickly washed and conditioned, then reluctantly shut the shower off.

In the full length mirror, she looked at herself for the first time since Niall had brought her to his home. "Oh, my, God." No wonder he could totally keep his hands off of her. She was a hot-mess.

Chapter Three

Niall's wolf beat at his skull as he got his first glimpse at Alaina's body. Not that she wasn't perfect in every way, his body reminded him in an obvious reaction. Niall adjusted his dick before he risked permanent damage. He and his wolf were in complete accord, wanting to hunt down those who had caused the damage to the woman in his bathroom. His deck wrapped around the entire back and one side of his house in an L-shape. When she'd stepped out of the tub, he hadn't meant to look, hadn't expected to see her. She'd stood up like Aphrodite coming out of the sea, and then he'd seen her bruised and battered body. His canines dropped, his fur had erupted from his skin, and it took all his control to call his wolf into submission. Niall had never had that reaction before. Never. He'd seen his friends busted up, bleeding and needing medical attention, but he'd never lost control of his wolf. He didn't like it.

Even now his gums ached with the need to shift and hunt. He curled his hands into fists, his nails had retracted, finally. He thought about calling Z and Cora, and asking them to come and get the unknown woman. An image of her on his floor, cowering in fear, put an end to that call before he could even pick up his phone.

He listened to her moving around, the sound of her bare feet approaching the sliding glass doors gave him a few extra seconds to compose himself. The steaks had taken only a few minutes to defrost and a few more to sear on the grill. Baked potatoes would've taken too long, and he was exhausted, yet wired. Her pert little nose sniffed the air as she walked down the steps onto his patio.

"Have a seat and I'll get the steaks out. Do you want any condiments?" Damn, he almost asked her if she wanted a condom. He thought of the words he'd said to his brother Zayn just a short while ago. If he could keep his own dick in his pants for the duration of her stay it would be a miracle, much less his fangs. The last thing he needed was a mate who didn't know who she was. He pictured the smirk Zayn would have while he recounted his exact words to him. Lord save him from little brothers with attitudes, who would have no problem saying *I told you so,* or in this case, *Keep your dick in your pants and your fangs to yourself.* Niall shook his head at the image of himself saying those ominous words to Zayn when his son had accidentally bitten Cora.

"I think I usually do, but these smell fantastic." She indicated the plate with the meat piled on it.

Niall nodded, worried if he opened his mouth he'd embarrass himself and say something about how good she smelled. Walking back inside he grabbed the bowl of pasta salad he'd made the day before, for him and Nolan.

"I hope you like pasta salad. It's my son's favorite, and one way I can get him to eat broccoli and cauliflower."

Her big brown eyes flew up to his. "You have a son? Where are he and his mom? Your wife?"

He gritted his teeth, the familiar ache like a knife to his heart. "Nolan is with his grandparents. My wife passed away many years ago."

"I'm sorry."

She looked on the verge of tears. The last thing he needed or wanted from this woman was her pity. "It was a long time ago. Let's eat before our steaks get cold."

They'd eaten their steaks, him two and her one and demolished what was left of the pasta salad, when he heard one of his pack members howl to let him know all was clear. The sound, reassuring to him, did just the opposite to his companion. Her shoulders stiffened, the chair she was in skidded across the deck, and she was on her feet in a fighters crouch.

Niall wasn't sure what to make of her reaction, other than she must be remembering the attack by the three rogues, and worried they were near.

"Easy, it's okay. I won't let anything hurt you."

Her chin trembled. "Can we go inside now? I want to go to bed."

He placed his hand on the back of her head, making her look up at him. "Everything will look better in the morning."

She snorted. "It's almost morning now."

Her inherent humor always seemed to break through. "Yes, but if you pretend it's not until you open your eyes, it'll be whenever you wake up."

"Is that what you do?"

Niall thought about his answer. "It's what I try to do." He tugged on her hair. "Come on, let's get some shut-eye. I don't know about you, but I could use a few hours of rest. I lugged a woman around the woods tonight."

"Hey!" She laughed. The joke got the desired effect, and got her moving forward.

He held the door open while she carried the empty bowl and he brought their other dishes inside. They worked together to load the dishwasher, and when he led her back to his room, intent on sleeping in the guest room, her hand on his arm stopped him. "Will you stay with me, just to, you know, sleep. I don't think I could sleep alone, and I don't think I'm the kind of woman who sleeps around."

Her rushed words sent all the blood south to his cock. He knew he should tell her no, but damned if he didn't nod and follow her inside his bedroom. The room he'd never shared with his Emma. When she'd died he'd turned the guest room into the master bath and built on, turning the master into the new guest suite. They'd planned to build on and have more kids, but life didn't always do what you wanted.

"I'm going to grab a quick shower, why don't you climb in and get comfortable and I'll be out shortly." After he rubbed one out in the big stall, but he didn't say that.

She nodded and headed to the bed, while he went into the bathroom, closing the door behind him. *Fuck.* How was he supposed to sleep next to her and not touch? He imagined her skin beneath his fingers, his tongue, and his dick was ready to go out and say hello.

The sound of seams ripping had him slowing down so he wouldn't ruin a pair of comfy jeans. He tossed the ruined shirt in the trash can, stepping inside his state-of-the-art shower, and set the temp to just above freezing, hoping it would stave off his need.

Niall braced his hands on the tiled wall. The water did nothing to abate his hard-on. He imagined his mystery guest lying in the middle of his bed with her curvy body, and even the icy water couldn't cool his ardor. He grabbed some soap and washed quickly, but his cock had other plans. Picturing the gorgeous woman's hand wrapped around him, he pumped his fist up and down his shaft, closing his eyes.

It only took a few slides up and down of his hand, before he felt the tingling in his spine. He squeezed his eyes closed, locked his jaw in place to hold in the yell as his cum flew out the tip. The orgasm shook him, but still left him feeling empty. He'd rather be between the thighs of the woman in the other room. Not happening. She could be married.

Grabbing a towel he dried off and realized he'd not brought in anything to put on, used to sleeping nude, he opened the door, prayed she was sleeping. She had her back to him, the steady sound of her breathing reassured him she wasn't awake. Niall drew on a pair of boxer briefs.

He made sure the security alarm was set, eased into the bed, careful not to touch her. The bed was a super-king. He figured they could get through five or six hours without touching. He exhaled as he relaxed into the soft bedding. His eyes closed, sleep usually coming easily to him.

Niall's eyes flickered open, the sound of breathing interrupted his attempt at REMs. Orange blossom and ginger tickled his nose, making his mouth water for a taste. He stacked his hands under his head to keep from reaching for her, exhaustion be damned.

She rolled into him, her head finding his shoulder as naturally as if it did it every day. He unlocked his fingers, wrapped his arm around her shoulder and brought her closer to him. Niall figured this was what hell was like. Being so close to heaven, but not being able to touch, or suck, lick, or kiss. *Yeah, he was in hell.*

* * * *

She woke to find herself snuggled up against a very warm, hard body. She blinked, trying not to let the man holding her know she was awake, wanting to look at him while he slept. The good Lord was in a great mood when he created this man. His reddish-blond hair was cut in a short spiky do that even in repose stood on end. His beard was the same color, making her hand itch to run across his jaw. She thought he'd look more boyish when he was sleeping, but he still looked fierce. Like the alpha she knew he was. However, she didn't have a clue who she was.

"Good morning, babe."

His voice should come with a warning label. She knew he could smell her arousal, she just didn't know how. Rubbing her legs together she said. "Morning, Niall."

"We need to get up, or we won't be getting out of this bed for a long time."

A little devil made her lift her leg and run it up his thigh. "I think something is definitely up."

"You don't want to start something, little girl, you can't finish." Niall's hand held her leg against

him.

She felt him twitch against her inner thigh. From the feel of his dick, he was definitely size appropriate. The man was large all over. Lifting her head up, she saw desire in his laser blue eyes. “I don’t know who I am.” Until she knew who she was, where she came from, she couldn’t give herself to this man. Although every fiber of her being wanted to see if he was truly as big as he felt.

“Come here.” Niall took the decision out of her hands, and pulled her up his body. “I’ve been dying to taste you, just a taste.”

Bending her head, she licked at the seam of his mouth. His hands tangled in her hair as his mouth crushed hers to him. His cock was trapped between them, separated between her borrowed sweats, and his thin boxer briefs.

She was five rubs away from coming. Gah, she wanted to come with him inside her.

With a growl, he flipped them, pressing his body into hers. She moaned into Niall’s kiss, smoothing her hand up his back to his neck.

He rocked between her legs, and she was seconds away from coming. Niall separated their mouths, his breathing ragged. “Shit, we need to stop.”

A whimper escaped her.

He buried his face in her neck, breathing deeply while she stroked his shoulders.

"You're right," she said without conviction.

Niall laughed. "You should try sounding a little more convincing."

Could she come by his deep voice whispering across where her neck and shoulder met, she wondered. "Hmm, I think you are the one on top, big guy."

Niall thrust his hips. "I've got your big guy, but you are also the one with her legs wrapped around me, not that I'm complaining." He lifted his head and upper body up, holding himself on his elbows. His smile letting her know he enjoyed their positions.

She traced the tattoos on his chest and down both arms. She was sure she loved a man with tattoos. Did she have any? "Do I have any tattoos?"

"I don't see any sleeves like mine, and last night all I saw was a whole lotta bruises." Desire turned to worry as he looked at his body lying over hers. "Fuck, babe, am I hurting you?"

She was amazed to realize that no, she wasn't hurting anywhere, not even her arm. Shaking her head she unlocked her legs from around his hips.

He rolled off before she could answer. “Let’s get up and eat some breakfast, and then we’ll go see about looking for your phone and keys.”

Nodding, she got off on one side of the bed as he jumped from the other. The flex and play of muscles on his body was a work of beauty. The man had more tattoos on his upper back as well as his chest and both arms. She really wanted to see if she had any, and if she didn’t, she was getting one the first chance she got. When she’d looked herself over last night she hadn’t thought to look for anything other than damage.

“Why are you staring at me like that?” Niall asked over his shoulder.

“I love your tattoos.”

He quirked one eyebrow. “Don’t go off halfcocked and get one, just to get one. You need to think about your ink and make sure they mean something special to you.”

“Do all your tattoos mean something special to you?” she asked, watching him stroll into his large walk-in closet.

“Yes,” he answered, but didn’t offer any more explanations.

His shortness left her with a sense of loss. *Not*

going there girlie. You don't even know who you are. "Heck, I may have a boyfriend, or fiancé, wherever I'm from." The whispered words jolted her. Panic at the unnamed man threatened to send her running off into the woods.

The next thing she knew, Niall was crouched in front of her.

"Breathe, you're safe. What happened?" he asked.

Trying to come up with a plausible answer, she ducked her head. No way in hell was she going to tell him what she thought. She was adding up the clues, and not liking what she came up with. Battered and bruised and left for dead, could only mean a couple things. She was running from something or someone. Did she have an abusive husband, or boyfriend she was running from? Either way she couldn't stay here and bring her problems to Niall and his pack.

She swallowed the huge lump in her throat, tried to control her heartbeat. "I just panicked at the thought that I don't remember who I am." Not a lie. "Did one of your friends bring my car here?"

Niall's blue gaze stared her down, and it took everything she had not to look away.

"They towed it to the garage in town."

"Did they find my purse in it?" She was getting tired of cowering in the corner, but with him now looming over her, she had no choice.

His head cocked to the side. "Actually, no. They said the inside had nothing in it so they didn't try to jimmy the lock."

"Fuck, shit." She raked her fingers through her tangled hair. "Could you please give me some space?"

Far from giving her more space he closed the few inches separating them. Warm breath fanned over her lips, creating a delicious tingle. She licked her bottom lip, and then sucked it inside her mouth.

"You are going to drive me insane. You know that, don't you?" Niall's mouth covered hers, taking instead of asking.

Damn man could kiss like a rock star. He nibbled and then sucked her lips, one at a time, making her think of other things he'd do with his mouth. By the time he lifted his head, she wasn't sure what they'd been talking about. She looked at the bed a few feet away, and contemplated how long it would take them to get undressed and him inside her.

"Don't look at me like that or I'll have you and me both stripped in less than sixty seconds."

She opened her mouth to tell him she had no

clue what he was talking about, then she remembered werewolves could not only smell a lie, but arousal. She was so turned on, the neighbors could probably smell her. Niall's blue eyes flashed electric blue, a clear sign his wolf was close to the surface. Again, she wondered how she knew about werewolves. Had the person she was running from been a wolf too? Instinctively she knew she was safe with Niall, but something kept her from telling him she was aware of what he was.

"I need to use the bathroom," she said.

He nodded and gave her space to get up, offering her his hand. She didn't think it was smart to refuse his help with his wolf so close to the surface. Her palm was swallowed up by his much larger one, yet they fit together. She released him almost immediately.

"I'll just be a few minutes." She stepped around him. Her borrowed sweats held up by one hand as she made her way into the large master bathroom, shutting the door for some much needed privacy. "Keep your hands to yourself woman, or you'll be getting screwed six ways to Sunday without knowing if you're a card carrying member of the V-club," she mumbled under her breath. She looked at her appearance in the mirror after using the facilities. The woman staring back at her didn't jar her memories. Dark brown hair, brown eyes, a straight nose that clearly had never been broken, and a face that would be considered pretty by many.

She noticed her own clothes had been placed on the counter. The silk thong, and somewhat matching bra had heat blooming in her tan face. With a shrug, she pulled his white T-shirt off, followed by the too-large sweats. They still held a hint of his unique fragrance, a tinge of patchouli and citrus and all Niall. Standing naked, holding a strangers clothing like a lovesick fool, she felt like an idiot. She tossed the clothes in the hamper, shaking off the need to inhale his scent one last time.

Pulling the panties and jeans on, she realized her shirt was clean but had rips and holes in all the wrong places. "Obviously, this material doesn't do well after falling down a cliff, and then being washed and dried."

She pulled her hair into a messy bun, brushed her teeth with the toothbrush Niall was kind enough to leave out, still new in the package, which made her wonder how many overnight guests he had. She looked at the dirty clothes basket, contemplating pulling out the shirt she'd worn to bed, then thought she'd just ask him for another one to borrow. Mind made up, she stepped out of the bathroom.

Niall had his back to her. He'd dressed in a pair of jeans that hung low on his hips with a leather belt. A chain attached to his wallet disappeared around the front, with a black T-shirt with the word Chaps on top and a motorcycle in the middle. The tight fit of the shirt molded to his muscles, which tensed as soon as she opened the door.

She cleared her throat. "Can I borrow another shirt? I'm afraid this one is playing peek-a-boo with my boobs."

He turned to look over one shoulder. "You're trying to kill me, aren't you?"

"No clue what you're talking about, but I really can't go out like this." She indicated the shirt she had on." The bra said thirty-four double D, and that was without padding. She'd guess her age to be mid-twenties to late twenties at the oldest. Her girls were definitely real, and firm. The strategic rips and holes in the once cute top were showing off the pink and black lace bra, making her comment abundantly clear.

His growl didn't scare her, quite the opposite, a

fact his sensitive nose was sure to smell.

He stomped around her, coming back with another black shirt similar to the one he had on. "Here, put this on."

"Yes, sir. Do you want to turn your back, go in the other room, or watch?" The imp in her couldn't resist teasing him.

Niall still held the shirt in his hand, but instead of handing it to her he draped it over his shoulder. "Baby, you play with fire, you are bound to get burned."

"What..."

He didn't let her finish, his hand ripped the already ruined shirt in half. "So damn beautiful." His head bent, suckling her through the lace cups.

She was pretty sure she was going to come right then and there. His hands came up and held her by the ribs, bringing her up to his much higher level. She wrapped her legs around his waist, locking her ankles behind his back.

He pulled the cups of her bra down, exposing her nipples. His mouth switched to the other breast, tongue teasing the tip before he nipped with his teeth. The sensation went straight to her clit, sending her closer to the edge. He brought his hand under her ass, the other around her back supporting her, pushing her pelvis into his groin. Whimpers escaped her throat as he continued to suck and bite on her left breast. So close, was the litany running through her mind.

Niall trailed wet kisses to her right nipple, biting down harder on the tip, sending her careening into a hard and fast orgasm. She yelled out his name, holding his head against her, wishing he was inside her.

His rumbling growl reverberated against her.

She loved the way his arms wrapped around her, holding her like she was precious.

"I'm sorry, I didn't..." Niall began.

Tugging on his hair, she covered his mouth with her own. He claimed her like she did him, taking his mouth in a deep, endless, soul searing possession. *Mine. Mate.*

She wasn't sure who was speaking in her mind, but the words made her pull back.

"No regrets." She bit his lip, making him bleed a little. The sweet coppery taste was like an elixir she wanted more of. "That's going to be my tattoo."

He nodded. "Let's get going. Hopefully we can find some clues."

He didn't say what they both were thinking. They were both banking on her miraculously remembering who she was and where she came from. He let her slide down his body, every inch of him was hard.

When her feet hit the ground, she stepped back and away from temptation wrapped up in six foot three of tattooed male yumminess.

Being the smart woman she was, she didn't mention the fact her tiny thong was soaking wet, thanks to her orgasm. It was his fault for his amazing talent with lips and teeth and tongue. She shivered with just the memory of how it felt to have him nuzzling on her. The thought of how it would feel to have him between her legs had heat rushing through her, threatening her resolve.

Chapter Four

Niall adjusted his dick. Her scent had man and wolf ready to claim her as their mate, but he was coherent enough to step away from the alluring temptation. He didn't think he'd bitten her hard enough to cause a worry, not like his brother Zayn had dealt with when Nolan had bitten Cora. Their situations were completely different. Nolan was an innocent child who'd been injured and had accidentally bitten the good doctor, causing the first bite in the change. His brother Zayn was the one who couldn't keep his dick and fangs to himself, and then turned the woman into one of them, taking her for his mate. Niall was older and wiser. He was alpha and wouldn't be getting an accidental wolf for a mate like Zayn, no matter how badly he wanted to fuck her.

Her scent had intoxicated him when she'd come from his sucking on her luscious breasts. No woman had ever done that before. He wanted to reach between her thighs and stroke her, bring her essence into his mouth and see if she tasted as sweet. Instead, he took a step away, followed by another. He picked up the shirt that had fallen on the floor and tossed it her way, not trusting himself to get close enough to hand it to her.

"I'll fry up some bacon and eggs, while you...um get finished." He waved in her general area.

Call him a pussy for rushing out of the room. He didn't give no fucks. He beat feet into the kitchen. The large space made preparing scrambled eggs and bacon quick and easy. His cell sat on the charging dock, showing he hadn't missed any calls.

After calling his son to see how his night was, and hearing all was great, Niall hung up and pulled the eggs off the fire. His stainless steel stove had eight burners, and he'd long since learned the art of cooking a fast breakfast on the fly. The toaster dinged, popping out four slices, adding to the others he'd already toasted and buttered. Within minutes he had breakfast done and was waiting for his sex-on-legs guest.

"Smells delicious. Can I help?"

He tipped his chin toward the side-by-side fridge. "Milk, OJ, or coffee?"

"Coffee and OJ. You can't eat bacon without having orange juice."

Her brown eyes sparkled, reminding him of his favorite woman, Payton, when she was happy. The image made him pause, but his guest already turned around. She'd tied the shirt in a knot at the back, giving him a glimpse of her tattoo-less waist. Her jeans were snug as hell, riding low on her curvy hips. She had an ass that was made for holding onto when going for a long hard ride. When he'd held her ass, each cheek fit perfectly in the palm of his hands, the same as her breasts. He was definitely an ass and breast man. Perfect was the word he'd use to describe everything about her. Dangerous.

"Do you want any jam?" she asked, her head in his fridge.

His mind went straight to the gutter and stayed there. "No," he said more harshly than necessary. "I mean, no, thank you."

Her rounded ass was enough to make a grown man get down on his knees and salivate. Watching her wiggle had his dick hard as a pike and his brain not functioning on all cylinders. She brought his favorite raspberry jelly out and sat across from where he stood at the granite counter. He was glad the top kept her from seeing just how hard he was.

"I clearly love bacon and scrambled eggs. I keep seeing a woman who looks very much like me cooking them for me."

She even looked sexy when she talked with her mouth half-full. “That’s good.” He pointed his fork at her.

“My mother makes the best lasagna, ever. She doesn’t put that gross ricotta or cottage cheese shit in it though.” He shuddered, making her laugh.

“Not a fan, huh?”

Niall raised his eyebrows. “If you tell me you like it, our association is over.” He grinned.

Her tongue peeked out to lick a crumb off the corner of her lip. “No, that is some nasty stuff for real. Lots of mozzarella and sauce and I’m a slave for some good pasta.”

He thought of being licked by her, or him licking her, either would work for him. His new favorite flavor was going to be orange blossom and ginger.

They cleaned up in no time, and were heading out toward the woods where he’d found her. He’d packed a backpack with water and snacks. Every good Boy Scout made sure they had provisions before heading out on a hike, and he had to keep up the pretense.

She stayed right behind him, her close proximity making man and wolf put her safety first. He took his duties as alpha seriously, always thinking of the pack before himself. The only ones who came before pack were his family, but this little woman had somehow moved up in his rankings, and he didn't even know her name. He was so screwed in the head.

His nose picked up the scent of an unknown wolf near the cliff edge. The trace of the intruder was hours old, but he sent a mental call out to Jett. Their wards had been breached and he hadn't been warned. His next mental call was to Emerson, all the while, he kept a tight hold on the woman trailing him, with his hand firmly clasping hers.

Technically the area they were in wasn't necessarily on their land, but close enough there should have been some sort of disturbance, unless the wolves knew exactly where to step and where not to. He sent a visual to his pack.

The attack from the wolves a few months back had put them all on guard, but they had no clue if the other wolves knew exact details of their property lines. If they did, they may also know their strengths and weaknesses.

"Wow," she said. "I fell down that and lived to tell the tale?"

Man and wolf both snarled, making the woman take a step way too close to the edge. Niall reached out and pulled her into his arms. "Yes, you were lucky." The image of her lying, broken and bleeding was burned into his brain. His wolf rose to the forefront, wanting to claim their mate. Niall pushed him back.

"Do you think my phone or purse is down there somewhere?"

She was obviously unaware of the war waging within himself. "Stay here and I'll go see."

Her gorgeous eyes widened, flecks of amber shone in the milk chocolate depths. "You're going to leave me...up here, alone." She swallowed audibly.

He couldn't help himself. He stepped closer, tipped her chin up, claiming her lips in a kiss that took both their breaths away. Niall almost forgot what he was going to do. Lost in the sweet taste of the woman who fit him as if she was made just for him, he had to force himself to pull away. "You'll be fine. I can be down there and back up in no time." He didn't mention he'd shift, if he had to, into his other form. There was something about her that called to him, both of his sides.

She nodded, but the fear was still present in her gaze.

He handed her his cell phone. "If something

happens, hit the number one. That's my brother Zayn's direct line. He will know how to find you and me. Not that I think we will need him, but to make you feel better. See that tree right there." He grabbed her hand and walked the few feet to the spot in question. "Keep your back to this here tree, that way you are blocked from three sides." The roots had spread out leaving a spot just large enough for a small person to nestle against.

"I'll be fine, go."

Her heart rate had slowed down, like her mini-panic attack was abated. Niall bent and pecked her full lips before striding to the cliff edge. He could see where she'd slid off the night before, and followed her descent over. Once he was out of her line of sight, he shifted to his partial wolf in order to scale the side with more ease, paying close attention to the branches and debris littering the sides. The ground was a good fifteen to twenty feet down, and he was still amazed she hadn't sustained any real injuries. He took his time scouting the terrain, looking for her cell and purse, anything that would lead to her identity.

A shaft of sun shone through the trees, making the ground near the edge of the hill sparkle. Niall strode to the spot and found what he assumed was her phone. When he tried to turn it on, it was completely dead. He spent a few more minutes kicking leaves out of the way, and using his nose to scent the area, looking for traces of her familiar smell. When he couldn't find anything else, he began the climb back up.

She still stood in the exact same spot he'd left her. "Did you find anything?" Hope laced her voice.

Niall pulled the iPhone out of his back pocket. The purple case with the diamonds on the back made her squeal. "Do you recognize this?" he asked.

"Purple is my favorite color. I think...no, I know, my mom bought me that case for Christmas last year. My name is Alaina Strop. Oh, God. My name is Alaina."

He caught her as she jumped into his arms, her laugh, one of relief and excitement bubbled out of her.

"That's a beautiful name, Alaina. Do you know where you're from?"

She closed her eyes in obvious concentration. "I live in Baltimore. I'm a teacher. I have no clue why I'm here though." Her chin wobbled.

Niall couldn't handle seeing her happiness

disappear. He palmed her ass, and yes, each cheek did fit perfectly in his hands, lifting her until she had her legs around him. "Hey, one thing at a time. It'll come to you. Once we get your phone charged you can call your mom, or boyfriend."

Alaina shook her head. "I don't have a boyfriend."

He wanted to fist pump the air, but that would mean he'd have to release her. That wasn't happening anytime soon. "Good," he growled.

She pulled him down to her, murmuring against his lips. "Yes, good. Now, kiss me."

Fuck, yes. Any protest he had at taking advantage of her flew out the nonexistent window. He kissed her deeply, feeling her roll her hips against him. Niall began to rock his hips, walking them backward with her wrapped around him. Her hips churned, making him harder.

Grinding against the apex of her thighs, he moaned as their excitement built.

The tree was at her back, stopping him in his tracks. He used his arms to protect her, pulled his lips away to see if she was with him. Her expression mirrored his, joy, passion, wonder, and excitement. He catalogued every nuance of her gorgeous face and feared he'd never grow tired of looking at her—not even when they were in their hundreds and were too old to make cubs. The imagery put him on edge.

"What's wrong?" she asked.

"Nothing," his voice sounded raw to his own ears.

"Bullshit, Niall. One minute you were ready to fuck me. Now, you look like I was asking you to marry me. Believe me when I say, this is a no strings attached thing. I'm not expecting anything from you." She smiled up at him, even though the words hurt to say.

Her hand lifted to touch his beard-stubbled jaw, but he caught it. "I'm still ready to fuck you. I just...don't want to harm you." He could give her pleasure, more pleasure than she'd ever experienced before, or ever would again.

"Then we are of the same accord. I don't want you to hurt me either. Don't make me promises you can't keep, and since I'm not asking you for anything, we are golden. So, where were we?" She pulled her hand free, then ran it through his short hair.

He released her long enough for them both to shimmy out of their clothes. She was so damn gorgeous that she took his breath away. Standing in the woods in nothing but her tan skin, skin he wanted to lick from head to toe, Alaina Strop was without a doubt one of the most beautiful women he'd ever seen. Her hair hung halfway down her back in dark brown waves, her eyes were a milk chocolate with amber flecks and her skin had a golden glow. A wood sprite come to life. Niall swore he was looking at a real life goddess, or royalty, as she stood proudly in front of him. He felt a niggling in the back of his brain that he should know something, but her scent called to him. *Mine.*

He deserved to have some happiness, the ultimate expression in the form of being with a woman who ticked off every box. Niall didn't worry about protection, knowing he couldn't catch diseases, nor did he carry any. He also couldn't impregnate a woman who wasn't his mate. However, for Alaina's sake, he pulled a condom package out of his wallet, slipping it on before he could forget. Hurt flashed in her eyes for just a second.

"I want you inside me, Niall," she whispered, and pressed up against him.

"You are going to kill me, woman," he swore.

He pressed her back against the bark of the tree and lifted her up. "Put your legs around my hips."

She did as he told her, biting her lip to keep from crying out. Niall wanted to hear her scream out her pleasure.

He aligned his cock to her opening, the slickness a testament to how ready she already was. He pushed forward finding her tighter than expected. Bending, he kept a hold on Alaina while he snagged his shirt off the ground and put it between her soft back and the tree. Once he had her protected he used one hand under her to keep her up, and the other he snaked between their bodies to strum her clit.

The little bundle of nerves didn't need a lot of attention before she was gyrating against his cockhead, taking him in a little farther. "So tight," he ground out.

He pinched her clit between his forefinger and thumb, sending her into a fast, hard, orgasm. Her intense brown gaze jerked to his, mouth opened on a silent scream as she relaxed her pussy muscles and he thrust upward, penetrating her.

* * * *

Alaina leaned her head back when his huge cock entered her. Holy hell, he was too big. She held completely still. Her mind and body tried to come to grips with the fact she'd just given up her V-card, and she hadn't started with an appropriate size.

"Why didn't you tell me you were a virgin?" Niall jerked her hair to get her attention.

Could she tell him her insatiable lust blinded her. It was a new flaw and only came out when in his presence clearly. "I'm sorry." Her voice wasn't as strong as she hoped.

He chuckled. "Sorry? Baby, I could've hurt you, but sorry isn't something I am."

"I can't seem to control myself around you," she confessed.

"Do you have these same problems with other men?" he asked.

Alaina couldn't believe they were having this conversation with him buried to the hilt inside her. "Obviously, not." She squeezed her inner muscles around his dick.

"Good, don't. I happen to like these urges you can't seem to control," he grunted.

Smiling, heart beating faster, she wrapped her legs and arms around him a little tighter, rubbing her clit against his groin until he had no choice but to move or be left behind. She kissed him desperately, needing him to want her like she wanted him.

The dominant way he reached back and grabbed her wrist, pinning them to the tree above her head, fucking her hard turned her on. His pelvis ground against her, his balls slapping her ass, hitting her clit each time he pushed into her until she had no choice but to come again, exploding into a bliss unlike any she'd found alone.

He groaned and shuddered against her as his hips continued to pump, his fingers of one hand clung to her ass with bruising force, as he began filling the condom with his seed.

When he released her hands, she snuggled her face into his neck, licking the tendon, an urge to bite down swept over her.

A twig snapped in the distance. Niall went perfectly still.

Alaina jumped, forgetting where they were, locked in their own cocoon of a lovers' embrace.

Niall reached back and unlocked her legs. "Get dressed quickly," Niall said, disengaging their bodies before bending and slipping into his own clothes much quicker than Alaina.

He cursed, making her look back up at him. "What's wrong?" Alaina wished she had a way of washing up. She envied Niall's ability to just slip the condom off, toss it away and he would be clean, where she had a mess and nothing in the woods to...

"The condom broke." His harsh words jolted her.

She shrugged, hurt at his tone and accusing look. "I get the shot." When he looked at her like she was speaking Swahili, she explained about the birth control shot. "I started getting it a while back, which is really none of your business, but since you were my first and seem worried, I can tell you I have no diseases. Now, how about you?"

Wriggling into her panties, and then her pants, she didn't look at Niall again. The silence stretched for several long seconds.

"I don't have any diseases."

"Good. Can we drop it then?" Somewhat decent she was ready for the walk of shame.

"Are you embarrassed for what we just did?" he growled.

Alaina's eyes flew up to his laser blue gaze. "Good Lord, no. I thought you were."

"I'm not, but I didn't want you to be. I'm fucking this up and my...friend is not far from here. I didn't want him to see you naked."

She pursed her lips. He was going to say pack

mate, but stopped and she knew it was because he didn't think she knew about wolves. Still, his words and actions made no sense to her. Was he or wasn't he upset that the condom broke? Did he think she'd make him marry her if she got pregnant? Again, the thought of marriage frightened her. The last memory she had was of going to her class to teach in Baltimore.

A sharp pain stabbed behind her eyes when she tried to remember teaching that day. Sucking in a sharp breath, Alaina reached up to rub her temple. Niall's hand slid into her messy hair making her moan as he massaged the back of her head.

"What is it?" he asked.

"I had a vision of me going to class. I can remember sitting at my desk helping a student who couldn't figure out the program we were working on. Her name is Jay, a really sweet girl, and then this pain began."

Niall's warm lips touched her forehead. "Don't force it, babe. It'll come to you. Let's see what Jett has found." He left her side momentarily to scan the area, always within sight of her. His friend Jett arrived within a few minutes, long strides eating up the distance. Jeezus, did all the men in Mystic look as good as the three she'd encountered so far?

Alaina gulped, eyeing Niall as he narrowed his angry glare at her. Looking up at him, she raised an eyebrow, wondering why he was angry now. Her body throbbed and ached from their recent bout of tree sex. She always joked with her friends that her dream man would have to be able to have wall sex with her. Niall clearly fit the bill, although it was tree, not wall, she figured it was close enough. The man was a threat to her sanity with his muscular, tattooed body, reddish blond hair, and his smile...lawd, she swore her panties were in a perpetual state of dampness from that alone.

"You going to introduce me to your mate, al...Niall?"

She didn't think the man she'd just given herself to was going to answer Jett, his jaw had a visible tick indicating his displeasure. Alaina wrapped her arms over her breasts that were still raw from where he'd sucked and bitten them. The image brought heat to her face and arousal flooding her once again.

Both men flared their noses and she was aware they could smell her, damn their enhanced senses.

With a groan, Niall prowled back to her. "God damn it, you are enough to drive a sane man fucking nuts." One hand fisted in the back of her shirt, the other ran up her spine.

Alaina's skin came alive, need growing again, melting away her insecurities.

Running her hands up his chest, over his shoulders, she stood on her toes, moaning when her hard nipples came into contact with his hard chest. Desperate to feel her nakedness against his, she pulled him down struggling to get closer.

Jett coughed, making Niall break away. His eyes narrowed and glittered as they looked at his pack mate. "Jett, this is Alaina. Alaina, this is my best friend, Jett." Pulling her next to him, Niall pressed a kiss to her temple. "Did you find anything?" he asked Jett.

Instead of being angry at his show of possessiveness, Jett's eyes danced with amusement. Grinning, Jett approached Alaina with an outstretched hand. A skull and crossbones ring was on his left middle finger, and like both he and Zayn, Jett had several tattoos. He ignored Niall's warning glare, clearly setting Niall's teeth on edge. "Hello there, gorgeous. I can see why Ny wanted to keep you all to himself. If you get tired of all his snarling, make him bring you down to Chaps tonight. It's ladies night, and we know how to treat the ladies. Right, Ny?" An undercurrent was being spoken, but she couldn't discern what they were talking about.

Shrugging, she looked up at Niall. "What is Chaps? I saw it on your shirt and this one." She plucked at the one she had on, drawing both men's attention. Niall and Jett growled.

Niall met Jett's eyes with what she would call a furious scowl, which seemed to amuse him even more. Turning back down to her, he frowned. "Surely you didn't travel halfway across the country without any clothes?"

"Torq made a key for her car and popped the trunk. She'd had a flat tire up the road and for some reason decided to cut through the woods instead of sticking to the road. Do you remember why?" Jett asked.

Alaina stiffened. "No. I'm not stupid, and I do know how to change a tire. Was there not a spare in the car?"

Jett shrugged. "Yeah, there was. You locked your suitcase and purse in the trunk, so at least you've got clothes and ID." His black gaze went from her to Niall and back again as if she'd lost her mind.

Her easy camaraderie with the two men

disappeared. Niall looked equally frustrated with the news, something they'd have to deal with as soon as they were alone.

"Did they bring her car to my place?" Niall asked.

Looking worried, Jett nodded. "I scouted from the road to here, and Bronx, along with a couple others, fanned out and couldn't find fresh tracks. No keys or phone."

Niall pulled her phone out of his pocket. "I found it down at the bottom where she'd fallen, but nothing else. Her missing keys are worrisome. I suggest you change all your locks when you get home."

Her heart ached at the impending loss of never seeing him again. Silly. She struggled to keep her emotions from showing or her scent from alerting them to how she felt. With the feel of Niall's body and his heat pressing against hers, it was hard for her to breathe, let alone think clearly, or hide the fact she was trembling.

"I'd like to go back to your house so I can shower and change into my own clothes, then I can be out of your hair." Both men stood well over six feet tall, making her feel small and insignificant. She'd shared her body with Niall, something no other man had the pleasure of, and now he couldn't wait to be rid of her.

Talk about a wham-bam-thank-you-ma'am. Hot tears burned her eyes, but she held them back. She remembered the way back and didn't need Niall, or any man, for that matter.

Before she could do more than take a couple steps, a hard arm came around her waist, lifting her off her feet. "Where the hell do you think you're going?" Niall's harsh growl reverberated next to her ear.

"Back to your house to get cleaned up so I can leave."

Setting her back on the ground, he barked an order to Jett. "Head to the club. If I can, I'll be there later. Did you leave her key at my place?"

Alaina couldn't look at either man, shaken by the rush of emotions, she fought for composure. Unnerved by her reaction, she tried to pull away from Niall. He shot a disapproving frown down at her, tightening his hold. He caressed her ribs, running his thumb over the underside of her breasts. She yelped and tried to squirm away.

"Hmm, are you ticklish?" His warm breath feathered her neck.

Uncomfortable with the way he took charge of her life, and her body, she batted his hand away. "It sounds like you have things to do, and I need to figure out...everything. Let me go, Niall." She didn't look at the man holding her like he owned her one minute, and then like he couldn't wait to be rid of her the next.

Chapter Five

Never. He silently vowed, agreeing with his beast. His wolf tried to push forward, wanting to claim Alaina right then and there. He restrained the urge to pick her up, carry her back to his home, and mark her for the world to see. Niall wanted to kick himself for his reaction over the condom. He hated the hurt he'd caused her, but it was the first thing that had popped into his head when he'd realized they were no longer alone.

She struggled against his arm, the terror in her voice had him marginally easing his grip. "Alaina, let me take care of you. We don't know why you were running, or who you were running from. I can protect you. Let me do this."

Her shaky indrawn breath undid him. The tingling sensation in his chest where his heart lay had him frowning down at her.

Without another word, Jett left, heading back the way he'd come. Niall figured he'd have some razzing from the guys at Chaps. He watched his friend leave, his long strides eating up the distance before he turned Alaina to face him. He adjusted his hold on her, shifting her body against his, showing her how she affected him. With an arm at her back and one beneath her legs, he lifted her in his arms and held her against him. "Let's get something abundantly clear, babe. I don't want you to leave. I can read your body language like a book. What we shared wasn't just some romp in the woods for fun, where I now send you on your way."

Alaina drew in a shaky breath and bit down on her bottom lip.

The faint hint of her blood raised his hackles. Leaning down, he ran his tongue along her lip until she opened for him. "You made your lip bleed." Licking the coppery sweet flavor away, sealing the small wound with his tongue, he eased her into accepting his kiss.

She grabbed him, wrapping her arms around his neck with a cry of surrender.

Niall tried to be gentle with her, tried to tame the feral intensity of his beast. Most women found his rugged looks, and uncompromising behavior, in and out of the bedroom a turn-on. As he held Alaina, he found himself straining to be different. His hands were firm, yet tender where he kneaded her flesh through the denim.

Blinking up at him. "You can't keep picking me up and carrying me around like this, you know," she whispered.

"Sure I can," he replied with a teasing wink, turning and walking toward home.

She smiled. "I'll get fat and lazy, then you won't be able to carry me."

Her tone was playful, but he marveled at the thought of her being big and round with his cub. First, he'd have to petition the pack to allow him to change her, then approach her with the news of what he was.

He'd loved it when Emma was pregnant. Every moment Nolan was inside his mate was an experience he'd relished. Emma was a wild wolf though, and he'd understood that. Had promised her he wouldn't curb those tendencies. If he had insisted she not run alone, she might not have been killed by a hunter all those years ago, leaving him to raise their son alone.

"What's wrong?" Alaina asked, running her finger between his brows.

Niall winced at the dark thoughts. "I was just

thinking about having to go into the club tonight. I hate to leave you all by yourself."

She was staring at his lips. He wondered if she was thinking of kissing him. Niall didn't want to make love to her in the woods again. Her first time should've been on a bed, his bed, with soft music and candles. The next time he would make sure she got the hearts and flowers, even if his heart wasn't available. He'd make sure she never knew.

"I'll follow you into town. I need to find a hotel for the night, maybe even the weekend. I'll call my mom on Monday."

Gritting his teeth to hold back his retort, Niall kept walking. "You won't find a room available for a hundred miles or more. This is the month of the bikes, babe. Have you ever heard of Bike Week in Sturgis?"

She nodded her head.

"You teach school, right?" Again, she nodded. "I'm assuming your classes just started. Well, Bike Week is the same week every year, and the bikers start pouring in weeks in advance and stay for weeks after."

At her puzzled look he explained that their club was in Sturgis and catered to the bikers and locals.

"Oh. Well, I guess I can just head out and drive till I find a vacancy."

He was getting a sinking feeling in the pit of his stomach. He needed to do something to get her to stay. "Alaina, I want you to stay with me for the weekend." Niall was smart enough not to say *forever*. It was too soon, and he didn't want to run her off. Shaken by the thought of her leaving and never seeing her again, Niall stopped in his tracks. "Stay with me, babe. I promise to be a great host and rock your world."

"What about your son?"

"He's with his grandparents. Do you know what that means?" He began walking again. "We've got the house to ourselves all weekend." Niall glanced down to see how she reacted to his words.

Her flawless skin glowed, cheeks pink from desire she couldn't hide. He couldn't wait to see the flush spread across her body when he got her home and naked. He'd been hard since the first time he'd caught her scent and found her injured, the smell of her wrapping around him, pulling him toward her as if she had him on a leash. He should be enraged, or annoyed, instead he was hard.

"Don't you have to work tonight?" she asked.

"Not for hours," he said. A primitive hunger and possessiveness fought to break free inside him, wanting to claim Alaina Strop.

He circled the front of his house, raising his head to the air. The smell of several of his pack mates overlaid his and Alaina's. Her compact rental sat next to his large four-by-four truck, looking small in comparison.

Setting her on the ground next to his truck, he pressed the keypad and got the envelope Jett had left with the key Torq had made for her rental. His boys had even coded a keyless remote just in case she'd had one from the company.

"Let's get your stuff out of the trunk, then go inside. I have plans for the next two hours." He popped the hatch. Her suitcase was as colorful as the woman, with pink and purple flowers all over it. He smiled and hefted it out, while she grabbed her purse that was neatly tucked to the side.

"Shower, and then I'll feed you."

Her mischievous look amused him. "Yes, you will." His cock throbbed, the need to sink into her heat once again inflaming him. His fingers itched to stroke the skin he'd already discovered was smooth as velvet and soft as silk. He wanted to slide his fingers through her hair while she knelt before him, wanted to feed her his cock and watch her suck him.

The dirty things he imagined doing to her, a virgin up until recently, should be illegal.

He took her bag, holding onto her hand the entire way into his bedroom. “Take your shower while I make a phone call.”

She fisted her hands at her sides, but nodded.

Reaching out, he pulled her to him. “I'm fighting a primitive urge to throw you down and fuck you senseless. First, I need to check in with my brother. That'll give you a moment to catch your breath, but don't think I'm not hurting so bad right now, I'm aching.” He placed her hand over his bulge. Every part of his being was tense with a hunger unlike anything he'd ever experienced in his entire thirty-seven years. Not even when he'd been with Emma.

He shook off thoughts of his truemate. The need to stake his claim on the woman in front of him overrode everything else. He bent, taking her lips in a hard kiss. There was a primitive quality to it, but there was nothing he could do to change how he felt.

Not giving her a chance to respond, he lifted his head and walked out of the room.

The sound of the shower coming on gave him the

chance to check in with his pack. His first call was to Zayn and Jett.

"I need to make this quick boys. You got any news for me?" Niall asked.

"How's your girl?" Zayn asked.

"Her name's Alaina, and she's great." Pride rang in his voice.

Jett cleared his voice over the line. "I noticed you were pretty acquainted with the young lady. What's your plans, boss?"

"You got something to say, Jett?" Niall kept his voice low, his hackles raised at Jett's question.

"She doesn't seem like one of the chicks from the club is all I'm saying, and there is something familiar about her. I'm not pressing in on your territory, Alpha, I'm just saying don't play around with her. I could see the innocence written all over her face, if not her body, anymore."

Niall growled, his blood boiling. Chaos erupted inside his mind at the thought of his pack mate interfering with what he considered his.

Reminding himself that this was Jett, his best friend, Niall took a deep breath. "I'm not playing shit with her. I've never felt anything like I feel for Alaina, not even with Emma. It confuses and pisses me off, but it excites me too. Now, that is the end of my sex life that you need to know. I appreciate you thinking about Alaina, but she's my concern, not yours."

"Don't fuck up the way I almost did, bro. That's my advice to you," Zayn said.

Jett laughed. "Nobody can fuck up the way you did. Besides, Ny is the smartest one of us. I just...you didn't even notice I was there until I was almost on top of you. I purposefully stepped on that branch, you know. What if I'd been one of the rogues?"

Shit. He'd been so consumed with getting inside Alaina, and then once he was, everything around them ceased to exist. He'd never had a problem putting the pack and their welfare before anything else, except Nolan. His son would always come first.

He lowered his chin to his chest. "Fuck, I don't even know what to say, except I was out of my mind."

"Do you remember what you said to me when we had our *talk*?" Zayn asked.

Niall waited, knowing Zayn would eventually get to his point.

"You said the greatest feeling in the world was being locked inside your mate, and you were right. When I'm with Cora, the world could melt away and I wouldn't even notice."

"I wasn't locked inside her. She's not my mate." He didn't say the word, yet. His plans for the weekend were to woo her, show her how good it could be between them. After he made her fall in love with him, he'd tell her about shifters, and hope she wanted to be one. If not, he'd be talking with Payton and having her do some fey magic. Alaina would walk away from the weekend with a memory of them having a brief affair, while he feared she'd take a piece of him with her.

"Whatever you say, Ny." Zayn laughed.

Clenching his hand, Niall gave them both a few instructions and told them he'd see them at Chaps. The shower had shut off a few minutes earlier, and he was impatient to get to Alaina. He went into one of the guest suites and took a quick shower, washing off the dust and dirt from his climb down the cliff. He got a cold chill thinking how close she came to death, and how lucky she was to have made it out relatively unscathed.

By the time he entered his bedroom, she was still in the bathroom. Niall turned the bed down, lit a few candles and shut the curtains, encasing the room in semi-darkness. He'd made certain his security alarm was set, but he opened his senses, making sure he couldn't detect anything out of place.

She opened the door, the smell of orange blossoms and ginger became stronger as she walked out. Her smile was hesitant, but welcoming. Niall wanted to close the distance between them.

* * * *

Alaina felt wonderful after taking a shower, anticipation for Niall and what he did to her strummed through her veins. She wondered if it was normal to want a man as much as she wanted Niall, or maybe it had to do with him being a shifter. She shrugged the thought away since none of the shifters from her home pack ever did anything for her. Most of the men followed Roger Strop like he was the king, and she supposed he was, since he was the alpha.

One look at Niall Malik and she was ready to hop onto any flat surface and offer herself to him, again and again. She wondered if there was a line of women who suffered the same addiction, then thought it better to not think of him and other women. Just thinking of him and some faceless woman had her growling like she'd seen the she wolves do back home.

"Come here," Niall said with a tilt of his head.

She didn't even hesitate as she eliminated the few feet separating them. The large red towel she'd put on was knotted in the front, and was large enough it covered her from her chest to knees. The way Niall's nostrils flared, the heat in his blue eyes, was like she'd been standing before him stark naked.

"Hi." Alaina wished she knew something sexier to say.

His lips tilted up. "You're so fucking gorgeous. Your scent makes me want to lick you from head to toe."

Goddess, how was she supposed to respond when he said things like that? She watched his nostrils flare, knowing he could smell her arousal. Heck, she wasn't a shifter and she swore she could scent it herself.

Alaina pressed up on her tiptoes, his neck the closest thing she could reach, and licked a long line up to his earlobe. "You taste good, too."

He was dressed in a pair of loose sweats, so when he lifted her by the waist, she wrapped her legs around his bare midriff. The instant her core met his hard stomach, they both groaned.

Alaina swore she could come if he would only

allow her to move a slight fraction, but his tight hold kept her still. "Please, Niall."

"Oh, I'll please you, but not yet. This time we're going to make it to bed, and I'm going to make up to you for the first time."

"What was wrong with the first time?" She looked into his eyes.

"It was your *first* time. It shouldn't have been in the woods up against a tree, for the love of all," he growled.

She laughed at his outraged look. Heat from his body making her own temperature rise. He was holding her lower half against him, and began walking toward the bed. Alaina stared at his lips. Really, men shouldn't have such full lips.

"You didn't hear me complaining, did you?" Smiling, she did what she'd fantasized about. She captured his full bottom lip between hers and sucked. The taste of mint exploded on her tongue.

Niall's gaze turned fierce, and then she felt a cold breeze on her back. She didn't have long to ponder why before he was laying her down in the middle of the bed, taking over the playful kiss, turning it into a seduction of her senses.

The flicker of several candle lights illuminated

the room, giving it a sense of romance, along with the red sheets and the scents from the candles.

A rumble against her chest had her toes curling.

He lifted her hands above her head, holding them in one hand. “Keep your hands up here. I’m going to do right by you this time.”

She couldn’t look away from him, nor could she hold still. “I want to touch you too.”

“Not yet. I need you to let me take care of you first. You gonna deny me that?”

Her mouth was suddenly dry. She shook her head, wanting anything he gave her.

Arching into his caress, Alaina moaned when he took her breast into his mouth. Arcs of pleasure flowed to every vein in her body, waking up senses she didn’t know she had. “Oh, Niall, yes.”

Niall kept her legs pinned together, preventing her from moving. His chuckle let her know he knew exactly what he was doing to her. She couldn’t wait to see what he did next.

“I promise you are going to come so many times you’ll lose count, I’m in charge, baby.”

* * * *

Niall loved the rosy hue that covered Alaina from head to toe. He held his breath, moving slowly to see if she complied with his wishes. Her hair fanned out over his red pillow cases, a strand of it caught in her mouth, and he laughed as she blew it out with impatience. She was the most beautiful woman he'd ever seen, each dip and curve of her body beckoned to him. With her soft smile, the graceful, fluid way she moved, reminded him of the sleek jungle cats. The alpha wolf that lived inside him wanted to claim her as did the man, but they needed her to know what they were. What he was first.

He pinched one pert nipple between his fingers while he sucked the other one into a hard point. She bucked against him, her moans of pleasure exciting him. He bit down hard enough to get her attention, stilling her movements, but not hard enough to cause pain. The scent of her arousal increased. His mate enjoyed a little pain with her pleasure.

Her eyes fluttered closed as he switched to the other breast, giving the same treatment to the neglected nipple. Her heartbeat was like a drum, throbbing through her body into his, jarring not only her but him, creating a rhythm his took up. He'd never experienced a connection quite like what he had with Alaina. Like the blood in his veins flowed in the same path as hers.

He shook off the unwanted thoughts and concentrated on the here and now, like the bow of her mouth and her lush breasts that were every man's perfect fantasy, fitting into his hands like they were made just for him. Niall wasn't the sort of man who allowed anyone or anything to own him, not even Emma. He forced his mind away from the past. He waited for the pain to rip into him, but aside from a slight twinge, the expected agony never materialized.

Her gaze met his, held him captive. He couldn't look away from the amber eyes. "What's wrong?" she asked.

He frowned. The beating of their hearts no longer in tune, the rhythm was off, no longer calling to him. Cold settled over him, a lonely existence where he was alpha, and father to Nolan, but he wanted more.

Niall nipped her flesh, her pulse pounded faster. There was no way he was going to let her draw away from him, no matter how much she wanted to. He knew now she was meant to be his and he wouldn't stop until he made her his in every sense of the word, not ever, not unless she denied him.

She smiled up at him, running her fingers through his hair, her brown eyes seemed to take on the multifaceted shade of the flames, only more. "Quit thinking and do what you promised or I'll have to take care of myself, Niall."

Her whispered words drifted through the room like a promise or a dare. His own heart stuttered. Alaina's hips moved under him again. She was so soft and warm, melting for him. He needed to taste her essence.

One last kiss to her breast, and Niall began moving down, licking and nipping a path across her flat abdomen. The flex and play of muscles showed she worked out, but was soft in all the right spots. He dipped his tongue into her neat little belly button, eliciting a giggle from her. Perfection. She breathed out, a soft airy puff.

He could track her heartbeat again as they began to align into the same rhythm, soothing his wolf. He actually felt her in his veins. Leaving little kisses, he moved to the top of her mound, spreading her legs to make room for himself. Her self-conscious move to keep them closed was one he didn't like. His beast rose up and growled. "Don't hide from me, Alaina. Everything about you is beautiful. From your head, to your pretty pink pussy. Goddess, you're wet."

She took a gasping breath at the first swipe of his tongue across her folds. He sent up a small prayer of thanks that she was sent to him. He smiled when her thighs tried to squeeze his head and felt her fingers brush through his hair, scraping along his scalp. Her touch a mixture of both pleasure and pain, sent a small current of electricity from his head to his belly, straight down to his cock, tightening his balls, coiling heat in his groin.

Desire rushed from her to him in waves. She beckoned to both man and wolf like a siren's call. Every single rule he'd made went out the window with a single smile. He wanted her in every possible way, and he would have her. Body, heart, and soul.

Another swipe of his tongue and the flavor of oranges burst in his mouth. He lapped at the juices, the sweet taste mixing with ginger became his favorite treat.

Niall used his thumbs to pull her lips apart, staring down at her exposed clit. The hood had already allowed it to peak out. He licked around the little nub, never quite touching where she needed. He looked up, seeing her eyes squeezed shut, her mouth open while she bit on her bottom lip. Fucking beautiful. She was so fucking gorgeous she took the very air he breathed away. Her eyes popped open. She must have felt his penetrating gaze. Keeping contact with her brown eyes, Niall licked his lips, watching her focus on his tongue, and then brought his mouth back down to her glistening pussy. He fastened his lips around the little bundle of nerves begging for attention. Her scream of pleasure was music to his ears.

She tightened her fingers in his hair. He allowed her to hold him. She was already branded on his mind, and he wanted to make sure he was on hers as well. Using one hand to hold her open for his lips and tongue, he speared two fingers into her. Heat. He was surrounded by her wetness and heat. He pumped his fingers in time with his sucking, flicking his tongue over her clit at the same time.

It only took him a few pumps and he felt Alaina's inner muscles begin to flutter.

"Niall, oh, I'm coming."

He continued to pump his fingers, loving how her body twitched in little aftershocks. "I could become addicted to watching you come."

"Hmm, I think I like that addiction."

He swiped his tongue through her folds and

pulled his fingers out slowly. Niall rose up and placed one hand next to her head, their noses almost touching, his lips brushed against hers. He barely touched her, but it felt like a benediction. Her mouth moved, a warm puff of air, feather light, a promise more intimate than he was prepared for. He opened his mouth over hers, taking the kiss to new heights.

Niall used his other hand to line his dick up with her opening, running the head through her wetness first. He watched for any signs of soreness before he slowly entered, feeling her clench down nearly had him coming as soon as he was all the way in.

"Look at me, Alaina." At once her eyes popped open. "Stay with me." He wanted his touch to bring pleasure, only pleasure.

"I'm with you, Niall," she replied, as if it was the most natural thing in the world to say.

Moving his hips back, he set up a slow pace. Her arousal made penetration easy, but she was still tight. He relaxed his arms and let his chest brush her breasts, their pulses pounded in unison, tension coiled deep. He bent his head and captured one nipple between his teeth, tugging and then laving it until she was begging him for more. Her nipples acted like a direct conduit to her core. His gaze still on hers, he leaned up and then over to the other breast and sucked as much of her flesh into his mouth as possible.

She moaned, sending flames leaping into his body, burning hot and bright. He swore it was a flash-fire that started in Alaina and bled into him. Niall didn't stop to ponder the implications, he switched to the left breast, using his teeth again and switched back to the right, doing the same.

Niall couldn't believe the sensations he was experiencing. Each time he gave her a touch of pain, an echo ricocheted through him. A scrape of his teeth or a stroke of his cock drove her insane with need, fueling him with the same urges.

He sank as deep as he could, his breath hissed out. "Fuck, you're gonna kill me, babe." The words came out between clenched teeth. He'd never had to fight to keep from losing control.

She whimpered when he moved too hard, but a heartbeat later and she was moving with him, begging him to go faster. He reared back and knelt between her spread thighs and began to surge harder and faster. The tether he had his wolf on broke free, setting a relentless pace he prayed she could handle.

With every stroke it became harder to keep his

beast in check, flames shot down his spine as her sheath tightened around him, or maybe it was his cock swelling. Either way he was close to coming, driving deeper, closer to ecstasy with her pleasure and his engulfing them both in desire so intense he wasn't sure where she left off and he began. He was being too rough with her, but she answered with cries for more.

He raised her legs onto his shoulders, spreading her wider. Around them the candles burned, tiny red and gold flames licked upward toward the ceiling. Niall caught glimpses of his surroundings, but he couldn't stop, even if the world would've dropped out beneath him. He felt his body swell and reached down to rub circles on her little clit.

His lungs burned, and the sweet smell of her arousal hit while her inner muscles gripped him like a thousand tongues working, licking along his shaft. Niall let his head fall back, suppressing a howl while she milked him of his seed. His orgasm tore through him like vicious waves that ripped him apart and put him back together again.

Chapter Six

Alaina was sure there were fireworks going off in the room while Niall made love to her. She pulled her legs down from his shoulders, and then tugged him down to her.

"Easy, I don't want to squish you," Niall whispered into the quiet room.

"I have complete faith you will protect me." She smiled up into his blue eyes, knowing they'd have to get up soon.

Niall shifted to the side, his cock sliding from her with the movement. "I need to go to our club, Chaps, in Sturgis tonight. You want to come hang out with me?"

Her heart turned over at the hesitation in his voice, not because she didn't think he wanted her to go, but because she could hear he didn't think she wanted to go. She slid her leg up his thigh, loving the way his hair roughened leg rubbed her. "I'd love to go with you. Should I take my own car just in case you're going to be really late?"

"Nah, if you get too bored I can have one of my

guys take you home."

"What should I wear?" Nerves settled into her stomach.

He grabbed her ass and pulled her on top of him, the movement bringing her face to face with him. "The man in me would say what you have on is perfect."

A pulse beat in her core at the heat in his gaze. "Pretty sure there are laws against women walking around naked."

"Actually, you could get a license to walk around with a thong and pasties covering these gorgeous nipples. However, I find myself not wanting anyone but me seeing you like this," he growled.

She was surprised to see his blue eyes turn their alpha shade. "Yeah, I don't think I have the balls to wear that anyway. I do have something I think would look great, and not make me stick out like a neon sign."

His brows rose. "As long as you're sufficiently covered, we're solid. This," he squeezed her ass, "can only be seen by me."

When she would have laughed at his words, he fisted his hand in her hair and sealed his lips over hers, ending their conversation. Alaina wouldn't have argued, although she wondered how he reacted when other women shifted from human to wolf, if he turned the other way, or thought it was okay because they were shifters.

Niall made thinking an impossibility as he lifted her higher on his body, bringing her back down on his rock hard shaft. She'd think about his words and the reasoning behind them later, much later.

By the time she took a quick shower she was still questioning going into town with Niall.

Too nervous to walk out of his bathroom, Alaina stood looking in the full length mirror inspecting her outfit. Black faux leather leggings, and a grey off the shoulder top with a lace back that hit her just below the ass and hugged her from her breasts to hips. Her charcoal grey ankle boots had two inch heels giving her a couple inches, with the spiked straps that wrapped around them, she thought she would fit right in.

Figuring she'd been in there too long, she twisted the knob and stepped into the bedroom. Niall was sitting on the bed, looking good enough to jump. "Hi," she said.

"Fuck me running." Niall's eyes looked her up and down. "Come here." He pointed between his spread thighs.

She was happy her shaky legs didn't show as she made her way to where he indicated.

Niall placed his hands on her hips. "Babe, I'm not so sure it's a good idea for you to go with me."

Alaina's heart broke. She swallowed the lump in her throat and tried to step away from him.

"Whoa, it's not because I don't want you there. I'm just imagining the riot you're going to start and all the heads I'm gonna have to bust."

"Right." She laughed, drawing the word out.

"If we had more time I'd show you just how serious I am." He took her hand and placed it on his crotch.

"You're so full of crap," she said, but ran her hand along his length.

He held onto her as he stood in one fluid motion. "Come on woman. If you keep rubbing me, we'll be late and then the guys will give me shit." He led the way out of his room.

Once inside the garage he handed her a helmet. She pulled a hair tie from her wrist and pulled her curls back in a ponytail behind her, then strapped the skull cap on.

The Harley rumbled to life beneath Niall. Alaina

swore she could come from looking at him alone. She wasn't sure how she'd make it riding behind him for the hour plus trip into Sturgis. His knowing smirk let her know he was aware of exactly how she was reacting. Damn, shifters sense of smell. She wondered when he was going to reveal his nature to her, and then worried how he'd react when she told him she already knew. That she had secrets of her own.

Niall patted the seat behind him. Eyeing the bike she lifted her leg and swung it over, happy she had stretchy leggings on, making the maneuver easy. Riding behind Niall was going to stretch her self-control to the limit, if she didn't behave she could cause him to wreck.

She shouldn't have worried. The man handled the big machine like he handled everything else she'd seen—with complete competence and utter control. As they wound their way down the hills and curves, he'd instructed her to hug him tight and follow his lead. She found herself wrapping her arms and thighs so tightly around him at first she feared he'd not be able to maneuver the bike. His deep chuckle had vibrated against her front, but within minutes into their journey she'd begun to relax and enjoy the ride.

By the time they'd pulled up behind the bar he co-owned with his brother, Alaina wasn't ready to end the ride.

"Give yourself a moment before you try to stand, babe. Trust me, I've seen a lot of first-timers face plant when they hop off." Niall took his skull cap off and hung it on his handle bar.

Alaina assumed he was the expert and listened to his advice. He'd already put the center stand down. Now, he held his hand out, so she unclipped the strap holding her helmet on and gave that to him. Using her hands, she finger combed her hair after removing the band at the back.

The music from the bar could be heard through the closed door, its heavy throbbing beat echoed down the alley. Night had fallen during their journey, but the lights from the streets lit up the parking lot.

She felt steadier, and taking the hand Niall offered, she climbed from the bike. Her legs definitely had a little wobble when she placed them on the gravel. She was grateful Niall was there to hold her. Of course, he used the moment to bend his head and covered her mouth with his. His kiss was demanding and forceful, just like the alpha Niall was. He pulled back, until his breath fanned her lips and took a deep breath. “Let’s go before I fuck you right here.”

He rubbed her back in a soothing motion, like he was fighting his beast. Alaina almost wanted him to do just that. Every instinct in her told her to let him claim her, to bind their souls right then and there, but she didn’t want to force him into a bond until he knew everything.

She nipped his bottom lip. “Let’s go, big guy, before I drop my pants and beg you to fuck me.”

His low growl was more animal than man, but Alaina pretended not to hear.

The back door to the club opened, making Niall and Alaina both turn to see who had interrupted them. Jett stood with his hands on his hips, and a knowing grin on his face, staring at them.

“Yo, think you wanna come and help out at the bar, or stand out here all night?” Jett asked.

Niall raised one hand and flipped Jett the bird, wrapping his other arm around Alaina and propelled her toward the door. “Fuck off, Jett. You’re just jealous ‘cause you ain’t getting any pussy."

Jett snorted. “Dude, I get more than my share. I need a stick to beat the chicks off my jock,” Jett said holding the door open for Niall and Alaina.

“Sure you do. Why you out here looking for me

then?" Niall asked as they passed Jett.

"The bands getting ready to start and they asked me to fill in for their drummer who's too fucked up to play. We need you behind the bar."

Alaina felt Niall stiffen before he relaxed. "It's gonna be hard to beat chicks off your jock if you're behind a drum kit."

"That's what you think. I'll have a line of them waiting for me between sets." She looked over to see Jett making a comical face. He had a really obscenely long tongue that she was sure the ladies enjoyed immensely, and then she noticed the piercing as he stuck it out and showed Niall exactly why the women would be extremely happy.

Niall pressed his lips to her ear. "Stop looking at his tongue as if you're fantasizing about it or I'll cut it out," he growled.

She nearly stumbled at his words, looking up to see if he was joking and saw real heat in his eyes. Standing on her toes in the middle of the hallway, Alaina wrapped her arms around Niall's neck and licked his closed mouth. When he didn't open immediately, she sucked his upper lip into her mouth and then did the same to the bottom. His mouth opened and she took full advantage, licking inside, dueling with his tongue until he took over. She submitted to him, but she still fought for a little control, her nails scraping at the nape of his neck even as she melted into him.

He used his superior strength to turn them, forcing her against the wall, kissing her over and over. His kiss was smoldering, overpowering with such passion that she felt tiny sparks of power sizzle in her veins, as if her fey side was waking up and welcoming him. She tasted the faint coppery flavor of blood and wasn't sure if it was his or hers, but she welcomed it as it raced through her bloodstream straight to her core. A tiny orgasm shook her and she cried out, arching into him.

His wolf was close to the surface, almost impossible to control. She wasn't sure how she knew that, but she did. Each time she tried to pull back, Niall became more aggressive. Alaina gave herself over to him, right there in the middle of the crowded bar in the semi-privacy of the hallway, uncaring if Jett was watching or if a hundred eyes could see her and Niall, she turned her head and gave Niall her neck.

The action seemed to pull both man and beast back, and Niall buried his face against her exposed throat, breathing hard. "Son-of-a-bitch, I'm about ready to fuck you where we stand or cum in my damn jeans," he groused.

Alaina ran her hands down his back soothingly. "Well, I just came in my miniscule thong, right here where anyone could have seen."

"Shit, don't say that so loud." He bit down on the tendon of her shoulder.

The off the shoulder top would show the mark of his bite, and Alaina felt oddly proud to walk around with his mark on her.

* * * *

Niall was so horny he had to hold Alaina in front of him for a few more minutes, taking deep breaths to steady his racing heart. When he believed he had himself under control he took a deep breath, then wished he hadn't. The scent of her arousal permeated the air. Every wolf in the place could probably smell her sweet scent. He wasn't kidding about her causing a riot, only he wouldn't be just busting heads, he'd rip throats out of anyone who dared touch what was his.

"Go to the bathroom and clean up, then come to the big bar and find me. I'll have one of the girls watch for you." He thought of having one of the wolves from the pack wait outside the ladies room for her, but nixed the idea out of fear he'd have to kill one of his own if they looked sideways at Alaina.

"Good idea," Alaina agreed.

He pointed to the closest ladies room and then told her where she could find him. Once he made his way to the bar, he located one of his waitresses, Lisa, and asked her to go wait for his girl. The Spanish beauty smiled, said something he pretended not to hear, and then sauntered off to do his bidding. He watched her go. She was wearing what the rest of the waitresses wore, with a twist. A pair of ass-less chaps with a pair of boy shorts underneath and a crop top with the bars logo on it. Some of the ladies chose to wear thongs, while some went for tight jeans. Niall and Zayn didn't care what they chose to wear under the chaps, but he definitely appreciated the view.

"Hey, boss, who was the chic you were all but screwing?" Torq asked.

Turning to his friend he saw the humor he didn't try to hide.

"I think there's a toilet that needs to be cleaned, Torq. You want that job?" Niall smiled.

Torq raised his arms. "Nope, you know what. I

didn't see or smell anything."

Niall laughed, lifting the heavy countertop and walking behind to help serve drinks. He and Torq worked well together, but tonight he figured he'd only have half his mind on the job since Alaina would be there.

"Man, you need to chill. You're all but growling. Actually, scratch that. You are growling, you just haven't showed fang, yet." Torq nudged his shoulder.

Torq wasn't quite as tall as Niall, but he was every bit as built, and was one hell of a scrapper when it came down to a fight in skin or fur. Niall trusted the other man to keep his head if Niall lost his. That reason he saw was walking toward him with Lisa. The two ladies were chatting like old friends. He was glad he'd never tried to get in the waitress' pants, especially when Alaina looked up and smiled at him, as if she was reading his mind. He shook his head, unable to control the grin that crossed his face. One day he'd have that connection with her, if she accepted him and his wolf.

"You are so whipped," Jett said, slapping his back. "I'm thinking the man who's notorious for giving no fucks, has just found something to give a fuck about."

Years of discipline kept him from ripping his friend's arm off. He hadn't heard Jett move behind the bar, which made him angry. Jett's words were spoken too low for anyone but him to hear. Just as he was opening his mouth to respond he smelled the unique scent of Alaina and he shut his mouth as she approached.

"Hi," Alaina said nervously.

Niall nodded, not trusting himself to speak.

"What can I get you to drink, darling?" Torq asked.

Alaina looked from Niall to Torq. "A Long Island Iced Tea, please." She reached into her back pocket and pulled out a fifty dollar bill.

Torq shook his head. "This one is on the house."

She smiled at him, then looked at Niall for confirmation.

He turned away from her to grab a couple beers for customers, and by the time he looked back, she was sipping on her drink with her back to the bar. Her body language was screaming hurt, but he didn't trust himself to go over and talk to her without losing focus on his job.

When the band walked out on stage, with Jett the last to go up, the crowd went wild. He lost sight of

Alaina as she wound her way up to stand at the front of the stage.

Niall motioned Lisa over to him. "Keep an eye on Alaina for me." He nodded at the front of the bar where the band was warming up. Lisa gave him a saucy salute but did as instructed.

Bronx was by the front door acting as bouncer, at six foot five, he was a big bastard most humans didn't want to fuck with, drunk or sober. He caught Niall's eye and made a motion that he had his eyes on the front as well.

He didn't have to speak on their private path, as their alpha, they knew what he wanted.

Jett started hitting the drums to a fast beat. The rest of the band caught up, while the singer started belting out the lyrics to one of the crowds' favorite songs, *Bad Girl Friend* by Theory of a Deadman.

The night went by in a blur. Every half hour or so he'd catch a glimpse of Alaina shaking her fine ass on the dance floor, or at the bar getting a refill. Not once did he smell her arousal, keeping all the men around her from losing an arm or hand.

A new scent reached him, a group of unknown shifters had the hair on the back of his neck rising. He noticed Bronx standing, instead of perched on top of the stool. Niall nodded for Bronx to follow them. He called out to Zayn and the rest of the pack, putting them all on alert. An unneeded warning as they all came to stand by the bar. Twins, Raydon and River, crossed as one, their dark stare menacing as they stalked up to the counter, standing behind him. Next to come was Fallon, usually the most laid back of the group, looking ready to kick ass, and ask questions later.

"Let's see if they do the right thing and approach me before we head their way," Niall said.

Niall watched the three men's heads swivel their way, catching their eye, the leader indicated they follow him. They were all big men, but none as big as Bronx, nor did they look nearly as tame. The first was a bonus, the last a worry.

"How's it going? You boys just passing through?" Niall asked, keeping his tone neutral.

"Something like that. We're on vacation, thought we'd stop in and get a drink. You got a problem with that?"

The guy speaking looked Niall up and down. Their clothes screamed average working man, their posture showed they weren't afraid to throw-down if it came to it.

"We won't have a problem as long as you realize this is my territory. You plan on staying, you talk to me. You got a problem, you talk to me. Is that gonna be an issue?" Niall let his eyes shift, letting the other men know who was alpha.

"I think I've seen all I needed to see here. If I have need of you, I'll let you know. What did you say your name was again?" the leader of the group asked.

Niall smirked. "I didn't."

Confusion crossed the shorter man's features. He'd probably be considered handsome by most women, but Niall's dickhead meter went off.

"This music must be addling my brain. My name's Rickard Willard. We'll be staying in Deadwood for a few days. Mind if we drop in from time to time. The eye-candy is quite nice." He turned to watch one of the waitresses walk by in a pair of ass-less chaps and panties, licking his lips like a hungry wolf.

"Don't mind at all as long as you keep in mind most of the clientele are human, and as such you keep your nature hidden." Niall nodded at the crowd.

Rickard scoffed. "How can you stand to be surrounded by so many of them?" He made it sound as if humans were disgusting.

Niall shrugged his shoulders. “They help pay the bills and are good for many things.”

The other pack members laughed and added a few comments. Rickard promised to keep his nature hidden and not alert humans to their presence, but when he turned to leave he lifted his nose, scenting the air.

“Can I help you with something else?” Niall asked.

Lisa walked by with a tray full of drinks, not able to miss bumping into the big man who stepped into her path. The bottles and glasses slid backward, but Torq’s fast reflexes kept the tray from spilling on her, instead the drinks crashed to the floor. The heavy smell of alcohol wafted up.

“You stupid bitch. Look what you did,” Rickard roared, raising his hand.

Bronx grabbed Rickard’s wrist. “I wouldn’t do that if I were you.” His blue eyes flashed fire and a promise of retribution at the two men with Rickard.

They all watched as Rickard tried to break Bronx’s hold on his wrist. If Rickard had been human his bones would’ve been crushed to dust. Lisa stood without moving a muscle, realizing she was in the middle of something. Torq bent and whispered in her ear, she nodded then scooted around them.

Niall didn't take his eyes off any of the men. The music was still pumping, and he was thrilled that his woman had taken herself to the front of the crowd to listen to the band. The last thing he needed was another pack thinking he had a weakness. He shook off thoughts of Alaina, and focused on the trio of idiots. "I think it's time you boys left."

Having let go of Rickard, Bronx stepped next to Niall and crossed his arms over his wide chest.

Rickard looked at Bronx's tattooed arms and chest, a sneer lifted the corner of his lips. "Yeah, I do believe this isn't our type of establishment. We'll be seeing you boys real soon."

Turning, the trio walked out without looking back. A sign that they weren't scared of Niall and his pack.

"Raydon, you and River go see where they are staying and report back. Try not to be detected, and don't get in a tussle with them. I have a feeling they want to fight, and while I'm all for a good brawl, I like to know what we're fighting for first."

"Why you gotta take all the fun out of everything?" River asked with a smile that showed the dimple in his right cheek. His twin had the exact same dimple in his left one. The Boone twins were eerily identical, people couldn't tell them apart most of the time.

"Go follow the dickheads," Niall said.

He shook his head as Raydon and River saluted him.

"Boss, I'm sorry about dumping that tray," Lisa came up to his side.

Niall wrapped his arm around her shoulder and gave her a hug. "No worries, little sister. It was the asshat's fault not yours. Did you get hurt?" he asked.

She shook her head, smiling up at him.

He could read the real affection in her body language. She looked at him and the other guys as big brothers. "Get back to work." Niall gave her one last hug, and kissed the top of her head.

* * * *

Alaina made her way back to the bar, hoping Niall wasn't waiting on another customer. Each time she'd gotten a refill he'd been busy, and she hadn't wanted to seem clingy. Torq would make her a new drink, smile his blindingly white smile that probably made most women drop their panties right there on the bar. The last thing she expected to see was her new friend being embraced by Niall. Sure, they weren't exclusive. Heck, she was only planning on staying for another day or so, but he could've at least not brought her where he clearly had other women.

She promised herself she wasn't going to cry or make a fool of herself, nor was she going to lash out and let him know she saw him. Making up her mind, she headed for the same door she came in. She kept people in between her and Niall, not wanting to see him, or let him see the hurt she wasn't able to hide just yet.

Outside she took a few deep breaths. The fifty dollar bill she'd stuffed into her back pocket still blessedly there. She wished she would've insisted on bringing her own vehicle instead of riding in with Niall, but then she'd never have experienced the freedom of riding on a motorcycle. Of course, now she'd never be able to climb on another one without thinking of the blasted man again.

At close to one in the morning the streets were still packed with people. It was easy to get lost in the crowd as she walked down the road, letting the humid air fill her lungs. Her boots, which looked great, were definitely not made for walking long distance. She noticed a tattoo shop across the busy street. Several artists were busy with clients, from what she could tell. An overwhelming urge had her crossing the road without looking either way. She heard horns blaring, but couldn't seem to make her feet stop moving. The goddess of the moon symbol on the window calling to her.

"You looking to get a tattoo?"

Alaina jumped at the deep voice next to her. She looked up at the man with long blond dread locks. He wasn't much taller than her, with tattoos covering both arms and every other available inch of skin she could see. "I think so."

He shook his head. "No. When you know you want one you come see me. Don't think so, know so. Ink is permanent, not a temporary thing. My name's Chris, and this is my shop, here's my card. When you're ready, give me a call. I'll be gentle."

She looked down at his card with the flying pig on the front as his logo and back up at him. "Thank you, Chris. I definitely want one. I'm just not sure what I want, yet. Flying Pig?"

Chris laughed. "When pigs fly was something I was told one too many times when I was growing up. I thought it was fitting." He indicated his shop. "You all alone, chica?" he asked.

For some reason Alaina didn't sense any reason to fear Chris. He was definitely a good guy. "Sort of. I caught my...friend with another woman. Not, like with her, but... it sounds stupid now, but at the time it didn't look stupid. You know what I mean?"

Nodding, Chris led her into his shop. "The green-eyed monster popped up and bit you is what you're saying."

One of the tattoo artists raised her head. "That bitch. She pops up every now and then just to torment me. I cunt punch her and she leaves me alone."

"Damn, Angela, you are one mean bitch." Chris looked over the art Angela was putting on the back of her client.

Angela held up her tattoo gun. "You got that right, Chris. Girl, you let me know who I need to hurt and I will."

Alaina laughed. The woman named Angela couldn't weigh more than a hundred and twenty pounds soaking wet, but she looked like she meant business with her tattoo gun in hand. The guy lying on the table turned his head toward Angela and whispered something too low for Alaina to hear, but it made Angela blush, and then the woman bent back over and started working on him again.

"You want to look through some books of tattoos?" Chris indicated the stack of albums. "My old lady is in the office and we can give you a ride home when we close or you can crash at our place if you need somewhere to stay." The sound of all the needles stopping at once was almost deafening.

"Oh, that's really generous of you." Alaina began, but stopped when a gorgeous redhead walked out of the backroom looking like she was about ready to pop out a baby any minute.

"Did I just hear you offer to take in another stray, my love?" The redhead walked up and tugged on one of Chris's dreadlocks.

The only sound in the shop was the song *Savages* by Theory of a Deadman and Alice Cooper.

"Hi, my name is Shelley, Chris's wife." She rested her hand on her stomach.

Alaina smiled at the fiery redhead. "Nice to meet you, Shelley. My name's Alaina, and I swear I am not poaching. I was in a daze and your hubby offered advice, and a lift. I think I overreacted when I saw my...fling...with his arm around another woman. Maybe I had one too many Long Island Iced Teas."

"Girl, those things kick my ass. How many did you have?" Angela asked looking up again.

"Maybe four or five. I can't remember."

Chris looked down at his heavily pregnant wife. "Either they were very weak or you are an alcoholic," Chris announced.

"What? How do you come to that conclusion?" Alaina asked.

Shelley smiled. "Because, after two of them, I'm on top of the bar dancing. On the fourth, I'm on the floor snoozing."

"Where'd you come from? Shelley and I'll walk you back. You can clear up the misunderstanding with your old man." Chris grabbed his leather coat from behind the high counter where a state of the art computer sat.

"Chaps down the street."

"Do you think your guy went to another bar looking for you?" Shelley asked.

"I doubt it. He and his brother own the club. I'm sure he hasn't even noticed I'm gone."

Again the silence, except for the sound of the music playing in the background was a little disconcerting.

"You're with Niall. Niall Malik?" Chris asked, his

eyes going wide.

Alaina nodded, unsure if that was a good thing or bad by the way everyone in the shop was acting.

"Holy fuck, woman. You left his club without telling him?"

Alaina turned to see one of the artists at the back who'd been working on a woman stand up. Alaina realized he smelled like wolf, he had the same woodsy scent as the rest of Niall and his pack, meaning he was friend instead of foe.

"Jory, watch your tone, boy," Chris chastised the young man.

"Sorry, Chris, I'm finished with this tattoo. I'll walk her back to Chaps and make sure my cousin knows she's okay."

Cousin was a loose term shifters used to humans when referring to pack members.

"Shelly and I'll walk with you if it's all the same. We need to stretch our legs. Right, Shell?"

"Oh, most definitely," Shelley agreed.

The young wolf cleaned up the woman he'd been working on, gave her instructions on how to take care of her tattoo, and then rang her up on the register. Within moments they all walked out the front door. Angela offered to come along and put the hurt on anyone, but Alaina turned her offer down. If she was going to be in town for any length of time, she knew she and Angela would've been good friends. Now, she had to head back to Chaps and hope her absence went unnoticed.

She and Shelley walked out first with Jory and Chris a few steps behind them. Alaina laughed at a story Shelley told her about Chris, and his obsession with tattooing a goat with six breasts on a client. "He's never going to find anyone drunk enough to let him tattoo that on their body," Alaina giggled.

"Girl, I have tried telling him that. But does he listen?" Shelley shook her head.

"How far along are you?" Alaina asked, looking at the obviously very large belly.

Shelley gasped. "What are you talking about? I'm not preggo."

Alaina sucked in a breath.

"Oh, God, I'm kidding. You should see your face. I'm seven months along." Shelley was laughing so hard she had tears in her eyes.

"That was so mean. Funny, but mean." Alaina bumped her hip.

They both stopped in their tracks when three men walked out of one of the bars.

The largest one blocked her path. "I knew I smelled trash in that first club we stopped at. Didn't I tell you boys I smelled used goods?"

Alaina pushed Shelley behind her. "Excuse us." She tried to walk around the three men.

"You don't know who I am? Do you, Alaina?" Rickard asked.

Shaking her head, Alaina looked over her shoulder to see where Chris and Jory were. Chris had caught up with them, but Jory was nowhere to be seen. A slight shake of his head let Alaina know Jory had gone for help.

"If you go with us quietly, we'll let your friends here live. Make a scene and we'll kill the freak and gut his whore while you watch she and the child bleed out, and then we'll still take you. The choice is yours."

"Why are you doing this? Who are you?" Alaina asked.

The leader grabbed her by the throat and brought her up to his level. "You wish to play stupid as well as be a whore?"

Alaina grappled with the hand around her throat. She had no idea who he was or what he was talking about. Whatever reason she had been running must've had something to do with the man standing in front of her.

She couldn't get air into her lungs, saw stars flashing in the distance and wished she hadn't left Niall because of her jealousy. Wished he was there to save her again. Goddess, she wished she had done so many things, but most of all she really just wanted the man to stop.

Heat traveled up from her toes to her stomach. She could feel it racing through her system like a golden beacon, soothing her throat.

"What the fuck." The man holding her dropped her like a hot stone.

Gasping, Alaina turned to Chris and Shelley. "Go, run." She raised her hand. A golden orb enclosed the couple and propelled them backward. The last of her strength was sapped from her, but she couldn't have lived if something had happened to Chris, Shelley and their beautiful unborn little girl.

"That was stupid, but Roger said you weren't very bright. By the way, *mate*, my name is Rickard."

Alaina looked up when she heard her stepfather's name. The man looking down at her with such hate knew her stepdad. Memories flooded her of the last time she'd seen her mother. Finding out the man she'd thought was her father but wasn't, actually was a blessing. It had explained so much while she'd been growing up. When he'd walked in and informed her that he'd planned to give her to another in his pack. Not because he worried for her safety, but because he'd always doubted she was his. She'd run. Now looking at Rickard she would rather die than become his mate. Her time with Niall showed her that being with a man, or wolf, could be beautiful. If that man or wolf, would actually love her, she didn't think she'd ever leave his side. However, she didn't think Rickard had the ability to feel anything except hate and the need to hurt others.

"I'm not your mate, Rickard. Roger is not my dad and he has no authority over me." It hurt to say the words from the damage to her throat.

"Hmmm, have you no love for your mother. Although she's a little older than I usually go for, I think your dad promised us all a go at her if you didn't comply. Ain't that right, boys?" Rickard squatted down to eye level. "So, what's it going to be, *mate*? You coming with us, or are we going back to take out our frustration on your poor old mama?"

"You're a sick bastard," Alaina spat.

Rickard backhanded her, making Alaina fall backward, her arm flying out to stop her head from hitting the sidewalk. She couldn't prevent the scream of pain from the agony of being hit by him. Panting, she saw a pool of blood from her mouth forming on the concrete. Damn, she wasn't sure she could handle too many more of his punches, and wondered if people passing by would stop to help and end up getting hurt.

Alaina tried to get up, knowing it was the only thing she could do or her mom would suffer much worse.

One of the other men helped her stand when she obviously couldn't do it alone.

"Make her walk without help." Rickard growled the words.

"I hate you."

Quicker than a snake, Rickard slapped her on the opposite side. He didn't let her fall to the ground. Instead he pulled her to him and licked her blood. "Good. I'll enjoy it so much more knowing you hate me."

Knowing she would anger him, but uncaring, she gathered spit and blood in her mouth and spat it in his face. His roar of outrage shook the windows around them, and then she was flying through the air. She sent up a prayer to the gods and goddesses to tell her mother she loved her, and asked that they take care of her when she was gone. She had many regrets, but her biggest was never telling Niall she loved him.

Chapter Seven

Niall looked around for Alaina. It had been way too long since he'd been able to see or smell her and an uneasy feeling was taking hold of him. The front door slammed against the wall, making Bronx jump up, and grab Jory. He was a young member of the pack, most definitely a beta, but a good kid.

"I need Niall, now. His woman is in trouble." Jory's words were rushed.

Leaping over the counter, uncaring who saw him, Niall grabbed the wolf by the collar. "Where is she? What's happened?"

Jory's eyes rounded, the unmistakable smell of fear wafted off of him, but he looked Niall in the face and explained what he knew. Motioning for the rest of his pack to follow, he raced out the same door Jory had come through.

His wolf recognized their mate's blood first, and then the sound of her terrified and pain-filled scream rent the air. Niall reacted without thought, half shifting, hurtling through the streets at blurring speed. Seeing Rickard's fist raised as if he was going to hit Alaina again, Niall struck the other man squarely in the side, both boots driving Rickard away from Alaina's prone form. He risked a glance back to check on his mate, who was being picked up by Bronx.

"This is none of your business. Leave now and I'll forgive your attack." Rickard wiped a smear of blood from his mouth.

The other shifter tried to step around, clearly thinking it was over. Niall made no sound, nothing to agree or disagree. For Rickard, he'd signed his own death warrant when he attacked Alaina, and Niall didn't care who was there to witness. He and his wolf were of one accord. He closed the small distance between them, jerking Rickard off his feet with the superior strength that came with being an alpha. "You touched what is mine. For that alone you are sentenced to death. You hurt my mate, and for that your death will be painful." That last came out more animal than man, but Niall couldn't call his wolf back and didn't want to.

Rickard must've finally realized he'd fucked up, his pupils became pinpricks as if he was trying to shift, but couldn't because of Niall's alpha status.

Jett stepped up to them. "Maybe we should take

this somewhere more private, Niall. We sort of gathered a crowd."

A low menacing growl came from Niall, his claws breaking free from the tips of his fingers. "Back the fuck off. He's mine to kill."

Bronx swore, and then he heard Alaina's voice behind him. Niall shook his head trying to clear his thoughts. Taking a deep breath he stared at Rickard. "Make one wrong move, and I'll gut you where you stand. Try to run and I'll chase you down and make you wish you were dead. Understand?"

He waited for Rickard to nod before motioning for Jett to take him. Once he felt more under control he turned slowly to face Alaina, fearing the look of horror on her beautiful face.

They stared into each other's eyes. Her look was one of hope, and something he couldn't define.

Alaina wiggled to be free from Bronx, making Niall's protective instincts surface.

"Easy, I'm putting her down now," Bronx said.

She moved toward him, no hesitation as she slipped her arms around his waist. "I'm so sorry I left like I did."

He felt her pain and honesty in her words, but didn't understand why she'd left. However, he wasn't going to discuss their personal business on the street with everyone around.

"Jett, you and Bronx bring shithead and the others to the sacred circle." He didn't care that she was hearing secrets. By the end of the night she was either going to accept all that he was, or he'd be paying a visit to Payton Glade.

The only indication that she heard was her soft inhale of breath. Her arms squeezed him tighter, and he felt a fist constrict around his heart. Niall put his arms around Alaina, hoping she could take his news with open arms like she accepted the man.

"You ready to go home, babe?" he asked, rubbing his beard stubbled jaw on top of her head. She really was too soft for him and his lifestyle. He was a wolf ready and willing to kill a man for daring to touch her, yet he couldn't let her go.

She nodded against him. "Yes."

Niall ran his hand down her back. "Are you okay? Where did he hit you?" He kept her anchored to him with one hand on her ass, the other he used to tilt her face up to him. Seeing her split lip and bruised jaw made him swear under his breath. "I'm going to knock every fucking tooth out of his mouth, and then I'm going to make him lay on the ground while I stomp his fucking head in," he said, his voice turning gravelly, more wolf than man.

She reached out and covered his mouth with her hand. "Don't. It doesn't hurt that much. Not anymore."

He couldn't scent her lying, which puzzled him. Her soft hand rubbed along his jaw as if soothing a savage beast, and he found himself nuzzling into her palm. "Let me get you home and cleaned up." Not making any promises of what would or wouldn't happen to Rickard, Niall bent and lifted Alaina. Having her close to his heart settled his wolf, allowing the man to take control.

"I sent Chris and his wife running. They own the Flying Pig tattoo shop down the street. Could you get someone to check on them?"

Being a man of action, Niall didn't pause in his quick strides, he sent a message to Jory, knowing the young wolf would check with the owners and get back with him.

He glanced around him, the streets were empty, as if no violence had happened. "Thank you for taking care of the civilians," he told Raydon and River. Power emanated from the twins, and he could feel the flow of energy they'd poured into the streets to get the people to evacuate the area in case Niall had killed Rickard. Each man held one of the men that had come with Rickard, both acting like they'd been forced to act on their alphas behalf. Niall would get to the bottom of the story, after he settled things with Alaina.

The ride back to his place took longer than any other time, yet passed by in a blur. His bike rumbled into the garage. Before he could help Alaina off, she slid across the seat to stand by the side looking nervous.

Without hesitation he went to her, uncaring of what tomorrow might bring. He needed to reassure himself that she was here, that she was okay and that she was his.

Heat burst through his veins at the first touch of his lips on hers, careful of her split lip. He walked her backward until they reached his Camaro, and lifting her easily he placed her on the hood without breaking their kiss.

Her legs wrapped around him, trembling even as they pulled him in closer to her. She moaned, ripping at the ends of his shirt trying to tug it off.

God, he needed inside her. "Do you like these pants," he asked between clenched teeth.

A pretty pink flush covered her face. “Yes. Don’t you?”

He was quickly losing the ability to focus on anything other than the need to get her naked. “I knew you were going to say that.” Moving back a couple inches he stripped her top and his, baring her gorgeous breasts covered in a matching grey lace bra. She lifted herself up, allowing him to pull the stretchy leather-like leggings from her legs, taking her panties with them. Her fuck-me boots had fallen off sometime during their short walk, which he was grateful for. Unsnapping the last article of clothing she had on, he let it drop to join the pile on the hood of his car.

His dick was so hard when he stepped back into the vee of her thighs. She locked her legs back around him, and he could smell her arousal.

The urgent need to mate with Alaina was tempered by the knowledge she was unaware of his nature. Niall swore he’d love her so good she’d accept all of him. He brought his hands up to her breasts, cupping and massaging, his fingers tugging on her nipples until they were hard little points.

She ground against his cock, leaving behind evidence of her desire on the denim. Her fingers moved between them, unsnapping the button and releasing the zipper in an excruciating slow slide. He growled a low warning, letting her know he was close to the edge.

"I'm just being careful not to injure you here," she murmured, brown eyes laughing up at him.

He tweaked her nipples a little harder, more of her orange blossom and ginger scent flooded the air attesting to her excitement. "Me too." His voice was gravelly with need. "I think I'm in need of something to eat, and you are just the treat I need."

Pulling her to the edge of the car, he dropped to his knees and with her legs over his shoulders, Niall licked Alaina like a favorite treat. He loved hearing her scream out his name as he plunged his tongue in deeply and drew more of her sweet flavor into his mouth. He found himself growling, more wolf than man as he devoured everything she gave. Taking little nips of her inner thighs, he licked and sucked until she was thrashing, her breaths coming in ragged little gasps as her orgasm crashed over her.

Only then did he stand and force her head back with one hand in her gorgeous brown hair. "Alaina, look at me. Watch me while I take you." He held his rock hard erection in one hand.

Her breasts heaved with her exhalations, but she complied, looking at him. She moaned as he slowly entered, her pussy rippling along his shaft making him groan.

"Oh, fuck. I don't think...shit, don't move." Niall tried to still her hips from moving up to meet him. He loved how responsive she was, how her body seemed to be made just for his. He pulled back and plunged deep, kissed his way to where her neck and shoulder met and bit down just hard enough to hold her in place. She cried out, screamed, jerked upwards and rotated her hips. Her arms came up, locking around his neck and held him to her. Small teeth, sharper than he'd have thought, bit into his neck, making his wolf howl.

There was something magical happening, but Niall couldn't think past the roaring in his head as his orgasm began. He let it take him, let his control slip, excited in the ability she had to make him, the alpha, lose all control. He felt her body clamp down on him, her pussy milking, squeezing, and taking everything his had to offer.

The orgasm ripped through them both, her passion filled cries overflowed his mind with pure love and joy. Niall's mind and heart sang with love that he savored. Ecstasy unlike any he'd ever known shook him to the core, and instantly he felt guilty.

Very slowly he unlocked her legs from around his hips, and slipped from her body. She had a wondrous smile on her face that made him want to bend over and kiss her. The fact he'd put the look on her face, made him want to wrap her up in his arms, and take her inside and do it all over again.

Yo, Niall. I hate to bother you, but I've got three strange shifters I think we should deal with sooner, rather than later. Jett's voice came over their private path.

Give me a half hour. Niall cut the connection with Jett and then opened one to his brother.

Zayn, I'm going to need you at the sacred circle. Instead of leaving the path open he closed it off as well. He needed to speak with Alaina, otherwise he was going to need to make a call to the Glades. The only person who could make her forget all about him and his kind was Payton, but that was only if she couldn't accept what he was. His heart threatened to shatter if she denied him.

"What's the matter, Niall? You're scaring me," Alaina said.

"We need to talk." Niall bent and grabbed his

shirt off the ground and pulled it over her head. His jeans were still undone, but he quickly stuffed his half-hard dick inside and fastened them.

She pressed her lips together. "That is never a good thing to hear come out of a guy's mouth. Listen," she held up her hand, "I know this is just a good time and I'm not expecting anything..." she squeaked as he picked her up and carried her into his house.

"Oh, a good time for sure, babe. Now, you listen. I've got a lot to tell you, and I need you to really listen and keep an open mind. Okay?"

He'd taken her into his bedroom, gently laying her on his big bed, and crawled in beside her.

Alaina looked up at him. "This sounds serious."

"I don't want you to leave. Not now, not ever. I know we just met, but...I'm not a normal human male, Alaina. I've never felt what I do for you for anyone, and I admit it's making me feel guilty as hell. I loved Emma, she was my wife, my mate and Nolan's mama. If she'd not been killed I'd still be with her, and that's the truth. However, fate had other plans, and I was blessed to be given another chance with love. I'm not expecting you to say you love me. Not yet. You're human so you need time to grow these feelings, but I knew from the first time I scented you that there was something special. I'm screwing this all up, aren't I?"

Alaina laughed, turning into his arms immediately. "You love me?"

Her hair spilled over his chest like silk. "Are you laughing at me, woman?"

She shook her head. "I think I fell in love with you when you first growled at me."

Hearing her talk about his growling he realized he needed to tell her the rest. "There's something else you need to know." He took a deep breath. "Alaina, I'm not just a normal human. I'm also a wolf shifter. I am alpha of my pack."

Alaina pressed kisses along his neck. "Hmm, that is cool."

Niall was amazed at how well she was taking his news, and then felt the heat of her skin. He was sure he'd not bitten her and worried the other shifter had. She glanced up at him, nuzzling him with her face, but he didn't see any signs of the mating heat.

"Do you understand what I'm saying, Alaina?" he asked.

"You're a wolf and a man. Will you show me what your wolf looks like?"

"Promise you won't freak the fuck out?"

She held her right hand over her heart. "I promise."

He got up off the bed and let the shift take him. Where once he was a man, now stood a big red wolf. Alaina got up on her knees and motioned him over to her. He was puzzled by her lack of fear, but his beast enjoyed her easy acceptance. The feel of her soft fingers brushing over his sides had him nearly panting and rolling over in submission.

"Goddess, you are a big fellow." She nuzzled against him again.

In his shift he was three times the size of an average wolf and bigger than most other shifters. He chuffed softly, letting her pet him a couple more seconds.

There was a disturbance in his mind even with his blocks up. *Niall, we got a problem. One of the guys got away and you're not going to like this, but I think we've scented more rogues in the area. If the rogues find the shifter before we do it could definitely spell trouble.* Jett warned.

How the fuck did one of those fuckers get away from you?

He cried like a bitch and said he had to take a

leak. I let him out of my sight for two seconds. He was faster than I anticipated. Through their link, Jett's voice held disgust.

Niall wasn't sure what the hell was going on, but something was off. Jett was one of his top enforcers for a reason. Nobody else could have broken through his blocks, but Jett did with ease. Jett had gotten his nickname because he was fast at everything, including running, on two feet or four. There was no way Jett would've let the wolf get away, unless there was something else going on.

Shifting back to human, he brushed a kiss on top of Alaina's head. "I need to take care of those men who came here to hurt you." He stopped her words with a kiss. "Stay inside the house. If you need anything call me. Don't open the door for anyone but me or my brother Zayn." He wrapped his arms around her, kissing her one last time.

* * * *

Alaina watched Niall stride from his bedroom. He loved her. Her lips felt bruised from his kisses. Her mind began to whirl at his admission and what that meant for her. He didn't let her explain to him she already knew all about shifters, or that she wasn't quite human either. Would he still want her knowing she was part fey, part wolf and had no real abilities like other wolves? Sure, she healed faster than humans, and had heightened senses, but compared to shifters she was normal, or average.

She worried her already healed lip. Fear for her mother had her jumping off the bed and rushing to her cell phone. Indecision warred with common sense. Rickard was the man Roger wanted her to marry and he was here in Mystic. What would he do to her mother if he found out that his puppet wasn't coming back to him?

Looking down at her cell, she tapped on the screen to bring up her emails. She hadn't thought to see if her mom tried contacting her. Of course she didn't think she was running from her dad, or step-dad. She scrolled through several pages until finally finding one from her mom. Opening it with dread, she read the short text. Her relief was palpable to hear her mother had been able to escape from Roger. She wouldn't tell Alaina where she was, but promised to email her every day and would call as soon as she got a burner cell. The last part of the email made her laugh. Her mom's love of Sons of Anarchy made her pick up all sorts of useful, and some not so useful information. The last email was sent yesterday, making Alaina worry that she hadn't received one today. She'd give her mom until tomorrow before she got too upset.

For now she had to figure out how to explain to Niall that she knew about shifters, and then tell him she was part fey and part something else. She'd always assumed she was part wolf, but now she wondered who her real dad was and why her mom ran off with Roger. The thought of her biological father being worse was a nightmare she didn't want to contemplate.

She decided to take a quick shower and be somewhat presentable when Niall came home. After scrubbing the grime of the day off, she went looking for her clothes in the garage wearing another one of Niall's T-shirts and a pair of shorts. She loved his rock band collection of shirts and couldn't help but wonder if he'd miss them if she stole a few.

With her earbuds in, she stepped into the garage, flipped the lights on and sang along with Avenge Sevenfold's *Dear God*. The song's chorus was one of her favorites and she belted it out like she always did.

Alaina danced around the hood of Niall's

Camaro, memories made her blush when she thought about what happened there earlier. She came to a halt, nearly dropping her phone when she noticed a small red wolf lying on the floor of the garage, right on top of her clothes.

He lifted his head, beautiful, familiar blue eyes blinked at her.

"Hi there, little guy. My name is Alaina." She squatted down to eye level with him and held out her hand to the wolf so he could smell her, showing him the top of her hand. Niall's scent would probably be gone from her skin, but he could still tell she meant him no harm.

"You must be Nolan. Your dad has told me so much about you. He had to leave to take care of some pack business, but will be back shortly. Do you want to come inside where it's warm?" Alaina figured she'd let him know she knew all about shifters.

The air shimmered and then a small version of Niall stood before her. "You sing really pretty, and you smell nice."

Alaina was glad she'd taken a shower. Shifters' keen sense of smell would have made this first meeting really awkward, or more awkward. The little guy looked at the pile of clothes and then at her in his dads shirt.

"Did you have an accident?" he asked.

She scooped up her pants and panties in one swoop, the bra and shirt next instead of answering him.

"Did your dad know you were coming home?"

Nolan fidgeted. "My grandma and grandpa had company show up. I thought I'd just come home, but then I found the door locked and I couldn't sense my dad, and I got scared."

She reached out and grabbed his hand with her free one. "Come on. I'm sure it'll be fine. Do you know their number?"

The little boy looked back toward the door leading outside. "Maybe I should go back. They're probably really worried about me."

Her heart turned over at the panic in his voice. "I'm sure they are, but they'd be more worried if I let you go traipsing off this late. Here, call your dad." She handed him her phone.

"You have his number?"

She nodded solemnly. "Yep, he programmed it in, just in case I needed him."

Blue eyes so like his dads sparkled up at her. "Cool. That means he must like you. I told him he needed to get a mate like Uncle Zay. Have you met him?"

Alaina was amazed at the kid's quick acceptance. "Yep, I've met him and Cora. Do you want to call your dad?"

He shook his head. "I'm really hungry. All that shifting burns lots of stuff my dad says." He blinked up at her, squeezing her hand. "You're really pretty. Don't tell Cora, but I think you're even prettier than her."

Niall was in so much trouble when his boy grew up. Alaina walked with the future heartthrob of the country back inside the kitchen. "What sounds good to eat, little man?"

His whole face lit up. "Can you make macaroni and cheese? It's my all-time favorite, but I don't want to put you out." Nolan licked his lips and hopped up on one of the barstools.

And just like that, she felt herself being wrapped around a seven year old boys little finger. Looking through cabinets she found a bag of macaroni and placed a pot on the gas stove to boil for the pasta. Inside the fridge she located a block of Nolan's favorite cheese, and within fifteen minutes she'd prepared his *all-time* favorite snack to perfection. He even let her have a small helping and asked if she wanted to watch a movie with him. How could she turn down a movie with a cutie like him?

By the time she'd cleaned up the kitchen, Nolan was already asleep on one of the leather couches. She grabbed a throw off the end and covered him up, brushing his hair back with her hand. "You are so damn cute. I could fall in love with you too." She brushed her lips over his forehead, grabbed another throw and curled up on the end of the couch, feeling absolutely content.

* * * *

Niall raced into the clearing, anger churning in his gut. He hated to leave Alaina before solidifying his mating with her. His wolf wasn't happy and neither was the man. Jett stood in the middle of the circle along with Zayn and two of the men from town, but not the one who'd hurt his mate.

He shifted before he'd landed on two feet, making his wolf snarl and rage at the loss of revenge. "What the hell happened? Where is Rickard?" He looked at the two lesser wolves cowering between the twins.

Jett shifted on his feet. "There was an issue while he was taking a piss. I took my eyes off of him for two seconds. I didn't think he would try to run, not with so many of us." Jett looked up. "I won't make excuses, and I'll understand if you want to invoke a discipline."

An audible feminine gasp had Niall swinging around toward the far side of the sacred circle. He zeroed in on the young woman hiding behind a clump of trees. "Come here, now," he roared.

When she didn't immediately comply, he went to go after her.

"She didn't mean any harm, Niall. It's my fault." Jett grabbed his arm.

"Your distraction allowed the man who tried to hurt my *mate* to get away."

A chorus of gasps filled the night.

Anger showed on Jett's features, but his voice was low and steady. "You're right. I'm sorry, alpha." Niall took a deep inhale recognizing the truth of his best friend's words. "We'll discuss this later. For now, we have more pressing matters to deal with. I need you to go with me to track him. Bronx, you and the twins stay with the other two. Don't let them escape. I want answers as to why they were here." He shifted again, uncaring if he hadn't addressed the elders who'd come.

Rickard's scent zigzagged across the woods. The man wasn't as stupid as they'd thought. Niall was kicking himself for not realizing he'd fucked up by misjudging an enemy. When the shifter's trail began leading him back to his home, his wolf's hackles went on high alert. A familiar and unwelcome smell hit him as he crossed his lands. Nolan. Gone was the leader of the pack, replaced by the father whose child and love of his life was being threatened.

Jett, my boy's scent is fresh along with Rickard's.

I noticed. Don't worry, we will save them. Jett's calm implacable words came through their link.

Cora and I are coming in from the other side. Zayn said.

Niall altered his trajectory so the light coming from the driveway wouldn't illuminate him when he got close, while Jett's midnight black coat would blend into the night.

From what he knew of the enemy, he'd expect Niall to come at him from the front. Unlike Rickard, Niall wasn't predictable. He moved through the trees, heading for the back of his home. Alaina had opened his bedroom window and he motioned to Jett, silently communicating he was going in that way. His wolf was too close to the surface to speak any other way.

Even now, he had visions of finding one or both of the people he loved broken and bleeding. His vision turned red, but he shook off the images. Making his way through the house on silent feet, praying Rickard didn't notice his scent.

"You think your boyfriend is going to save you?" Rickard's laugh grated on his wolf's ears.

"Why would you want to mate with me? Roger is not my father and this isn't the stone ages anymore. It's not done in this day for a...man to marry off his daughter, or step-daughter to another man," Alaina's said.

Niall paused to listen for his son's heartbeat. *Nolan, where are you?*

Dad, I'm scared. Laney saved me. She woke me up and had me hide in my toy box. There's a bad guy here. I heard him hit her, Dad. Nolan's voice quavered. *I was gonna help, but she made me pinky promise to stay inside and said you'd be mad if I didn't listen to her.*

You did good, Nolan. Stay where you are and

don't come out unless me, Uncle Zayn or Aunt Cora come get you.

What about Laney?

Niall closed his eyes. He wasn't sure how to answer that. Wasn't sure if Rickard would be able to use her to get to his boy. Even the strongest could get pushed to do things against their will. He thought of Jett, his strongest enforcer, and silently asked Alaina to forgive him. *No, Nolan, only me, Uncle Zayn and Aunt Cora. Love you, buddy. Now, stay quiet no matter what you hear.* He cut the connection with Nolan and shared his son's whereabouts with his brother.

Through the hallway he could see Rickard had shifted to human and was shaking Alaina.

"Where are your fucking keys, bitch?"

Alaina jerked on her arm. "They're in the bedroom, in my purse."

Rickard's head bent and he sniffed her neck. "He hasn't marked you. You were good enough to fuck, but not make you his mate. Now, I have to take you back and mate a used whore. Maybe I should sample what I'm getting first, hmmm?"

"You're a sick bastard. I'll die before I let you touch me." She reared back and tried to kick him.

"Oh, little bitch, trust and believe that is the plan. I won't be shackled with you for life, nor will I be putting my cubs in you. Fuck you for sure, but I'll make damn sure my seed don't take root."

Niall watched him lick Alaina's cheek, but he waited, knowing Alaina realized he was there and was leading Rickard to him. He crept backward not willing to allow the man to enter his room too far. This was the room he'd made love to his future mate, and nothing would sour those memories.

He could hear their footfalls, Rickard's heavier set, and Alaina's almost imperceptible ones getting closer. Finding himself forced to wait didn't sit well with Niall.

The door swung open, exactly as he'd anticipated, and in a flash he pushed Alaina toward the other side of the room. Her lithe body was prepared and rolled, coming back up into a fighter's stance. Goddess, he fell more in love with her.

Alaina, I'm going to force him out of the house. I want you to get into my truck and get out of here.

Not gonna happen.

He projected an image of him snapping his fangs at her, but didn't have time to argue. Displaced air signaled the other man shifting into his wolf, meeting

Niall in a clash of dominance.

Niall was more than ready for him, ducking in his wolven form, barely missing the lethal claws. He raked his own at the underbelly of Rickard, knowing it would enrage the wolf. Nipping at the flank, Niall maneuvered his opponent near the open window so that the next move would easily get them into the position he wanted.

Rickard cried out in a mixture of anger and pain. The bastard looked around, once again looking to use Alaina as a shield or to inflict his own brand of damage, Niall suspected. Rickard's roar, when he noticed she was no longer in sight, gave Niall the moment he needed, and he struck hard and fast, hitting the other wolf with the flat of his head in the side of the ribs. They crashed through the window, glass shattering around them.

The coppery scent of blood filled the air.

He came up, shaking shards of window debris from his fur and eyed the other wolf. Pouring all the hate he had into his attack, Niall didn't let Rickard regroup, he snarled and slashed. More of the other man's blood poured down his paw, a kidney was shredded, and he rejoiced.

By the time Zayn and several others from his

pack arrived, Rickard had curled into a whimpering ball of fur. Niall shifted back to human, but didn't clothe himself completely. He squatted next to Rickard. "You will die for your sins against my family. Shift. Now!"

Slowly Rickard obeyed his command, becoming man again. His wounds were even more severe in his human form. Niall grabbed him by the back of the neck and pulled him to his feet, thrusting his face into the other man's. "What have you to say for yourself?"

"She is my mate by right. Her father gave her to me. He's my alpha," Rickard gasped.

"What the hell are you talking about?"

"I can answer that." A woman who was an older version of Alaina stepped from the woods with Emerson and Payton.

Rickard lunged for the newcomer, halting abruptly when she raised her hand and a bright golden orb surrounded him.

"Who are you?" Niall asked.

"My name is Adalynn, Alaina is my daughter."

Niall jolted. The woman who wielded fey power very similar to Payton was Alaina's mother. That would make her related to his Emma. She'd lied to him. A lie by omission was a lie all the same to him.

He wanted to roar with agony, but he had to put on the alpha face.

Jett, take Rickard back to the circle and wait for me there. Take everyone with you while I deal with this mess.

Niall, don't do something stupid. Let her explain. Remember she didn't know who she was until recently. I'm sure she was going to tell you. Zayn tried to reason with him.

When I want your advice, baby brother, I'll ask for it.

Aren't you the one who advised me on my love life?

Niall had yet to lock inside of Alaina, and now he didn't think he'd ever experience the sensation again. He'd told Zayn being locked inside his mate was the best experience in the world, and when his first mate had died he thought he'd never know that feeling again. The woman he thought would be his mate came out with Nolan, his son was extolling the awesomeness that was *Laney* to his grandparents, but he could feel her eyes on him. He turned away from them, looking up at the moon.

"Dad, are you okay? Laney saved me. You should

have seen her."

"I was trying to tell you when you got called away," her soft voice came from behind him.

He held his breath. "That's convenient."

Emerson picked up Nolan, taking him over to where Payton stood, giving him and Alaina space.

"Fuck you, asshole. At the very least turn and face me. I know you can scent if I'm lying, so do it." Her words were barely over a whisper.

"How do I know you aren't using your fey powers to manipulate me?"

Several female growls rang out.

Alaina shoved him in the chest. "I don't have any powers."

Everything in Niall stilled. "What do you mean?"

She shrugged her shoulders.

He looked up to see Emerson walking off with Nolan. "What the hell is going on," he croaked.

"Dad, you need to fix this," Nolan yelled, his lower lip quivering.

He cursed their shifter hearing. "Buddy, I will talk to you in a little bit. Go with your grandparents." His son nodded, but he saw tears in his son's eyes.

"I need to take care of pack business. When I finish we will talk," he said looking down into her brown eyes.

Space. He needed to get away from her and the smell of orange blossoms mixed with ginger. The cloying scent of the other wolf was overlaying everything with his coppery blood as well making Niall's wolf howl. Hearing she was not human like he'd assumed, he wasn't sure which way was up and which was down. Without looking back, he shifted. He'd take care of Rickard and the other two men, then he'd deal with Alaina.

At the clearing, Rickard and the other two pack members were on their knees in human form.

"Were you able to contact their alpha to confirm their story?" he asked River.

River kicked the one closest to him. "This one actually called his *alpha* and told him they'd failed in their mission. He left it on his voicemail, but immediately received a text back." River turned the phone around to show Niall what it said.

Niall whistled through his teeth. "Looks like you boys don't have a pack unless you bring the prize home. Unfortunately, that's not going to happen."

"You can't just kill us. We have family," one of the men cried.

The old Niall would've felt a twinge of guilt. The

new Niall saw the way the men had looked at the women in his bar. Seen the way they'd stood by while Rickard was ready to hurt or even kill Alaina without once thinking of stopping him. Their death warrants were all but signed, sealed, and delivered. He fought for control.

Pack law would be invoked, and nobody would blink an eye, or think it wasn't his right, since Rickard went to his home where his cub was present. Even though he hadn't claimed Alaina yet, he'd made it clear she was his, she carried his scent. Rickard chose to ignore all those facts.

He pictured her face, the hurt he'd inflicted when he'd left.

The elders signaled they agreed with him and pack law would be passed down. He motioned for them to release Rickard. "You have two choices. Die on your knees or on your feet."

Rickard stood, his wounds beginning to heal. At six foot three Niall was a big man, but Rickard was a little taller and almost as brawny, black hair cut military short and not a tattoo in sight. He wore a pair of khaki pants and a polo shirt for crying out loud.

The exact opposite of Niall.

Niall lunged forward, not allowing the man a chance to take a swing. His fist connecting with enough force to send him flying through the air.

Rickard's eyes widened, his mouth opened, begging for mercy.

None would come for him. Drunk on bloodlust, Niall pounded all his pent up fury into Rickard who turned on his stomach and tried to crawl away. With a yell, Niall planted his booted foot in the middle of the other man's back, and reaching down he gave a vicious twist.

All went quiet around him, not even the forest creatures seemed to breathe. Bodies shuffled after a few minutes. His heartbeat returned to normal, and then he felt Emerson's presence next to him. "Come on, son, it's time you went home," Emerson Glade said.

Niall nodded.

Chapter Eight

Alaina hugged her mother. "Mom, what are you doing here?" She pulled back and looked at the other woman. She was a towering woman next to Adalynn, but looked very similar.

"Sweetheart, this is my sister Payton."

She released her mom, feeling the power both women had. An immense sense of weakness, of being the only one with nothing, overwhelmed her. Like a petulant child, she let go of Adalynn. "Why didn't you tell me? I thought you were fey and I was just a half fey and a defective shifter, but obviously there's more. What's going on?"

Her mother dabbed her eyes with her hand. "I did it to protect you. Roger would have killed you had he known. I...did the only thing I could think of."

Payton scowled at her. "What your mother did was endure years of abuse in order to give you what she thought was a better life, and at a great cost to herself. Look at her," Payton said indicating Adalynn. "Does she look like a fey at full strength? She hid your nature, even from you, in order to keep you safe."

"Don't Pay. I should've told her. Roger was—is a bastard. You have no clue." Her mom shuddered. "The man who fathered you is even worse, but I didn't realize it until I'd fallen head over heels in love with him. When I overheard him talking to some of his pack members, and the things they'd planned for me, I latched onto Roger. I know it was wrong, but he was the lesser of two evils. I did the best I could," Adalynn sobbed. "I was your birth father's truemate, but I used my fey magic to hide myself, and you, from him. I manipulated so much it drained me for all these years, but I'd do it again. What he'd planned for me would've killed both of us, before you'd even had the chance to be born."

"Mom, I'm sorry. You were the best mom in the world." Alaina hugged her.

"There's more, sweetheart." Her mom's tear filled voice broke her heart. "Roger's truemate had died the year before I'd met him. I used his loss and broken heart to my advantage, knowing I resembled her and he wouldn't turn me away. I am far from innocent."

At some point she was going to need to find out who her real dad was, but right now her nerves were too raw from Niall's rejection. "Mom, go and we can talk later."

Her aunt nodded. "She will recover her strength now that she is home. I will make sure of it. Are you coming with us?"

Alaina looked at the drill sergeant of an aunt and saw true love and worry etched on her face. For better or worse she needed to stay and face Niall. "I have to talk with Niall first. I'll call you when I...I know what is happening."

"Something else you should know. Niall's wife was my daughter Emma. She was taken too soon from this earth, but I believe the All Mighty has a way of balancing things out. You, my child, are just what he needs. Don't let him run roughshod over you." Payton bent and kissed her on both cheeks.

Unable to speak with the tears choking her, Alaina nodded. A golden orb appeared to surround both her mom and aunt and then they were gone. She really wished she wasn't the weak link in the equation, but if Niall could accept her with all her faults she would too.

"That was truly a lovely homecoming wasn't it."

She jumped at the sound of Roger Strop's voice. "What the hell are you doing here?" She looked around for his enforcers, wondering how her mom didn't scent him.

He tsked. "Are you looking for help?"

"You should leave before Niall returns."

Roger laughed. "He doesn't want a liar any more than I do."

Her mind whirled. "How did you find us?" She was stalling for time, hoping Niall came back.

"When the little bird flew the coop, I let her think she got away and followed. She thinks she's smart, but she's nothing except a stupid bitch who's outlived her usefulness," he spat.

"Clearly, she outsmarted you for twenty-five years. She's not a fey with no powers like you thought?" Alaina edged closer to the forest while they were talking.

His expression darkened. "I sensed something, but I assumed it was her lack of abilities, not her tampering with them. When I get my hands on her, I'll make sure she suffers before I kill her. You, on the other hand, I'm going to enjoy killing quickly."

Her tone softened. "Don't you have any feelings for me at all? You raised me as your child." She hated the whine, but she only wanted to be loved by her father.

He shook his dark head. "Why would I have? You

couldn't shift. You were a girl, and you had no talents except you were pretty. I couldn't fuck you because I thought you were mine, but that's no longer true." Roger's face twisted in a sinister smile. "Now, I can do whatever I like, and then I'll end your sad existence."

"You'll have to kill me before I'll let you touch me, you sick fuck."

"No," he said menacingly. "That is where you are wrong, Alaina."

"I'll fight you with every fiber of my being," she said just as menacingly.

"Oh, you have no idea how much I enjoy a good fight."

She swung around, and ran for the woods. She'd thought she could throw him off by angering him, but she could smell by his scent he was getting excited and that was the last thing she wanted. His maniacal laughter followed behind her and then she knew he'd shifted, the familiar sense of displaced air, signaling a shifter's change.

Power ebbed and flowed in her veins, unfamiliar, yet soothing, giving her strength and speed.

Unwilling to glance backward, she swore she could feel the hot breath on her neck. She screamed.

The trees on each side of her shook, leaves falling as she passed them in a blur of unnatural speed. Branches broke too close to her, making her stumble, and then the big black wolf was on her in a flash.

Alaina rolled with the huge animal, knowing if he got his fangs into the back of her neck he'd jerk her around like a rag doll. She hit the trunk of a huge tree, grunting at the pain, but fought to breathe through the ache. The impact sent Roger tumbling off, giving her a moment of respite. He got to his feet shaking it off and glared at her through huge wolven eyes. She thought of trying to run for it, but he'd be on her in seconds. A low hanging branch caught her attention, and she made up her mind. Jumping to her feet, she swung up and ascended as fast as she could, scraping her bare legs on the rough bark.

The way her luck was going her blood was going to coat the forest. Roger paced at the base of the tree, leapt at the branch and snarled. Just as she was prepared to watch him shift and come after her, the most beautiful sight she'd ever seen came barreling through the woods.

Niall. Goddess, he was beautiful as a man and wolf.

Roger turned to meet Niall's charge, clearly

unprepared for the younger man's ferocity.

He showed no mercy coming at Roger with all the alpha strength and power that Alaina admired from the beginning. The fight between the two men was short and swift, and she was suddenly aware Niall hadn't wanted to battle with Rickard, had in fact only been playing with the other wolf. His actions gave her hope for a future.

She stared down at the man who she'd thought was her father and felt no remorse for the loss of his life.

"You coming down, or do I need to come up and get you?"

Suddenly, Alaina was aware she truly wasn't sure if she could get down. Licking her lips she thought about how she'd gotten up. "I think I'll just stay up here for a little longer if you don't mind," her voice had a slight quiver to it.

"Hold tight, babe, I'm coming to get you."

Oh, shit. The tree shook as he started scaling it. Alaina didn't think it would hold up under all their weight. She inhaled sharply and held it. Maybe if she didn't breathe the branch she was clinging to for dear life wouldn't break. She giggled.

"I am not that big, woman," Niall said just below

her.

Two more branches and he'd be right next to her on the twig. "I'll come down to you."

He studied her face then nodded and held his hand up for her. She'd have to release the death grip she had, but she trusted Niall to keep her safe.

Placing her palm in his, she scooted down to the larger limb he stood on.

"Goddess, you scared ten years off my life."

* * * *

Jett followed the trail of the woman who'd caused him to allow Rickard to escape. He really couldn't blame her though. He'd caught her scent and instantly his wolf had stood up and howled. The fact she'd smelled like spiced honey wrapped in sin should have been enough to warn him she was trouble, but he never was one to listen to common sense.

He'd ignored her, thinking she was far enough away as not to be an issue, knowing she was canine and somewhat familiar, and then he'd smelled rogues heading her way. The prisoner became a nonissue to him, even though his alpha had entrusted him to watch over Rickard. His main focus, only focus, became finding the woman and insuring her safety until common sense kicked in.

Turning back, he'd planned to ask Bronx to watch over Rickard only to find the wolf had escaped. By the time he'd alerted Niall, he couldn't find any trace of the elusive woman, or the rogues except a faint trail of their scents. When his alpha had shown up and he'd realized she'd returned, Jett was ready to put himself in front of her, only to realize she had disappeared without a trace once again. His frustration rose at one woman's ability to evade him so easily.

But Jett wasn't one to give up easily. He shifted seamlessly into his wolf, going to the last area he'd scented her. His hackles rose at the overlying smell of other wolves trampling her uniqueness. Several paw prints showed him there were at least four other wolves that had tracked over hers, and he hoped she hadn't come with them in an attempt to draw him out. By the indent of the different prints, she was clearly a small wolf next to the males, especially his own, much larger paws. He'd wager she was light as a feather, and had it not rained earlier in the day he'd have had a hard time finding her prints at all.

He shook his head and continued to track the other wolves back the way they'd come. From the looks of their trail they were either all together or they were following the female. The latter made him and his wolf growl.

When he got close to the highway he noticed several sets of tire tracks and fresh oil from a leaky car. Whoever had been parked there had an older vehicle that needed maintenance. Still that elusive, sweet spiced honey could be smelled under all the other odors, making him want to howl at the moon. Jett breathed deeply, memorizing the female, because he wanted to know her when he found her. There was no doubt in his mind he would find her.

The moon overhead shone on an object not far from where he assumed the female would've gotten out. Jett's instincts had him crouching in the shadows, blending into the darkness and waiting. An hour later his patience paid off. A fifty-seven Chevy pickup came rumbling up, its neon purple color in no way trying to blend in. He wasn't sure if it was coincidence or not until the driver's door opened, and he was hit with the smell of sweet honey. The driver couldn't be seen until she stepped around the back of the short-bed. His breath stalled in his throat.

Her hair gleamed in the moonlight, dark brown with streaks of purple, like her vehicle. He shifted, his dick instantly hardening. Jett couldn't believe he was aroused to the point he was just by looking at a strange woman, and she was possibly the enemy.

He stayed downwind, watching to see what she was going to do.

"Fuck me running, where the hell did it go?" Her husky voice had his balls quivering in his jeans.

She walked around the vehicle and then he heard her exclamation of *ah hah*. She bent over in jeans stretched tight across a firm backside that he could envision in all sorts of dirty scenarios.

Jett memorized her plate number, turning to watch as she walked back to the driver's door. She stopped, looked longingly toward where he stood in the woods, and then got behind the wheel. He knew she couldn't have seen him, but his heart still did a little pause, his dick jerked at the thought of her looking and liking what she saw. His little vixen liked being watched, did she?

The sound of the pickup sputtering to life brought his protective instinct out, making him shift. He'd follow her down the hill until she hit town, where she'd at least have cell service, just in case she needed to call for help. Tomorrow he'd find out all he could about his little purple loving wild wolf, and why she was hanging out with a bunch of rogues.

* * * *

Niall saw her trying to pull back from him, not physically, but mentally and he wasn't going to allow it. He realized she had been telling the truth, and even if she hadn't told him right away, they were still learning about each other. If he wasn't willing to give her the benefit of the doubt he didn't deserve her, and he damn sure wanted her. Wanted to be good enough for her. Before she came along he was only half alive. He'd always love Emma and be grateful for the time they'd had together, but their time was over. Niall looked at the bent head of the woman who was his light. Her insecurities, because she didn't think she was good enough for him, were in every line of her body.

He tugged her head up with one hand fisted in her hair. "Do you realize you're in our tree?"

"What?" she asked, staring at their surroundings.

"Come on, I'll explain when we get down." Niall swung her up in his arms, leaping the last fifteen feet with ease. “Look,” he said.

The moon shone overhead illuminating the area, showing her where they were. He was amazed to find she’d climbed the tree where he’d first made love to her.

She looked around and asked what he knew she was thinking. “Where is—Roger?”

While he’d climbed up to get her he’d had a couple enforcers come and remove the wolf’s body, not wanting to traumatize Alaina.

“He’ll be taken care of. I’m sorry for being an asshole earlier. I’d promise to never be one again, but that’s asking a lot. I can say I’ll try really hard not to be.” He held her by the hips.

She raised her chin. “I really was going to tell you.”

“I believe you.”

Her uncertainty was like a knife gutting him. “Let’s go home so I can take care of you. You’ve got to be freezing. There’s more to being a shifter and mating, but I think you know that, right?”

She nodded, struggling for a reply.

“I want that with you. You are it for me. I know you think you’re flawed, but to me you’re perfect. Everything about you is perfect. If you let me, I’ll show you just how perfect. I'm not sure how my bite will affect you since you're half fey, but I want to mark you so every shifter knows you are mine."

"Oh, Niall, I love you." She kissed him. "Are you sure?" I mean what if our children can't shift? I mean, do you want children with me?" She bit her lip.

He picked her up and carried her back home. Not just his, but theirs.

The door to his kitchen was busted open from where Rickard had obviously broken in. He stepped over the mess and concentrated on the shapely body he held in his arms.

"Are you going to carry me around forever?"

"Thinking about it." His voice came out a growl.

Stunning. She looked damn stunning wearing his T-shirt, he thought as he gazed down at her beautiful face. Dark brown hair hung in a messy disarray around her face and shoulders, her breasts, high and full, that fit perfectly in his palms, were outlined in the thin material and he itched to cup them.

He made the way to the master suite, kicking the door closed and remembered the window had been busted out during his fight with the other wolf. Exhaling when he saw someone had boarded up the damage while he'd been gone.

"I'm sorry about that." Alaina pointed to the window.

"Hey, it's not your fault." He loved having her breasts pressed against him. "Are you sure you want to be with me for the rest of your life, Alaina?"

His question seemed to catch her off-guard. "Of course I'm sure, unless you've changed your mind."

"Do you truly believe I'd ever let you go after climbing a tree for you?" he joked, walking into his bathroom.

She shook her head. "No, I guess not. Of course you're not a cat, so heights don't scare you."

"We are definitely nothing like them damn cat-shifters." He shuddered for affect.

Alaina placed her hand on his chest. "Are you prejudiced against other species?" she asked, her hand caressing him, making him forget what they were discussing.

Niall set her on her dainty feet. "I just don't trust them, they make me sneeze."

Her delighted laughter pushed away thoughts of everything except getting his mate naked and clean.

"Goddess, I love you, Niall." Her hands went to work on his jeans.

Her words had his head spinning, and then she

knelt on the tile at his feet working the denim off him. She was wearing too many clothes while he stood naked with his cock pointing straight at her perfect mouth.

"You have too many clothes on, babe." He looked pointedly at the now dirty rock T-shirt that was too big, but looked amazing on her.

"We can remedy that." She gripped the ends and pulled the black fabric over her head, leaving her naked from the waist up. A slight shimmy and her shorts were off and in the pile next to her.

"I take back my earlier statement. You're exquisitely beautiful." Niall tried to pull her up.

"Mmm. I've been wanting to do this for a long time." Alaina reached out and cupped his sac, rolling his balls around in her small hand.

Every single fiber of his being tensed, but he didn't move. He wanted her mouth on him like he wanted his next breath. She released her hold on him and slid one hand up his length from root to tip, running her thumb over the head. His dick jerked, and liquid seeped from the slit, begging for release.

She ran her thumb over the top in a circular motion, spreading the moisture. "I love how hard you are. I want to taste you."

He growled in agreement.

Her head bent and she blew on his slick head, making his balls draw up tight. “Alaina,” he warned.

She giggled, and then she opened her rosy pink lips and took him inside. The head of his shaft disappeared and as she licked, the feel of her tongue swirling around and around, dipping inside the tip had him moaning.

He gripped the back of her head in a tight fist and swore he’d not force her, but then she teased him, going down a little further and sucking, only to pull back with a scrape of her dainty little teeth. She gripped his hips, and then took him deeper, sucking harder, humming in pleasure. The sweet smell of her arousal mixed with his own much muskier scent permeated the air, but he didn’t want to come in her mouth. Not this time, maybe next, or the next.

Niall gritted his teeth and eased her head back and she released his cock with a loud slurp and a questioning look.

“Let’s shower first, quickly, and then I want to be inside you when I come and mark you. I need to be inside you more than I need my next breath.”

Her brown eyes shifted to that strange amber he had seen before, but in the next instant she was leaping into his arms. “You say the sweetest things.”

With his hands holding her ass, he guided them into the stall and made quick work of their shower. He ignored his raging hard on trapped between their bodies, and the nipples that looked like taut red berries needing to be licked.

Once they were sufficiently cleaned he shut the water off, loving her infectious giggle and vowed to insure she always had a reason to laugh.

Back in the master bedroom he stood at the end of the bed and watched Alaina with her hair spread on his pillow, exactly as he’d envisioned.

“Touch your breasts, show me what you like.”

Her skin flushed a rosy hue from the tip of her toes to her beautiful face, but she did as he’d asked. Her legs parted, showing him how wet she already was.

He crawled up between her thighs, nibbling on her as he went. He bit her inner thigh gently, and then lapped at the folds of her pussy, enjoying her flavor. Bending her knees, he pressed them toward her chest.

Alaina grabbed his hair. “Niall, I need you in me. Please,” she begged. Even as she spoke he was lifting himself up her body so he was kneeling between her legs. Her pussy was pink and wet and so damn hot as he positioned his cockhead to her entrance.

Their eyes met and as she smiled up at him he pushed downward, she swiveled her hips and he went deeper and deeper still. Finally, when his balls rested against her ass, he held completely still.

Alaina rocked against him and that slight movement had him bending to take a nipple into his mouth, laving the taut bud with his tongue. She was so tight and snug around him, and when he lavished the same attention to both nipples her pussy clamped down even harder around him.

Unable to control the sounds of pleasure from escaping, the intense urge to come was riding him, but he needed her to come with him.

"Fuck me Niall, harder, faster damn it."

He pulled back and panting hard, he did just that. Hooking her legs over his arms, he opened her wider and began to thrust hard and deep.

The first pulse of her pussy clamping around him along with her widening eyes had his wolf howling in his head. He released her legs, and with a growl gripped her shoulders and fucked her in short hard thrusts. She turned her head, exposing her neck and he couldn't resist, didn't want to, and bit down. She cried out as she came, her orgasm cresting as his washed over him. His cock began to jerk inside her as he found his release and then the most amazing thing happened, he felt the knot swell, locking him inside his mate. He licked the small punctures in her neck, and rolled to the side to keep from squishing her.

"That was...oh, goddess," she whispered.

She shoved him onto his back. "More, I need more."

Niall could feel the link between them, his wolf recognizing his mate. He also sensed something else. His cock jerked inside her as she sat up. He could smell her arousal mixed with something more. She began undulating, around and around.

With his hands on her hips, he found himself guiding her, and even when the knot eased he was still hard and full inside her. Her movements became more erratic and then her eyes flashed from brown to amber, a low feminine growl escaped her parted lips.

"Need to mark you, make you mine too," she muttered.

Niall turned his neck giving her access. She was panting and so was he, and then she struck. He threw his head back, holding her to him as he felt her incisors pierce his skin. Another orgasm crashed through him, totally eclipsing anything he'd experienced. The warm rush of her pleasure bathed his cock, her pussy spasming around him had his heart pounding.

He sucked in air, holding his mate, his perfect wolf in his arms. She lay like a limp doll and rested her head on his shoulder. "I bit you."

"I know," he said with satisfaction.

"Is it normal to shift so soon after a first bite?" Her lack of energy made him feel like he was the king of the world.

Niall raised his head enough to see if she had her eyes open, seeing her with the brown he'd fallen in love with, he smiled. "No, it's not normal, but you're not just a normal human, my love."

She lolled against him. "Explain. I'm too tired to work out what you're saying."

He ran his hands down her soft as satin back. "Alaina, I think your wolf just woke and said hi to my wolf."

Alaina's head popped up. "What the heck are you talking about?"

Her abrupt movement caused his cock to slide out, which was a shame, but he figured what she really needed was to find her wolf. "For whatever reason your wolf has been hidden inside you, and now I can sense her. My wolf and I are of one accord, and your eyes also shifted during lovemaking." He shrugged. "Not to mention your teeth." He tilted his head to the side to show her the wound that was already healing, but to all shifters would forever be seen.

Niall sat up with Alaina's legs still straddling his thighs. He had to tell his dick to stay down, which made his mate laugh. "See, you can already read my thoughts."

"That's so cool. Can you read mine?" *Niall has the biggest dick I've ever seen. Well, except this one time at band camp.*

Mate, I will spank your ass.

Oh, my gawd. You can totally hear me. Oh, shit. How do we turn it off?

Niall kissed her nose. "I'll teach you that, but first don't you want to see your wolf?"

She fidgeted on his lap and he sensed her nervousness.

"We can wait."

Her heart pounded against his and she bit her lower lip. "No, let's do this." She scrambled off his lap. "What do I do?"

He sent her an image of what he thought her wolf would look like and then told her how to shift.

"You go first." She chewed on her thumbnail.

Climbing off the bed he stood in front of her. "Why don't we do it together? On the count of three. My wolf wants to see yours."

She stood completely still, and then eventually she nodded after a few long seconds. He connected with her on their private path. *I'm with you every step of the way, babe. When you're ready we do this.*

A deep inhale and then he heard her count in his head. He was right. She was a gorgeous wolf with beautiful brown fur, and amber eyes looking at him with awe. *I did it.*

Of course you did, and you are the most perfect wolf a mate could ask for. Want to go for a run?

Yes. Only I am not eating the Easter Bunny, just so we're clear.

She sounded so regal and with her head held high, her tail in the air, Niall followed her out the door and down the hall of his home. He couldn't wait for Nolan to find out he'd done exactly as he'd told him to do. Found a mate like his uncle Zay. If the goddess blessed them they'd have more cubs for Nolan to boss around, if not, they'd spoil the kid rotten. Niall had a feeling Nolan already had his mate wrapped around his little finger. Life couldn't get much more perfect.

The End

About Elle Boon

Elle Boon lives in Middle-Merica as she likes to say...with her husband, two kids, and a black lab who is more like a small pony. She'd never planned to be a writer, but when life threw her a curve, she swerved with it, since she's athletically challenged. She's known for saying "Bless Your Heart" and dropping lots of F-bombs, but she loves where this new journey has taken her.

She writes what she loves to read, and that is romance, whether it's erotic or paranormal, as long as there is a happily ever after. Her biggest hope is that after readers have read one of her stories, they fall in love with her characters as much as she did. She loves creating new worlds and has more stories just waiting to be written. Elle believes in happily ever afters, and can guarantee you will always get one with her stories.

Connect with Elle online, she loves to hear from you:

www.elleboon.com

www.facebook.com/elleboon

twitter.com/elleboon

Author's Note

I'm often asked by wonderful readers how they could help get the word out about the book they enjoyed. There are many ways to help out your favorite author, but one of the best is by leaving an honest review. Another great way is spread the word by recommending the books you love, because stories are meant to be shared. Thank you so very much for reading this book and supporting all authors. If you'd like to find out more about Elle's books, visit her website, or follow her on FaceBook, Twitter and other social media sites.

Other Books by Elle Boon

Erotic Ménage

Ravens of War

Selena's Men

Two For Tamara

Jaklyn's Saviors

Kira's Warriors

Akra's Demon's, Coming Fall 2015

Shifters Romance

Mystic Wolves

Accidentally Wolf

His Perfect Wolf

Wild Wolf, Coming 2015

Paranormal Romance

SmokeJumpers

FireStarter

Berserker's Rage

A SmokeJumpers Christmas, Coming Soon

Mind Bender, Coming Spring 2016

MC Shifters Erotic

Iron Wolves MC

Lyric's Accidental Mate October 20th, 2015

Contemporary Romance

Miami Nights

Miami Inferno

Miami Blaze, Coming Summer 2016

FireStarter

SmokeJumpers - Book 1

Elle Boon

Chapter One

Keanu Raine walked a few feet from his team, letting his inner fire control him. The forest fire was all but burned out, but it was searching for more, and he knew it had found a new source. The living breathing entity of unforgiving heat that could engulf hundreds of acres, only needed a little spark to ignite all over again, only Keanu wasn't going to allow it if he could stop it. He ignored their questions knowing they were missing something. The hair on the back of his neck stood on end, never a good sign when you were in the middle of a huge forest fire. "Hey, did you guys hear that?" Keanu asked.

"Shit, man, this gobbler is a fuck nut," Brax McKay grumbled.

"Kea, all I can hear is my stomach rumbling."

Hal Aldridge grinned, his blond hair soaked with sweat.

"I swear something's not right." Keanu nodded in the direction of the burned out forest.

He couldn't squash the feeling of doom as he looked through the smoke. His inner fire leapt to life, sending his senses on high alert. A small blaze could easily turn into something much larger with the dry conditions, and in Keanu's opinion, it was a guarantee. They'd evacuated the surrounding homes, but it wasn't always a certainty all families would get out.

"I'm going to scout around a bit, since we have about thirty minutes before pick-up. You guys head for the zone and wait for my call. If I'm not there when the DC shows, I'll meet you at the next drop." He tapped the radio attached to his suit.

"Yeah, right, boss. I don't think so, I'm going with you," Hal snorted, moving to stand by him.

"It's cool. I'll go by myself. It's probably nothing." Keanu shrugged.

Hal shook his head. "Let's go."

The group of smokejumpers paused and Keanu nodded to Brax. He knew Hal would follow him regardless. They left the other six members of their team and headed in the direction that Keanu sensed the disturbance. The overwhelming feeling persisted. Someone was trapped in the middle of the blaze. He could feel it in his bones. They needed to locate him or her quickly, or there wouldn't be anything left to find.

Several minutes later, they stood on the outskirts of an already evacuated community. Keanu considered calling a stop to their search, fearing he was too late. There were towering homes to his right, less than a hundred yards away, and blackened earth to his left.

"Kea, if there was someone here, they must've gotten out."

Keanu wasn't sure how Hal knew he was searching for a person, but he had figured out early on Hal was every bit as sensitive as he was.

Hearing Hal mimic his thoughts about their search made his stomach drop. The other man didn't have to add *or they were dead*; nothing could've survived in the middle of the area.

Keanu shook his head, not willing to give up yet. "This way, I know I'm right." Turning toward the trees, he didn't need to check to see if his partner followed.

Burnt wood and grass surrounded them. Inhaling deeply he caught a scent so distinctive it made most people gag.

“My water tank is almost empty. If there’s a fire, and I’m not saying there is, maybe we should call for back-up.”

“There isn’t time. I smell burnt human hair.”

“Shit,” Hal swore.

Keanu led them into a thick clump of charred trees. With all the blackness surrounding him, he couldn’t see a thing, but he sensed a hot spot. A tingling deep inside wouldn’t let him ignore what he knew was a real threat. He rushed to the area before coming to an abrupt halt. A large section of land filled with tall dry grass had started to smolder.

“What the fuck? How the hell did we miss this?” Hal pointed. “Look.”

A small boy was nestled in the branches just above the flames.

“Hal, you climb and I’ll take care of the fire,” Keanu ordered, relieved to see his partner and best friend didn’t argue for once.

Stepping over the fallen branches and blackened areas, he inhaled the hot air into his lungs.

He continued sucking the flames into his body, relishing the feel of the warmth rushing through his system, while using the water hose attached to his pack to douse the hot spots.

By the time Hal had the boy on the ground, he couldn't sense any more flames. He coughed and gave Hal two thumbs up.

They made their way back to their teammates with the small boy cradled in Hal's big arms.

"What the hell?" Brax eyed the child.

Keanu grabbed a bottle of water from his coworker and chugged, while the rest of the group tended to the boy. His inner flame began to cool with the refreshing fluid and he accepted another bottle gratefully.

"Oh man, Kea. You saved the boy's life." Barry looked from the boy to Keanu.

Keanu shook his head. "Nah, I just got lucky. Hal got the kid down."

"Bullshit! Good job, Kea." Brax punched his arm.

Praise from his team made Keanu cringe. None of them were ordinary men, far from it, but he hated having attention drawn to him. He looked to the sky, happy to see their pick-up overhead in time to save him from unwanted admiration. They'd radioed ahead, alerting them to the addition. The first man took the child. Keanu was the last to leave the clearing. Giving his inner fire free reign one last time, he made sure they hadn't missed anything else. By the time they finished, he was sure the next team wouldn't have any surprises.

Getting into the DC-3 wasn't nearly as fun as jumping from one, Keanu mused as he was finally lifted up.

* * * *

Keanu stood on his deck gazing at the openness for as far as his eyes could see. He loved the smell of the mountains, the clean pine scent. It was very similar to his home with his grandparents. He raised his face to the sun, allowing the rays to warm him from the outside as his internal fire warmed the inside. Letting out a deep breath, he turned toward the fire pit in the corner and blew a puff of air on the logs, making them burn.

Smiling, Keanu stepped into his spacious kitchen and grabbed a bottle of beer from the fridge. Closing his eyes in bliss as he twisted off the cap, he tipped his head for a much needed drink. A platter of steaks and two potatoes wrapped in foil were on the counter, ready to be cooked. He grabbed the platter, stepped outside and placed them on the grill, then with another breath of air, the charcoals started to smoke and turn a fiery red.

"Yo, Kea. Where you at?" Hal yelled from inside.

"I'm on the deck. Grab a beer and come on out."

Hal ducked his head, avoiding the doorjamb, and joined Keanu on the deck with two bottles dangling from his fingers. Keanu took a bottle from Hal with a shake of his head.

"Oofta, I so needed this." Hal tipped his bottle to his mouth.

Keanu laughed and flipped the steaks. "Is 'Oofta' a real word?"

"Hell yeah, it's real. You can use it for just about any swear word."

Keanu stifled a chuckle. "Thanks, but I think I'll just say 'fuck' at least once in every sentence."

"Why doesn't that surprise me?"

"Fuck off." Keanu laughed.

They sat in companionable silence, listening

to the birds sing and the wind whistle through the trees. Keanu loved being outside almost as much as he loved women. He swore watching the trees sway was like watching a woman sashay as she led her man to bed.

"So, what did your grandfather want?"

Leave it to Hal to cut to the chase before Keanu was ready to talk about it. His grandfather lived at the top of the Cascades. It was only fifty miles away, but it could be another country.

Keanu shrugged. "Something is spooking him, and if you knew my grandfather, you'd know it was major. He scares the shit out of me and I'm a grown man."

"He didn't give you any hints?"

Keanu looked at the pit and sucked in a breath, making the red coals lose some of their glow, before turning to his best friend. "Nah. He needs my *expertise*." Keanu made air quotes, shrugged, and headed to the grill.

"So, are you looking forward to going home, boss?" Hal asked.

"Yes and no."

"We're going to miss you on the team. Not sure what we'll do without our very own fireman."

Hal laughed, his booming voice echoing in the still of the night.

"Real funny. I'm still on call in case of emergency situations, and you know Brax can bend things to his will." Keanu raised his eyebrows. The co-leader of their group had truly amazing and sometimes frightening powers, but Keanu wasn't going to tell him he thought he was great. The man already had a big head.

Keanu flipped the steaks and checked the potatoes.

"I'm going to miss my own personal barbeque-man." Hal had a frown on his face.

He flipped Hal off. He'd had the ability to make a fire out of air since he was a small boy. By the time he'd turned twelve, he'd learned to breathe the fire back into his body without much cost to himself, other than the need to burn off the energy one way or another.

After graduating from high school he became a fireman for the local fire department. Known as a fire-breather in the world of elementals, Keanu could create a small flame or a large roaring blaze, and in the next breath suck it back into his body. Of course, the larger the fire the more energy he needed to burn afterwards.

As a child, he'd hike for miles and freefall off a cliff into the freezing streams surrounding the Cascades. The adult Keanu found other more pleasurable ways to expel the effects, usually between the thighs of a woman.

"You need some help there, Kea?"

Keanu shook off his thoughts of the past. "Could you grab the salad and dressing out of the fridge?"

"No problem."

Within moments, Keanu had the steaks and potatoes on the table. It always amazed him the way the six foot four blond giant waited until everything was set before digging into his food. He'd slice his steak with exact precision into small cube-like bites, and then stab them with his fork, before chewing each piece several times.

Hal always consumed the meat first, then the carbs, followed by whatever was left, claiming he liked to eat the good stuff first. It amused Keanu to watch him. Being a man who loved his sweets, Keanu would skip the meal and eat dessert first when he could.

"Why are you staring at me like I'm some kind

of lab experiment?" Hal asked.

Keanu shook his head, raised his fork and pointed it at his friend. "You are the weirdest eater."

Hal raised his bottle. "I get no complaints from the ladies."

"Thanks for the visual, dude."

Ankles crossed, hands resting over his full belly, Keanu leaned his head on the back of his chair and stared at the darkening sky.

Hal kicked Keanu's feet on the ottoman. With a grunt, Keanu made room for the other man to stretch out his long legs, too.

"Have you ever had the feeling your world was about to get rocked?" Keanu asked without looking at Hal.

"Yep! Every time I take a lady to bed." Hal wagged his eyebrows.

"Shut up, dick," he laughed. "I don't mean like that. Besides, I don't get my world rocked when I fuck a woman, I rock *her* world." Keanu smirked.

"Man, you're so full of it. I heard Cathy calling you all kinds of names and none of them good." Hal punched Keanu's arm.

"Damn, she's one crazy-ass bitch. Seriously though, have you ever gotten a feeling nothing is gonna be the same again?" Keanu brought the conversation back around, avoiding the unwanted reminder of his ex.

Hal bumped his size fourteen feet against Keanu's before answering. He felt like a pussy for voicing his fears.

"I don't discount any mysterious crap. For real, my grandmother used to talk about the berserkers in my family, and how they came back every hundred years or some shit. I'm the first *blond giant* in over ten decades." He gave Keanu a pointed look. "My Nana's words, not mine. Sometimes, when I'm in the middle of a fire, I feel like another person is in my body. Ya know what I mean?" Color spread across Hal's face.

Keanu knew exactly what he meant. Every member of their Smokejumper group had special abilities. Hal was clearly a human wrecking ball. He just hadn't realized Hal wasn't always in control, or didn't feel like it at least. "I think we all feel like that to an extent. Have you talked to the captain about it?"

Hal pinned him with a look brooking no argument. "Nothing to talk about."

They fell silent. Keanu let the quiet of the night soothe his soul. One of the reasons he and Hal were such good friends was because neither man pried into the other's business.

"I'd better get going. You want me to help clean up?" Hal nodded at the dishes on the table.

"Nah, I got it."

"Hey, I owe you for cooking, but I haven't mastered the art of making anything other than Ramen noodles yet."

Keanu blinked his eyes. "Because you have the poor little boy look down to an art. You bat those baby blues and all the ladies line up to cook for you."

"Well, you just smile that bright cheesy-ass grin and the ladies are lining up to take their panties off for you. I think that trumps my free meals."

Both men laughed at the familiar argument, since neither man lacked for food or companionship.

They were opposite in looks. Keanu had dark hair hanging past his shoulders, dark brown eyes, and topped out at six foot. Hal was built more like a swimmer, and had at least three inches on him. Keanu had the physique of a body builder and spent his off-time working out or participating in extreme sports.

Brax, the co-leader of his team of Smokejumpers, recruited Keanu at twenty-two when he'd made national headlines. Now at thirty-three, he was ready to head home and settle down. Being seven years older than Hal, he considered him like a little brother. As the unofficial leader of the team it was his job to watch over the guys, but he'd taken Hal under his wing. Knowing he'd possibly done his last jump, and he and Hal would no longer be working together, Keanu already missed his friend.

He walked Hal to the door and watched as the big man took the stairs two at a time, before jumping into his oversized four-wheel-drive pickup. Hal waved one big hand out the window before executing a U-turn to leave. Keanu waited until the taillights disappeared down the long drive before going inside. After cleaning up the mess, he shed his clothes and stood under the rainforest-like shower he'd installed on his deck. Sighing, he closed his eyes.

* * * *

Cammie Masters loved the little town of McKinley Landing, and the way it was tucked into the side of the surrounding mountains. But, and this was a big but, she hated the way it had grown. The town used to be only thirty-eight hundred people. Since the pork plant had moved in, the population had almost doubled, and so had the crime.

Many of the residents of McKinley Landing were a mix of races, but she connected best with her mother's Native American relatives. Her red hair was the only thing that was different. When she was a child, she'd played with the other kids and wished she'd had their black hair.

The summer Cammie had turned twelve, she'd fallen in love for the first time. She'd climbed one of the big pines bordering the Cascade forests and her shoe got stuck several feet up, between two branches. She thought back to the afternoon that changed her whole life with fondness.

"I'm a big girl. I am not gonna cry." Cammie shivered, looking down at the ground from the tree she was stuck in. "Dang you, Mazey Otto," Cammie whimpered.

Mazey called her a fire demon because of her red hair. When she told her it didn't mean she was evil the other girl called her a liar. She hadn't intended to hurt the brat, she'd only wanted her to shut up. It wasn't her fault. Mazey was clumsy and fell down the stairs. Now everyone was calling her names, so she ran away.

Swiping at the tears dripping down her cheeks, she didn't want to admit she was crying. Cammie tried to wiggle her foot free, but only made it worse. The sound of something crashing through the trees caused her to nearly jump out of her skin. From her viewpoint, something really big was running straight for the tree—for her.

Cammie held her breath, closed her eyes, and prayed whatever it was wouldn't see her and decide she'd make a tasty snack. Her mama always said there were things in the forests that would kill and not to go into them. But Cammie loved the big pines, and the noises the animals made were her favorite sounds. Now, the wilderness seemed to stop and wait, like it knew a greater predator was in its midst.

The beat of her heart filled her ears. Cammie opened her eyes. Surely if the beast was hungry it would be growling or shaking the tree, right? Looking at the last place she'd seen the thing, she relaxed, or tried as much as she could with her arms wrapped around the trunk.

"Are you ready to get down?"

Cammie jumped. "Oh my God. Please don't eat me. I'll taste really, really bad. I promise."

A deep laugh had her looking at the speaker. He had to be the most beautiful person in the entire world. Long black hair and two dimples in his cheeks, if he was gonna eat her, he wouldn't smile at her, Cammie thought.

"I'm not that hungry." The gorgeous man snapped his teeth together. "Yet."

She shivered, and the tears she tried hard to hold back, dripped down her cheeks.

"I was only joking, don't cry. I'm going to climb up and see what's going on, okay?"

He didn't give her a chance to answer before he scaled the big tree like a monkey. She was a good twenty feet in the air. What had taken her at least fifteen minutes to climb, he did in less than five.

"Wow, you're a really good climber."

"Why thank you, my tiny damsel in distress. I'm Keanu Raine. What's your name?"

Cammie's brow furrowed. "Um...I'm not supposed to talk to strangers."

He held out his hand. "Well, since you're kinda stuck in this tree and it's getting dark, let's become friends."

Cammie gazed at the man she decided she would marry someday. He told her about himself, patiently telling her he was a local firefighter, and about his grandfather, the shaman of their tribe. Her mother was so gonna love him. Cammie adored the name Keanu, figuring it would go down in her diary as her new favorite.

"I'm going to be grounded for life if my mama finds out I was here," Cammie groaned.

"Let's worry about getting you down and then I'll take you home. I'm sure she's already worried about you."

She nearly fell out of the tree when Keanu pulled out a little knife. "Please don't hurt me."

"What? This?" Keanu held it up. "I'm going to trim some of the bark off between these branches, so we can get your shoe loose."

Watching closely, Cammie held completely still until the pressure eased on her foot. She jerked her leg, nearly kneeing her knight in the jaw.

"Thank you, thank you, Keanu." She wrapped her arms around his shoulders.

"All right, now we need to get down. I want you to climb on my back and hold on. Can you do that?"

"I can get down by myself. I got up here, didn't I?"

"Yes, little lady, you did, but you also got yourself stuck. Besides, it's my job to rescue people, so you'd be letting me do my job."

He made it sound like she was helping him. With a huff, Cammie wrapped her arms around Keanu's neck and held on for dear life.

He descended the tree like he'd been doing it all his life. She didn't want to let go when they reached the bottom and he obviously thought she couldn't walk. All the way back to town, he told her about his new job. When he told her he was leaving to become a part of a group called Smokejumpers, she wanted to weep.

Cammie decided she was going to be just like him when she grew up.

"Hey, Red, how 'bout you and me going out tonight?" Ted Grossman asked.

The question jarred her out of her memories. She used to consider Ted to be one of her best friends. Any time Cammie was in a jam, Ted was there to help pull her out. When her high school boyfriend had been cheating on her, it had been Ted whose shoulder she'd cried on. Luckily for her, Ted was also the one who had broken the news to

Cammie. Otherwise she may have made the biggest mistake of her life, since it was prom night and all.

Now, the thought of Ted and his new friends made her skin crawl. There was something about the three men he'd been hanging out with that didn't sit well with her.

"Um, not tonight, Ted." She smiled to lessen the blow.

Cammie tried to walk around the pack of idiots standing outside the bar. One of them grabbed her arm, making her flinch at the rough treatment. The hand wrapped around her bicep held her in place. She looked at the man, at his hand where it rested on her arm, and back to him. She raised her eyebrows. Ted gave her a beseeching look.

"Listen, you little bitch. You think you're better than us? Well, I have news for you."

She recognized Bob Thompson and his sneering voice immediately. "Guys, I'm tired. I really just wanna go home and get some rest. Why don't you go back into Sully's and have another beer?" Cammie looked at Ted, a guy she used to consider a friend.

"Aw, come on, Cam. You can have just one drink. You know you're the hottest piece of meat in town," Ted said with a drunken leer.

Cammie shuddered. "Did you just call me a cow? No, don't answer that." She held up her free hand. "Seriously, I really appreciate your flattery, but I'm going home." Cammie looked pointedly at the hand still holding her arm.

"Let's go, Bob. I'll buy you a drink," Ted offered.

"You are a fucking pussy, Ted," Bob snarled.

Cammie had enough. Using Ted's distraction, she shoved her palm into Bob's chest, pushing him away, and twisted out of his grasp. He lunged, but luckily for her his friends dragged him back into the bar. His curses still rang in her ears. Tossing her ponytail over her shoulder, she shook her head and quickened her pace.

Walking to the firehouse yesterday had seemed like such a good freaking idea. Why hadn't she considered the danger of leaving at midnight the following night? She decided to claim temporary insanity. With the string of fires, and one of her teammates injured, it worked for her.

She picked up her pace, pushed her bag over her hip, and tapped her pocket to make sure her phone was still there. She'd be totally lost without her iPhone. The hair on the nape of her neck prickled. Cammie glanced over her shoulder and saw a Jeep sitting idle at the stoplight. The late hour and the dark tinted windows didn't allow her to see the driver, and a shiver wracked her frame.

With some kind of pyromaniac running around, the last thing she needed was a stalker for crying out loud. The engine roared and she watched from the corner of her eye as the Jeep turned at the light. "Thank you, Lord Jesus," Cammie murmured.

Berserker's Rage
SmokeJumpers 2
Elle Boon

Chapter One

Felicity pinched the bridge of her nose and closed down the computer. "Thank God today is over." The final rush before prom had moms, and their teenage daughters, coming into the overpriced boutique to buy one of a kind dresses. The boutique, located in a strip mall, was in one of the wealthiest parts of Beverly Hills.

She'd let the other employees, most of whom were teenagers or college students, leave shortly after closing, while she did the end of the month total. Looking at the clock on the wall she grimaced. "Fuck a duck." Knowing it was going to be dark out, but figuring she was in a well-lit parking lot, not to mention the crime rate was almost non-existent, she grabbed the bank envelope and stuffed it into her purse.

From her office she saw the lights in the front of the store were set to low. After making sure the alarm was turned on she walked out the back, closing and locking the heavy steel door. She took two steps and then stopped at the sight of four figures wearing hoodies.

Felicity hugged the bag closer to her chest, calculating in her head the chances of getting back into the store, or making it to her car. She wished she'd listened to her parents and learned to use a gun, or taken those self-defense classes they'd went on and on about.

"Look at her. She's thinking about trying to escape, Danny." One of the thugs sneered.

"Shut up, asshole." The one she assumed was Danny began moving toward her.

Felicity decided a few thousand dollars wasn't worth her life, and pulled the bank envelope out. The credit slips and checks could be cancelled, she reconciled in her mind. "Here, just take it and go." She held it out as the one she assumed was the leader came toward her. They had masks with white skulls painted over their faces, making them appear even more frightening to Felicity. She locked her legs in place as he took, and then opened the envelope pulling the cash out.

He leaned down and sniffed her neck. "You really should've locked up and went home earlier. Don't you know it's not safe to be out after the sun goes down? Things go bump in the dark, little girl."

Looking up, she saw the coldest eyes staring down at her, and knew her life was over. No matter how much she wished it otherwise, these men had no plans to take the money and run.

"Why?" Felicity hated the plea in her voice, but couldn't help but ask the one word question.

The other three had moved closer, somehow maneuvering her into the darkened corner near the dumpsters. A perfect place to do God only knew what to her. Felicity looked around for an escape, or a weapon, but saw nothing but garbage and darkness.

"You want to know why we chose you?" One of the thugs asked, his voice grating. "You are always the last to leave. You may not be much to look at, but your body is kickin, and there is the added bonus of the money. We call that a win-win." Two of the masked men fist bumped each other.

"Wow, he sure is talkative tonight. I guess that means we get to kill this one, huh?" Felicity nearly fell on her ass hearing the feminine voice behind the mask.

"Awe, what's the matter, sugar lips? Did you think only men could do these sorts of things? Nah, I enjoy fighting and fucking just as much as these guys. Actually, I think I may get off on it more."

Thinking back to the string of crimes she'd read about, and how they'd found all the victims, made Felicity's stomach roll. She placed her hand over her mouth. "I think I'm going to be sick," she said. Her parents would be horrified that her body would be found naked, the way the other victims had been discovered.

"That's not going to save you, sugar lips." Felicity hated the woman.

"Alice, quit being a cunt and scaring our date." The one she assumed was Danny moved in closer. "Now, we can do this several ways. You can let us have our fun, or you can fight, and we will enjoy that even more. The difference is you won't enjoy option B nearly as much as us."

"What the hell, Dan, you got a soft spot for the ugly duckling or what?" Alice asked.

Felicity winced at the words tossed out by the woman. She had always been a plain Jane, and had been fine with it. Hearing that even her attackers thought she was ugly, but still planned...she couldn't finish the thought of what was coming. What she could do was fight and not let them have it the easy way. She'd rather die fighting than be alive while they did whatever they intended. Since they weren't expecting her to attack, she would go on the offense. She lifted the cross-body bag from across her chest, knowing it appeared light, when it fact it was heavier than if she had a couple bricks stored inside.

She watched Danny's eyes widen, like he was expecting her to strip for them. The other two men folded their arms across their chest, preparing to watch the show.

Well, Felicity would do her best to give them a show, even if it killed her.

"This is gonna be great. Look at her tits. More than a handful." One of the guys said, making Felicity shudder with his raspy voice, sounding like he'd already started anticipating what he was going to do to her.

Near the dumpster, she noticed a broken clothing rack with pieces of the metal pole lying off to the side. If she could ease closer to it she might have a fighting chance. With a yell she swung her heavy purse and knocked Alice in the head, and then hit Danny. Both were stunned, giving her a chance to lunge for the metal pole.

"Looks like our toy has claws." The last man spoke. His voice hissing, a snake-like sound that slithered along her nerves.

She held the weapon in front of her. "I don't want to hurt you. Just take my purse, my car, and the money from the store and go. I can't identify you, so just go."

Danny sighed. "She went with the hard way, kids. Let's do this then."

If she wasn't the one in their sights, she'd have appreciated their well thought out choreography. The way they fanned out, giving her no chance to escape. Again, she wished she'd learned self-defense or something useful that would've saved her. Instead, she held the metal pole like a baseball bat, because she was good at that, and hit the first person to come at her. The sound of metal hitting flesh and bone, followed by the grunt of pain, almost made her drop her it. Only too soon another body came at her, and she swung with all her might, hitting a hard male body, who grabbed her weapon and jerked.

The metal pole was ripped from her, forcing

Felicity to cry out in pain as the skin on her palms was ripped open.

"You stupid little bitch. You should've went with option A." One of the men grabbed her, jerking her close to his body, shivers wracked her frame.

She raised her knee and tried to hit the one holding her between his legs, but he threw her away from him. She scrambled on her hands and knees, looking for more pieces of the rack, when her foot was grabbed.

Pieces of dirt and gravel scraped against her hands and arms as she was pulled back. Felicity clawed at the ground, feeling her nails breaking off, screaming, and knowing nobody could hear her.

"Give me something to gag her." The leader's voice grated.

Being flipped onto her back, her skirt hiked up to her waist, Felicity felt tears running down her temples and into her dark brown hair. The smell of the trash, and the overwhelming scent of the man's cologne was forever imprinted on her brain as he straddled her, and shoved a piece of cloth in her mouth. She kicked and punched, trying to get the large man off her.

The feel of several hands grabbing her legs, and then her arms, brought a fresh wave of adrenalin through her. She worked the cloth out of her mouth with her tongue, and with the last bit of her breath, Felicity screamed, and screamed, until a fist came down, and still she screamed. She continued to scream, even when the man kept hitting her, telling her to shut up or else. Felicity heard bones cracking, tasted her own blood filling her mouth, and swallowed in order to continue screaming.

A stranger's yell broke through the blackness trying to swallow her. Pain wracked every nerve of her body, and then the weight holding her down was gone. She wanted to move, needed to get away, but couldn't. She let herself go where there was no pain, and prayed her parents knew she loved them. Darkness filled her vision. Broken, Felicity stopped fighting wishing she could see who the new man was.

* * * *

Hal rounded the corner and came to an abrupt stop. He swore he heard a woman scream. The hair on the back of his neck stood on end, and then he heard the sound again. He took off at a run, seeing the empty parking lot, save for one lone car parked under a security light.

The sound of the screaming was cut off, but he realized where it came from. In a darkened corner, he saw four figures surrounding what looked to be a woman's prone form. Rage filled his vision. The closer he came and saw the damage they'd done, Hal's grip on his control began to slip, making him see a red haze surrounding the four beings. He gave a yell that he knew was louder than the average man, making the attackers turn to face him, except the one still straddling the body.

He couldn't control his temper and didn't attempt to. His inner beast had free reign to do whatever it wanted to the animals responsible for killing the young woman, and Hal would rejoice in their pain. He felt his seams stretching and knew he probably looked like a monster to them. Again, he didn't care. Let them scream and beg for mercy. They wouldn't get any.

With another yell he ran, his arms extended, grabbing hold of two of the men. He threw them against the concrete wall and watched them slide down, their screams for mercy falling on deaf ears. The last one standing faced him with a glare, but it was the one bent over the downed woman who held his attention. Hal's sole focus zeroed in on him. Before he could stop himself he crossed the small space and knocked him off the woman. He landed with a sickening crunch against the trash can, a metal pole skewering him, blood pouring from his stomach. Hal's gaze went to the woman lying so still, gasping at the bloody pulp her face had become. He promised he'd make them all look just the same before he was done with them.

"Please don't hurt me. They made me do it." Hal stared at the outstretched hands, hearing the plea behind the mask.

Hal came to an abrupt halt at the soft feminine voice behind the mask. He shook his head trying to clear thoughts of rage running through his mind. A whimper and the sound of gagging had him turning to the injured female. He took a step toward the masked woman, and then more gagging had him spinning to help. While his back was turned the woman fled. Hal took a few calming breaths before making his way to where the poor abused woman lay. The berserker in him was trying to stay in control, needing to make everyone suffer the way the woman had, but with utter ruthlessness Hal pushed him back. Taking out his cell, he dialed 911, and explained to the dispatcher what had happened as quickly as he could, leaving out the fact he was a berserker, and did his best to save the young woman's life.

He wasn't sure how old she was, but from the look of her body she couldn't be more than early twenties. A connection to the unconscious woman threaded its way through him like the lifeline his nana had spoken about. *Mine.*

He shrugged out of his jacket, and covered her lower half up as best as he could. Her skirt had been rucked up and her panties had been torn off. Hal hoped she hadn't been raped, but he couldn't be sure he'd gotten there in time to save her from that injustice. "Hold on, *ma petite*. Help is on the way." The urge to brush her hair off her face was strong, but her injuries were so severe he stopped himself, barely.

In his rage Hal hadn't thought to check on the two men he'd thrown against the wall, or the one impaled on the pipe. He made a quick call to his team leader, Brax, just in case he needed him to bend some minds. The last thing he needed was anyone to think he was more than a human man.

"What the hell did you do now, Aldridge?" Brax

asked.

Hal told him what had happened, hearing the other man swear fluently in several languages, before he settled down. “I’ll be there in a few hours. Don’t say anything more than what you have to. You have PTSD. Do you hear me?” Brax’s tone turned serious.

“I’m a smokejumper, used to stressful situations. Do you really think something like this would cause me to have PTSD?” Hal checked for a pulse on one man then the next, finding they each had one, he relaxed. “I think I only killed one, Brax.”

“Oh, goody. Now, go back to the girl and make sure she lives.” Brax’s voice growled through the connection.

Hal was already heading back to stand guard over her. There was something about her that called to him on an elemental level. Before he’d taken a step away he noticed a bag. Figuring it was hers, he gathered it and the items nearby. Her wallet had fallen open and, seeing her face for the first time, he studied it as he walked back toward her.

“Felicity Evans, I wish I’d gotten here sooner, *ma petite*.” He liked her name. Liked her dark brown hair and the way it looked long and soft in her picture. Lying in such a disarray, Hal wanted to hurt the men who did this to her, all over again.

Shoving the wallet back inside the overly large bag he crouched down and waited. He'd used his shirts to brace her body on the side to keep her from choking on her own blood, his leather jacket was covering her lower half, leaving him half dressed.

The first responders pulled in with the lights flashing, followed by several police vehicles. Hal held his hands up, still in a crouched position, and shirtless. "My name is Hal Aldridge. I'm a firefighter. I came upon the scene when I heard a young woman screaming." He went on to explain what had happened, moving aside while they hooked an IV into Felicity's arm. The fact she never regained consciousness worried him.

"Was she awake when you found her?" One of the officers asked.

"No, other than gagging on her own blood, no." Hal felt a primal growl rise in his chest as they removed his jacket exposing her lower half. With reflexes too fast for most humans, Hal jerked the jacket back up her legs. "I don't know what they did to her before I got here, but you can respect her modesty, boy."

The paramedic mumbled an apology, however

his jacket wasn't removed again.

A lady police officer tapped him on the shoulder. "Did you do that to them?" She pointed at the three men.

"I'm not sure what happened, officer. I think I'm suffering from PTSD." He watched as they carefully transferred Felicity onto a backboard then into the ambulance. "Can I ride with her?"

"I'm going to need you to come down to the station for more questions, Mr. Aldridge."

"Am I under arrest?" Hal asked.

She sighed, sympathy in her gaze. "No, we just need to make a report."

"Then you can follow me to the hospital." He jogged over to the ambulance. "Can I ride with you?" He asked the paramedic.

"I'm sorry, there isn't room." The man said with way too much satisfaction.

Hal took a deep breath. "What hospital are you taking her to?"

He listened as they told him, making a mental note of the man's name. "Todd, can I tell you a secret?" When the man settled in on the bench, Hal continued. "I make for a really bad enemy. You treat her like she's the most precious thing in the world. If

I think for one second you didn't, I'll make what happened to her look like a walk in the park next to what will happen to you. Got it?"

"Excuse me, Mr. Aldridge. You shouldn't go around threatening people." The police woman whispered, humor lacing her words.

Hal turned to look at the police woman. "It's a promise, not a threat. I'll see you at the hospital." He nodded at the paramedic.

"How about if I give you a ride? To the hospital, not the station, scouts honor."

With a jerk of his head, Hal picked up his bloody shirts from where they'd been under Felicity's body. He shook them out and looked at them.

"Those are evidence, Mr. Aldridge." One of the other officer's tried to stop him from taking his clothes.

"I used them to prop her up so she wouldn't choke on her own blood. Why would they beat her so severely?" Hal didn't expect an answer.

The woman officer led the way to her car, speaking in low tones. "We've had a string of similar attacks in the area. Usually the vic is not so lucky, though."

"Excuse me? Did you see her face, or what was

left of it? There is probably not enough plastic surgery in the world to fix the damage done to her."

And that was the thing that bothered him the most. While she wasn't beautiful in the classic sense, he felt a connection to her. Her green eyes had such trust and intelligence that even the camera couldn't hide.

She waited for him to buckle up before pulling onto the road. "Oh, hun, this is Beverly Hills. Believe me, if she has money, she can get anything fixed, and be good as new."

Hal looked at the woman driving with such surety. Her name tag said Coleman. He hoped he never became quite so jaded. Even if Felicity was able to get all the corrective surgery to heal the outward scars, he wondered if her inner wounds could be fixed as easily.

Hal slapped the dash, making the lady cop jump. "Shit, who will call her next of kin?"

Officer Coleman patted his thigh. "You really are one of the good guys aren't you, Aldridge."

He couldn't imagine the phone call that was to come to her parents. Not even eight o'clock on a Sunday night, and you think your child is safe from the evils of the world, only to get a phone call saying just the opposite.

"Shit, one of them got away. A female. She said they made her do it, and then I got distracted when I realized Felicity wasn't...well...I turned my back on the female and she ran off. There was something about her, though, that didn't scream victim to me."

Coleman nodded her head. "Since we have two of the others, who hopefully aren't injured too badly." She looked at him out of the corner of her eye before continuing. "Maybe they'll give her identity up."

They followed the ambulance, with the sirens and lights flashing, all the way to the nearest hospital. Hal was pushed to the side while they wheeled Felicity in. The ER team seemed efficient and quickly called in a plastic surgeon. Hal listened and waited for Brax. He knew his captain could get a lot more information than he ever could, and for some reason it was immensely important that he knew everything about Felicity.

After a few hours, a couple walked in looking like they were worth millions of dollars. Hal ignored them, assuming they were there to see someone else.

"Excuse me, are you the young man who saved our girl?"

Hal's head shot up at the cultured voice. He got to his feet. "Hello, ma'am. Are you Felicity's parents?"

The woman looked nothing like the woman he'd rescued. Neither did the man, but that didn't mean they weren't related.

"Yes, my name is Felicia, and this is my husband, Rand. We owe you so much for saving our baby."

Rand and Felicia looked like supermodels.

Hal stuck his hand out and was surprised by the strong grip Rand had. Felicia looked at his hand and threw her arms around his waist. He looked over her head at Felicity's dad and saw tears in the older man's eyes. Both of the Evans clearly loved their daughter very much. Hal hugged Felicia and waited for her hiccupping cries to subside.

"Have you heard anything about her condition? They won't tell me anything because I'm not family."

"You're family now, son," Rand said firmly.

Hal wondered where they'd been, but didn't question what had taken them so long to get there. He watched Felicia walk to the desk with her husband next to her. Both with their backs straight as pins. Felicity's mother turned to Rand and murmured *oh thank God,* and then she broke down into tears again. He felt like a voyeur.

The wait for them to return was the longest three minutes of his life, but he made himself stand still instead of going to them and demanding information. Rand tilted his wife's face up and brushed her tears away with his thumbs, and then he nodded in Hal's direction. Luckily, he'd been given a shirt from Officer Coleman's workout bag. The woman kept a spare change of clothes, and liked men's T-shirts instead of women's. Why he was worried about being shirtless in front of these people, he had no clue, but there was something that made him want to impress them.

"They have her in a medically induced coma and stopped the bleeding. The doctors don't believe there's any brain damage, but won't know until all the swelling goes down. There's extensive damage to her...fa...face. She's going to need a lot of surgeries, and even then they don't know...oh my poor baby." Felicia buried her face in Rand's chest again.

Rand held Felicia closer. "They didn't rape her. There's no evidence of that atrocity. Now, we will just go one day at a time. She will have the best that money can buy."

Hal nodded, but knew all the money in the world couldn't blot out the physical and mental pain that she'd already suffered, and what was sure to come. He breathed a relieved sigh that at least he'd gotten there before they'd been able to rape her.

"How long will they keep her in the coma?" Hal asked.

"A couple weeks probably." Rand soothed his wife as she cried at his words.

"It will give her body a chance to heal." Hal wasn't sure who he was reassuring, them or himself. He was in California on vacation, and hadn't planned to stay for more than a couple extra days of sun and surfing with his buddies. Looks like he would be staying a little longer.

"Give us your information," Rand said.

Hal pulled out his card, handing it over without hesitation. A commotion down the hall had them all turning to see Brax coming their way.

"That's my buddy, Brax. I called him when I wasn't sure what was going on. He's my captain."

Mr. Evans studied the card. "SmokeJumper huh?"

With a nod, Hal waited for Brax. He made the introductions, and saw Brax's eyebrows rise. He wasn't sure if it was because of the obvious wealth or because of the too small T-shirt he had on.

"I've spoken with the Chief of Police. Your leather jacket, along with your shirts, are being released since they aren't considered evidence any longer. The one man who was killed, pardon my frank talk ma'am, has a rap sheet longer than my leg, and his fingerprints match those on one of the other victims. The other two are going to live, although I'm not sure how much they'll be good to society. They keep murmuring and rocking back and forth, or so I'm told. I think their brains are scrambled. Again, their fingerprints are all over several other victims, and they are running other bodily fluids to see if they match as well." Brax coughed and looked away.

"Its okay, Felicity wasn't raped." Hal slapped him on the back, making him stagger forward.

"Easy, boy. Remember your strength." Brax grimaced.

"Oofta, sorry." Hal ran his hand over his face. He hadn't realized how worried he was, or how much he depended on Brax.

Made in the USA
Middletown, DE
16 February 2017